EAST OF DALLAS

EAST OF DALLAS

The European Challenge to American Television

Alessandro Silj
with Manuel Alvarado, Jean Bianchi, Régine Chaniac,
Tony Fahy, Michael Hofmann, Giancarlo Mencucci,
Barbara O'Connor, Michel Souchon, Antonia Torchi

BFI Publishing

First published in 1988 by the
British Film Institute
21 Stephen Street
London W1P 1PL

Typeset by KC Graphics Ltd, Shrewsbury
Printed and bound in Great Britain by
St Edmundsbury Press,
Bury St Edmunds, Suffolk

British Library Cataloguing in Publication Data

Silj, Alessandro
East of Dallas.
I. Europe. Television programmes.
Influences of television drama series in
English. Dallas.
I. Title
791.45′094
ISBN 0-85170-225-2
ISBN 0-85170-226-0 Pbk

Contents

‘ . . . surrender to a culture which, however inevitable its global spread, must for as long as possible meet a show of resistance.’

Anthony Burgess in *Time for a Tiger* (commenting on the hiring of an American to teach at a British public school in the British colony of Malaya).

RESEARCH GROUP

Alessandro Silj, novelist and journalist (Italian correspondent for the *Irish Times*), has published books and essays on international relations, political violence, and communications. He is Secretary General of the Italian Social Sciences Council and a trustee of the International Institute of Communications.

Manuel Alvarado, academic co-ordinator for the Journalism and Communications Programme at Boston University's London base, has taught at London University, been a research fellow at the Broadcasting Research Unit, London and Director of the UNESCO global video flow study. He is also a freelance researcher and writer and has published widely in the field of the mass media.

Jean Bianchi, Director of the Department of Communications at the Catholic University of Lyon, France is also research associate at IRPEACS, Centre National de la Recherche Scientifique (CNRS) at Lyon-Ecully. Amongst other works, he has published *Comment comprendre le succès international des séries de fiction à la télévision? – Le cas 'Dallas'* (CNRS 1984).

Régine Chaniac, formerly with the research department of ORTF (French Television), is now in charge of the Studies Programme in the Research Department of INA (Institut National de l'Audiovisuel).

Tony Fahy is manager of the Audience Research Department of RTE (Radio Telefeis Eirann) and Vice-Chair of GEAR, the Group of European Researchers. He is co-founder of the Media Association of Ireland.

Michael Hoffman has since 1975 taught American literature and film, communications theory, television and cinema studies at the Free University of Berlin. Currently he is visiting scholar at Columbia University and New York University and is working on a comparative research project on public broadcasting in West Germany and the USA in collaboration with PBS, the Public Broadcasting System.

Giancarlo Mencucci is head of Verifica qualitativa programmi trasmessi (VPT) for RAI (Radiotelevisione Italiana).

Barbara O'Connor is currently lecturer in sociology and anthropology at the School of Communications, National Institute for Higher Education, Dublin. Her research interests include feminism, and culture and communications. She has published on the representation of women in film and television drama, on the female audience, and on gender in Irish society.

Michel Souchon, formerly Director of Studies and Research at TF1, currently holds the position of advisor to the Secretary General of Programming and Head of Studies and Surveys at Antenne 2. He has published *Petit écran, grand public* and other works on the sociology of the television audience.

Antonia Torchi graduated at DAMS, Bologna with a thesis on British Television in the 1950s. She is currently undertaking research on audiovisual languages and techniques at the Institute of Communications Studies, University of Bologna.

The following also attended some meetings of the working party: David Docherty, David E. Morrison, Michael Tracey (Broadcasting Research Unit), Morten Giersing (UNESCO), Elihu Katz (Hebrew University of Jerusalem, Annenberg School of Communications/USC), Mariano Maggiore (EEC), Giulio Carminato and Piero Dorfles (RAI).

Preface

My main concern in writing the ritual acknowledgments to all those who through their far-sightedness or absent-mindedness have made our work possible, is that I might forget someone, since the help and encouragement we received came from so many and varied sources, both institutions and individuals. This research, sponsored by the Italian Council for the Social Sciences (CSS), would never have started had it not been for the initial support received from RAI's Verifica Programmi Trasmessi (namely Nicola De Blasi and Giancarlo Mencucci).

The financial support of the EEC Commission made it possible for the group to meet regularly (twice a year). The group would like to thank Mariano Maggiore of the Directorate for Information, Communication and Culture of the Commission for the ideas and personal support he brought to those meetings he was able to attend. We wish to thank also UNESCO, which funded our meeting in London in March 1986, and Morten Giersing, who among other things put us in touch with the research carried out in Denmark by Anne Hjort. Finally a special word of thanks to our friends at Teleconfronto (above all to Ivano Cipriani and Stefania Brai) for having so generously hosted our meetings at Chianciano and more besides: in fact, this project was originally conceived at the first meeting of Teleconfronto and has always benefitted from the ideas aired at the Chianciano debates.

In conclusion, a word of reproach (instead of thanks) for the American networks, which we unsuccessfully tried to involve in the research and which, having received our subsequent request to provide information on European series they had broadcast, saw fit not to reply. Perhaps they thought they would hurt us by confessing to never having shown any. If this is the case, and we suspect it is, then this alone would be the best justification for our research. *East of Dallas,* after all, there is also Europe, and much of its television fiction is just as good as *Dallas* even if some Europeans seem to be convinced of the opposite.

Alessandro Silj
Rome, May 1988

Introduction

Objectives

The objective of the work, carried out between June 1984 and March 1987 by an international research team, promoted and co-ordinated by the Italian Council for the Social Sciences (Consiglio Italiano per le Scienze Sociali, or CSS), was to analyse the contents and narrative structures of television fiction in European countries. These were then to be compared to American series, in particular to the by now mythical *Dallas* (but not only *Dallas*), in order to assess the validity of the pre-occupation, repeatedly expressed over the past few years, concerning the possible consequences of the wide success which American fiction has achieved with viewers.

The debate on the success of American programmes, on its causes and its real or alleged effects, may be summed up in a number of statements and inferences. In short, television fiction programmes produced in the United States:

Statements	**(Inferences)**
are successful	(are more successful than European programmes)
represent models of American life and values	(these models are negative)
are successful because their professional standards are high	(in general, European programmes are less professional)

are also successful because of economic factors: the size of the American market permits a rapid amortisation of costs and programmes can be sold on foreign markets at highly competitive prices.

(it is possible to improve the quality of the European product by using American production techniques; since to produce a programme costs more than to buy an imported programme, the strategy of the European 'answer' should be based on co-productions and on the enlargement of the market.)

Up to now, these problems have been interpreted in three different ways. According to the first, essentially ideological, interpretation, television and in particular television fiction (only apparently apolitical) is an instrument of 'American cultural imperialism'. The second, which refers to the characteristics of the medium and its natural trends of development, believes that a progressive 'homogenisation' of the television product is now underway; that we are witnessing a determinism inherent in the very nature of the medium. Lastly, according to the third interpretation it is the law of the market that has led to the dominance of American productions. The ideological interpretation, quite apart from its validity in other countries of the world, seems hardly relevant in the political and economic context of Western Europe. As for the other two, they can be intellectually very appealing (the 'homogenisation' theory) or far too obvious (the economic theory).

Our work started out from the consideration that much has been said and written about *Dallas* and American television fiction and very little, on the contrary, about European programmes (the only exception being Great Britain). The debate has focused on 'the differences' between European and American television programmes and on national identities 'threatened' by an overdose of *Dallas*. However, a comparative analysis aimed at establishing exactly what these differences are, or how the distinctive traits of this or that national identity are represented on television and in fiction in particular, has never been attempted. Therefore, our project was above all a reconnaissance. We explored what was 'inside' the television series (plots, characters, values – explicit and/or implicit) of five European countries, Italy, France, West Germany, Great Britain and Ireland; then we compared this to American television series, especially *Dallas*. We also wanted to check how the public 'reads' these programmes. In short, we proposed to establish the validity of some of the 'inferences' listed above, and at the same time question some of the 'statements', since not all of them can be regarded as axiomatic.

When our research group came to decide which programmes to study in each of the five countries, we of course looked for criteria that would enable us to plug the data into some kind of comparative analysis scheme. Eventually our choice fell on programmes which told a family story (or at the very least where family relations played a significant role) and at the same time placed these stories in a wider social context.

Crime stories could have been another possible choice. However, we felt that this was a genre more standardised than others and therefore less liable to highlight the contents and narrative style particular to one country or another. The various typologies present in this genre seem to reflect the characteristics of its various sub-genres more than national differences. Moreover, and above all, in a police story social and personal relationships usually are less varied than in other genres and therefore these stories were less likely than others to provide significant answers to the kind of questions we were most interested in. Lastly, one of the five countries studied, Ireland, has not produced crime stories. The other criteria we used in choosing our sample were the following: the programme had to be part of a series (serial, series or mini-series); the stories had to be located in the country of production and be contemporary (from the end of World War II onwards). Only programmes produced between 1980 and 1985, broadcast during that same period at peak viewing hours, and with top audience ratings, were eligible. As for the size of the sample, we agreed on five episodes of national fiction in each of the five countries. The American programmes were to include at least one episode of *Dallas* (the same one for all five countries).

In fact, when we moved on to choose the programmes in each of the five countries, it was not always possible to respect all the criteria listed above. The difficulties encountered are significant in themselves, as they illustrate the differences in television programming between one country and another. In Ireland and West Germany, only two series were broadcast during the chosen period which fitted our criteria. What is important to stress here is that we found ourselves confronted with a panorama made of very different realities, above all as far as *genres* and *consumption* were concerned. For example, while soaps are the most popular genre in Great Britain, in Italy there are no serials, and mini-series are the rule. Moreover, it would be quite meaningless to compare the interaction between the British audience and a programme like *Coronation Street*, which has been on the air 28 years, and that between the Italian audience and *Quei 36 gradini*, a 6-episode series. Thus our research, initially geared to a comparative analysis of American and European television fiction, forced us to come to terms with some significant differences which exist between European countries. In this sense, it can be said that our landscape turned out to be more varied than expected.

Content Analysis and Narrative Structures

In an initial phase, following a suggestion by Elihu Katz, to whom we are grateful for having participated in our first workshop (Chianciano, June 1984), we tested the grid drawn up by Milton Rokeach for plotting instrumental/terminal values. However, the values listed seemed heavily geared to the ethic and lifestyle of American society; the grid did not list values likely, more than others, to denote the characters and situations recurrent in European television fiction programmes. In order to 'Europeanise' Rokeach's grid, we tried out some variations, but failed to reach meaningful results. As we proceeded, we became convinced that an out-of-context analysis of single values, i.e. the fact of pinning a positive or negative label on each of them independently from their relationship to other values, would not be particularly significant. In the end, what counts is the way in which the confrontation between opposite values is resolved. Reducing the content analysis to an operation of fractionalisation and identification of values, as American communication research often does one way or another, would be somewhat paradoxical in Europe, where in recent years theories of narration have been discussed passionately and at length.

Therefore, in elaborating our analytical tools, we tried to give the narrative forms their due – by looking at them not just as carriers of values, but as producers of values as well. It seemed to us that Jean Bianchi's proposal to combine this value analysis with that of narrative structures could produce useful results and, among other things, would be more in keeping with the nature and characteristics of the medium. Bianchi's grid was based on the obvious premise that, in filmed stories, values should be taken from both explicit narrative (action, dialogues) and other elements of the television language (camera, lights, etc). The problem then was to build a tool for analysis which would permit an integrated reading of: 1) the narrative structure: theme (story), characters, situations, duration and chronology, etc; 2) television (film) language: camera movements, sound track, *mise en scène*, etc. Accordingly, we worked with the following grid:

1	2	3	4	5	6
editing	place/time	characters	action	audio-visual language	stereotypes

For each sequence, we recorded the following: duration of frames and sequence, the place and time of the action, the characters, the plot (action/dialogue), as well as *mise en scène*, camera movements, sound track, special effects, etc. – focusing on how these various elements contribute to the connotation of characters and situations – and lastly, the stereotypes represented in the story (for example, Pietro in *Quei 36 gradini* is the good-natured and fatalistic Roman).

With regard to the latter point, we intended to check whether the presence of universal stereotypes was more evident in programmes geared to the international market as well as the relative importance of regional and national stereotypes in the definition of national identity. In retrospect, one must note that the results were interesting but not particularly relevant to our analysis. On the whole, this methodology was useful mainly as a key to 'enter' and find our way in the materials analysed. Furthermore, for each programme, a card was compiled comprising: 1) reasoned synthesis and overall evaluation of the episode; 2) for each main character: A) description of the character (salient traits), B) description of his or her relationships with other characters. Parallel to 1) and 2), a list of the values 'carried' by the episode on the whole and of those 'carried' by each character was to be added. However, it was agreed that we would not use a pre-determined grid of values (see above).

The latter operation was subject to long, hard discussions within our work group. Because of the subjective nature of the judgements obtained this way, some members believed it to be of little significance. Moreover, their use in comparative analysis would have presented obvious difficulties. By retrospectively rationalising on the nature of difficulties and doubts which emerged concerning this aspect of our work, one can say that it would, in fact, have been difficult and perhaps arbitrary to create a grid of values without first taking into account the content of the programmes which we were to analyse. Hence we agreed that each national research group should feel free to 'recognise' the values carried by the characters and situations in the programme (i.e. each time starting from the programme itself rather than from a prefabricated grid), in the belief that this method would bring out the cultural and social peculiarities of each country. This, we felt, compensated for the risk, inherent in such an approach, of making subsequent comparative analyses less accurate. Eventually however only three research groups (Italy, France and Ireland) carried out the value analysis.

The Audience

In order to ascertain analogies and differences between national programmes and American programmes from the point of view of audience perception, one episode of *Dallas*, the same one for all countries (Bobby's death), and one episode of a national series were shown in each country to four groups of ten people each, which represented a cross-section of the urban population (except for Italy, where work was done on eight groups). The research was carried out according to a methodology drawn up by Mesomark for RAI's Servizio Opinioni. Each group was shown the programmes (in two separate sittings, one for *Dallas*, the other for the national programme); the screening was followed by an 'open' discussion, guided by a moderator (motivational research) and finally, each member of each group was asked to fill in a questionnaire. The same questionnaire was used in every country, i.e. in Italy, Ireland and France. The research with audience groups was not carried out in West Germany because of lack of funds. The British group's decision not to participate in this part of the project was based on a critical dissociation from the proposed methodology. However, since no other proposal was put forward, we went ahead nonetheless. The work carried out with audience groups did, in fact, produce relevant information which contributed to our analysis on both *Dallas* and the national programmes.

In order to make up for the English absence in this part of the research, we used the results of a study published by the Broadcast Research Unit on American television series on British screens.[1] Furthermore, on the wider subject of how American television series are perceived by a non-American audience, we took into consideration the results of the research carried out by Tamar Liebes and Elihu Katz on various ethnic groups in Israel[2] and Anne Hjort's Danish study[3] as well as other available data. The results of this part of our work are significant, as they contradict many clichés often heard in recent years concerning the effects of American television series on foreign audiences.

Notes

1. Geoffrey Lealand, *American Television Programmes on British Screens* (London: Broadcasting Research Unit, 1984).
2. See Tamar Liebes, 'Ethnocentricism: Israelis of Moroccan Ethnicity Negotiate the Meaning of *Dallas*', *Studies in Visual Communication* vol.10 no.3, 1984; Tamar Liebes and Elihu Katz, 'Once upon a Time in *Dallas*', *Intermedia* vol.12 no.3, 1984; Tamar Liebes and Elihu Katz, 'Patterns of Involvement in Television Fiction: A Comparative Study', *European Journal of Communication* vol.1 no.2, 1986; Tamar Liebes and Elihu Katz, '*Dallas* and *Genesis*: Primordiality and Sensuality in Television and Fiction', in J. Carey (ed.), *Communication and Culture* (Sage: forthcoming); Tamar Liebes and Elihu Katz, 'On the Critical Ability of Television Viewers' in Borchers and Seiter (eds.), *Rethinking the Audience: New Tendencies in Tele-*

vision Research (Methuen, forthcoming); Elihu Katz and Tamar Liebes, 'Mutual Aid in the Decoding of *Dallas*' in Phillip Drummond and Richard Paterson (eds.), *Television in Transition* (London: British Film Institute, 1986).

3. Anne Hjort, 'When Women Watch TV. How the Danish female public sees *Dallas* and the Danish serial *The Daughters of War*' (Mediaforskning, Denmark Radio, 1985).

PART I

Dallas

1
The Production Context

Perhaps we shall never know the secret of the extraordinary success of *Dallas*. In the history of television, the Ewing saga has been a symbol and an encapsulation of its time. The name *Dallas* conjures up soap opera, escapist television, a Trojan horse in the cultural empire, television as the opium of the masses, the power and the organising ability of the American television industry, and so on and so on. One thing is certain: the success of *Dallas* will have done nothing to clarify the problems in which, rightly or wrongly, Dallas has been seen as the focal point of debate. On the contrary, it will have helped to confuse the issues. It is all the harder to arrive at an objective analysis when so many intellectuals and scholarly observers of television adopt such an ambiguous stance (attraction and revulsion) on a programme of universal appeal which – like Coca Cola – has won a devoted following in more than seventy countries, reaching out even to the remotest African villages. Critics have undoubtedly been swayed by the fact that the attention paid to *Dallas* has been generated by its overwhelming success, and it was this success which was the first to be analysed; the analysis of its content took second place. The critics were placed in a situation in which they had to assess a product when they knew in advance what the public thought. *Dallas* has thus become a sort of mystery object; it must, the critics felt, have qualities not immediately apparent, since success on such a scale would never have been predicted from anything the product *seemed* to be. And so it came about that critics more often and more readily directed their gaze at the mythical object rather than the raw material generating the process that led to the myth.

The generalisations aired as a result distorted the intrinsic nature of the product. Improbable meanings and consequences were read into its success. *Dallas* was elevated to the rank of an (admired and despised) archetype of American television, when in fact it was an innovation, the forerunner of a new genus, a product that did not trace its ancestry to the classic genera of American television serial fiction. Those genera, moreover, did not disappear when the new programme arrived. One looks at *Dallas* and says 'Aha! That is the epitome of television as an industry, a product planned and packaged down to the tiniest detail in the light of thorough market research.' In reality, the birth of *Dallas* was quite spontaneous: CBS wanted a series set in Texas, but had turned down a suggestion from David Jacobs, who promptly came back with another proposal – *Dallas*. And spontaneous it continued. It evolved pragmatically, its progress promoted by hazard and good fortune until it was transformed into something very different from what its authors had originally intended.

In this chapter we shall discuss the *Dallas* myth, but even more we shall discuss *Dallas* without its myth. We shall begin with a reminder of how this programme came into being (because the story is unfamiliar to many people): in a small room, in the course of discussions among three authors who had no inkling that their names would go down in history. We shall then outline many of the things that have been said about *Dallas*, from the judicious to the dotty, thus contributing a *bibliographie raisonnée* to the myth. Finally, referring to other people's research and to materials compiled in the course of our own, we shall try to interpret the *Dallas* viewing figures in Europe and elsewhere, comparing them with viewing figures for home-produced programmes, with particular reference to the five countries covered by the research. We shall report on instances of the '*Dallas* model' being imitated by televisions in other countries. What we shall not try to do is to verify the hypothesis that where *Dallas* has a regular following of a mass audience it is altering values and behaviour patterns. In other words, we shall not venture to measure the 'colonialisation effect'. What resources could one use today to conduct such an investigation? And even if it could be done, would it not be premature? Why should such research be directed towards *Dallas* – just one of the many manifestations of the television phenomenon that shapes our lives?

And, in the search for the villain of the piece, why point the finger at *Dallas* or its audience or both when the basic issues are the cultural and political choices made by the 'gatekeepers', the people in a country who hold the keys to the storehouse? The excuse usually made for importing rather than producing, as we know, is money – it costs less. But is this a genuine excuse, especially when it is advanced by such a body as a public sector television corporation? It is not denied that externally induced effects may be significant in a country, but the fact remains that this is above all a cultural problem common to all countries, an internal problem within each country.

Dallas: how it all began

This is our summary of an interview with Leonard Katzman, *Dallas* scriptwriter and producer, and other two scriptwriters, Bernard Lewis and David Paulsen. The interview took place in June 1983 and it was given to Sylvie Blum, for a programme produced by INA-TF1 entitled *Faire 'Dallas'* [*Making 'Dallas'*].

As we have already mentioned, the idea of *Dallas* and its main characters came from David Jacobs, who also wrote the script for the first episode. It was Jacobs who sold the idea to CBS and to the production company, Lorimar, which made the programme. This meant that Katzman, Lewis and Paulsen were involved in the project almost by chance. These three writers are freelance, but they are far from amateurs since all three are products of that teeming nursery of scriptwriters that grew up under the wings of the great American television industry. Lewis in particular can draw on the experience he acquired when he worked for a few years as managing director with CBS, where his job was to pick programmes likely to do well in the forthcoming season. 'Sometimes they worked, sometimes they didn't . . . if we had been able to predict it right . . . when I was there we would have had nothing but "hits" and there would have been no room for *Dallas*.'

Katzman, Lewis and Paulsen are a copybook model of how to work as a group. They discuss things together and decide on the outline story, plots and characters. Then they split up the scripting work.

Jim Davis and Barbara Bel Geddes in Dallas

Finally they come together again to read the thing as a whole. What takes up most of their time is joint discussion. Under production schedules, there are often only a few days for actually writing an episode. The stage at which CBS – which has to give its general approval – comes in is when the general story line for each series of episodes is mapped out, in other words once a year (since series are planned on a yearly basis). The executive producer, Lorimar, in the person of Phil Capice, takes part in the discussions on the initial story. The producers come in again when it comes to the editing as well as any final work needed on the dialogue and sound track. All the rest, including detailed work on twists and turns of the plot and the writing of the script, is done by the authors, working entirely on their own. Their only interlocutor and 'controller' is the viewing public. 'What matters is that the audience should believe us', is a recurring phrase in the interview. Above all, viewers have to believe in the characters, and to achieve this the story of the characters' emotional lives must be realistic. Each character must remain in character, whatever happens to him or her. What is not necessary, on the other hand, is that the audience should believe in the everyday details, and indeed the authors are not over-scrupulous about realism in the domestic background. One final point: it was public reaction, the reaction of an audience identifying with the emotional realism of the characters, that persuaded the authors to give up the series format in favour of the serial format.

Production times are tight, with a filming schedule of 7 to 9 minutes a day. Output is streamlined: one week's work per episode, with the directors carrying out to the letter what the script and producer require of them. The first twelve episodes in the year (a season consists of 28 episodes in all) are very important because the location work is done in Dallas, to place the story in its setting and give it a dimension that would be impossible in a studio. All the other episodes are shot entirely in the studio. 'With the first twelve episodes everything is planned down to the minutest detail' explains David Paulson, 'and after that we have an overall idea of where we want to go but, confidentially, we never know exactly how we shall get there nor what the end result will be . . . '

For the sake of simplicity and brevity, our summary of the interview with Katzman, Lewis and Paulsen combines the replies given by all three into a single account:

> In 1977, David Jacobs had suggested to CBS the idea of a series entitled *Knot's Landing*, but CBS wasn't interested.[1] What it wanted was a sort of present-day '*Giant*' rewritten in modern idiom. So Jacobs came back again with the idea of *Dallas*, and they liked it. In fact at the beginning what we had in mind was a sort of Romeo and Juliet. The two rival families are the Barnes and the Ewings. Pamela Barnes is Juliet, and the series was designed around Pamela in the role of the leading character. But Texas is a state of rough, tough men and any series in which a woman determined the lives of men wouldn't have lasted out more than six episodes. So it was decided to amend the story by making Bobby (the Romeo) and JR the main characters. And so the story started to evolve. It grew like a tree, with one branch being left to grow and another being pruned back in a search for what seemed the most suitable shape. What we found

ourselves with in the end was something very different from our original idea. In practice, what happened was that Larry Hagman gave the JR character an unpredictable dimension: he made him a 'baddy', sure, but a vulnerable baddy with whom the audience established a very strong love/hate relationship.

We couldn't say whether there is any rule ensuring success, but we are aware that nobody ever knows what the public will like. All we know is that it is important always to bear in mind that a programme is not created because *we* like it; it is created for the public. Of course, suspense is important. Each episode is made up of four 'acts', with intervals for the advertising, which means that each part lasts 12 or 13 minutes.

And we have to create a little suspense at the end of each act, to hold on to the viewers, to stop them changing channels. From this viewpoint, the first act is very important. It has to have a 'strong' finale. This is true of the second act as well, whereas the move from the third to the fourth is easier. At the end of the fourth act we obviously have to have a powerful piece of suspense to ensure that people come back and switch on next week. That's it, these are the basic rules for constructing a soap. If audience reactions can be researched over a fairly long period to find out what people want, then you can succeed. At the beginning, our only concern was to make sure that the series wasn't dropped during its first season. Now it has become an enormous success, it all seems extraordinary to us, there's no explanation for it.

At the beginning it was a story of a family and each episode was self-contained, a story on its own. Its popularity didn't really take off until the last episode in the first season, when Sue Ellen and the baby had a car accident. People wanted to know what would happen next, and we realised it was better to leave episodes open-ended. During the second year, we went on writing self-contained episodes, but we introduced ongoing elements more and more often. The turning point came at the end of the second year, with the attempt on JR's life. The audience wanted to know whether he would die, who tried to kill him and why. It was then that we decided to drop the series format and make it a soap. It was not such an easy choice and it was not so obvious as it might seem at first sight. Up to then soaps had only been relatively successful in the States. Nobody had ever tried out a soap based on one-hour episodes at the rate of one episode a week and in evening viewing hours.[2] Our stories are far more quick-firing than they are in traditional soaps, because the audience doesn't want to sit and listen to interminable dialogues as in soaps. This meant we had to switch over from the JR/Sue Ellen story to the Bob/Pam and the Lucy and the Ray stories. The problem was how to introduce a lot of information, a lot of information in a short time. This is what gives it pace, and the audience doesn't have time to get bored. Viewers don't go off and fetch themselves a drink from the refrigerator because something might happen in the thirty seconds they are away. The plot material we use up in a year would be enough to keep the traditional afternoon soaps or even the old-style soaps like *Peyton Place* going for five years.

In *Dallas* we don't talk about religion, partly because CBS wouldn't agree to it. Quite apart from that, who are the Ewings? They could be Catholic, Presbyterians, Jews – we don't say, it isn't important. We talk about people in general and obviously it's worked because people throughout the world watch *Dallas*, whatever their religion. We don't show any explicit sex and violence because CBS is very strict about such things, but also because it's not necessary: a hint is more telling than action.

Certain factors are universal and close to the hearts of people from every country. One of the reasons for the success of *Dallas* is that is shows a real family where there is a bit of everything, good and bad, where people quarrel and hate each other but then come together for the evening meal and can talk it over and even joke about it. And there is always a pinch of envy and greed and humour, so you can always find something of yourself in *Dallas*. Everybody needs love and seeks it just as Sue Ellen seeks it, although perhaps not quite in the same way. Everyone betrays people and is betrayed, and so you watch *Dallas* and you feel you're not so alone as you thought. But when we talk like this we are being more serious than we would like. We don't dabble in psychology, we don't think in the terms we have described, all we think about are the stories being told. We highlight those things that are important in a family: what happens between brothers, mother, sister and wives, in short the story of emotions. When the Ewings sit down to table, each one with his or her own secrets, they try to be nice and talk to each other, but JR knows something he's not about to tell Bobby, and Sue Ellen knows something else that Pam mustn't know, and Miss Ellie tries to maintain her position as head of the family. It is in these scenes that everything happens, and the audience knows exactly what each person is doing while the people in the scene don't know . . . this is

Linda Evans and John Forsythe in Dynasty

the essence of the story. This is what makes it a family story.

What sets the Ewings apart, of course, is that they are very rich. But they don't live in a fairy-tale castle. The house is large but not too large, and they don't have thirty servants or a chauffeur-driven car. The American middle-class viewers looking at *Dallas* can tell themselves that, with hard work and a bit of luck, the Ewing ranch is not altogether out of their reach.[3] People can imagine themselves there, eating breakfast in that type of place. They would not feel out of their depth at Southfork, they can identify with that way of life, perhaps with a few more worries about money matters but with the same emotional problems as the Ewings. It is very important not to build walls around the characters to keep the audience out. It is just as important that the characters should be consistent, because viewers must be able to believe in them. There we are, that's another rule: you must never lie to the audience, never start off a story in one way and then suddenly take off in another direction. This consistency does not exist, for example, in characters in *Dynasty*, which talks about the bizarre side of life, not ordinary things. We make an effort to talk about ordinary things and to push them to their limits. Of course JR is a totally amoral character, but his triumphs are always followed by disasters. In this sense, we have always tried to take a fairly moral line. Sue Ellen is an alcoholic who goes to bed with lots of men, but in the end she is likeable. Why? Because she loves that individual, and the only thing she really wants is for him to love her too. It's something the audience understands. If the audience understands the reasons why someone behaves in a certain way, if those reasons coincide with what the audience believes, the character becomes likeable. JR, every now and then, is likeable. Like in the 16th episode of the second year, when he finally realises the child is his own.

He gathers up the child in his arms and tears come to his eyes. Basically, people love scoundrels. JR is a marvellous example of a scoundrel because he does things that make you hate him, terrible things, but at the same time you're taken in, and when you realise, it is too late.

Every product, every story formula, sooner or later comes to a saturation point, particularly on American television. For a long time we had nothing but detective series. Then Westerns came in, and films about doctors. Today we have soaps. We think the public will soon be beginning to look for something else. But we bear one thing in mind: *Gunsmoke* lasted for twenty years, *Bonanza* for sixteen. It's quite a long time. Many series stop short at thirteen episodes, others are successful. It is difficult to forecast.

In this interview Leonard Katzman and his companions are undoubtedly speaking off the cuff, and the reader may have noticed a degree of ingenuity or over-simplification in their version of the *Dallas* story (although we should bear in mind that this is the authentic version). But it may also be true that some of the ingenuity is only on the surface or intentional, and some of the modest declarations may well be less sincere than they are intended to seem. With these reservations, what is most striking when we look at the filmed interview is the attitude of the three authors, who are as laid back as might be expected of people who allow themselves to be interviewed in their shirtsleeves, their feet up on the desk. They are mildly amused at it all: 'What, you come all the way from France with all those TV cameras to ask us about *Dallas*?' We see them on film, sitting around talking about their brainchild – a child spawned in the midst of beer cans and clouds of cigarette smoke, without too much racking of brains. . . almost by accident. As they talk about it they are still obviously and sincerely incredulous. Who would ever have thought it would turn out like this? Would success of this kind ever have happened to someone who was striving to achieve it?

It is this image of three authors talking about *Dallas* that we wanted to present (a trifle mischievously) before we go on to look at everything *Dallas* has succeeded in generating: from ideological disputes to semiological dissertations, from deeply felt analysis to populist enthusiasm and intellectual sarcasm. Could it be that such a tiny mouse has unleased such interest and attention? Perhaps the mouse was not so tiny as people had led us to believe, or perhaps the debate/confrontation/clash between the advocates and adversaries of a certain type of television had come to a head and *Dallas* appeared just at the right time and, for the very reason that it was successful, was taken as a symbolic object?

Notes

1. *Knot's Landing*, a story of four families, one of which is the Ewings, was in fact produced in the end, but only after *Dallas* had become popular. It is more sophisticated, more middle-class than the rival series, with more concern for social issues. *Knot's Landing* has met with only modest critical acclaim and, despite its clever use of the participation/identification mechanism whereby it has won a certain audience for itself, it has not managed to compete with *Dallas* and other more successful series.
2. Traditionally USA soap operas are afternoon shows, with 30-minute episodes transmitted daily.
3. The scriptwriters contradict themselves on this point, because elsewhere in the interview they say 'We believe that *Dallas* came just at the right time. It started in 1978, at the time of the second Arab oil embargo when Texas oilmen were being regarded with interest. The time had also come to show rich people. The economy was starting to be shaky. What happened was something like what happened in the 30s with the Fred Astaire and Ginger Rogers movies, those marvellous fairy stories in which a poor young girl is discovered by a very rich man, and people went to the cinema and, for two hours, forgot they didn't have enough to eat at home.'

2
What People Have Written About *Dallas*

It is hardly surprising that the first people to take *Dallas* – and soap operas in general – seriously were women. Attention has always been devoted to soap operas by television researchers, and the impulse for research has often been 'instrumental'. In feminist-linked cultural circles, the soap opera's success with such a broad female audience led many women researchers to study the imagination and pleasure linked with formats originally designed for, and exclusively aimed at, that audience. Among the many studies are those by Tania Modleski. In 'The Rhythms of Reception'[1] Modleski presents a quotation from Tillie Olsen:[2]

> 'More than in any other human relationship . . . motherhood means being instantly interruptible, responsive, responsible . . . It is distraction, not meditation, that becomes habitual: interruption, not continuity: spasmodic, not constant toil.' Daytime television[3] plays a part in habituating women to interruption, distraction and spasmodic toil.

Modleski disputes the theory advanced by Raymond Williams,[4] who rejects the concept that television programmes and advertising can be regarded as interruptions. On the contrary, she argues, the ebb and flow of daytime television reinforces the principle of 'interruptibility' that is crucial to the proper functioning of a woman in the home. In other words, the television experience is a profoundly decentering experience. In an essay on Baudelaire, Walter Benjamin has spoken of the 'art of being decentered', whereby the ordinary little man can make a job for himself in places like fun fairs, the jobs that flourish as unemployment grows. Daytime programmes too, says Modleski, and even more obviously soap operas, teach people to be 'decentered' (and it may be no coincidence that *Dallas* and its imitations have flowered at a time of economic crises and rising unemployment). In a sense the housewife is like the little man in the fun fair, unemployed but also perpetually busy. Her work, like the soap, is never done. Caught up in a variety of domestic and family chores, involved by her television programmes in the pleasures of a fragmented life, why ever would she wish to give her own life a clear sense and purpose? The many sub-plots of the soaps manage to keep her interested in several characters and their different destinies at the same time. If a story looks as if it is becoming too enthralling it is interrupted, by an ad or another story, which naturally takes up at the point where it was last interrupted . . . So the woman viewer continually has to gather the threads of unfinished stories again. Since, in the final analysis, advertising does no more than present the housewife with a mini-problem and its solution, the woman viewer will – after watching all the heart-rending unsolved dilemmas of the soaps – at least have the satisfaction of seeing *something* tidied up and set to rights, if only a stained shirt or a dirty floor . . .

The suggestion that the origin, structure and connotations of soap opera associated with a housewife's day hark back to radio broadcasting is repeated in many American studies.[5] They argue that the term 'soap' cannot be applied to productions scheduled during prime-time, where the visual is more important than dialogue (in other words, *Dallas*-type productions). In brief, the genre is characterised strictly by the times at which it is shown, the cheapness of the product and the type of audience. This is not the view taken by another 'historical' researcher, Dorothy Hobson, who places productions such as *Dallas* under the heading of soaps, although she acknowledges that it is a hybrid compared with the traditional formats.[6] According to Douglas and Wollaeger,[7] British and North American dramas (and perhaps those from other countries as well) can be grouped under two headings: one heading is seen as 'harmony' dramas, the other as 'disruption of harmony' (which can be broadened from the small group to society). By tradition, the soap opera as it is rigidly defined in previous studies comes under the first heading, whereas all drama productions in the broad sense come under the second. Most of the soaps produced in recent years, and the whole line of soaps inspired by *Dallas*, *Dynasty*, etc., combine both these characteristics – 'harmony' and the 'disruption of harmony'. In many cases they shed the over-verbosity, money is not skimped in their making, they go on the air in the evening and, as a result, are no longer aimed at a predominantly female audience. A combination of factors goes towards making the current product something different from, and more complex than, the original product, around which so many theories have been elaborated and to which so much thought has been devoted. The literature on *Dallas* reflects this complexity. It usually focuses on one aspect or another. Without claiming to offer a comprehensive bibliography, we shall try to list some of the thinking on *Dallas* that has been published at international level.

In mass circulation magazines such as *Time* ('TV's *Dallas*: Who-dunnit?', August 1980) or *Star* ('*Dallas* rocked by Miss Ellie legal battle', vol.12, no.25, June 1985), *Dallas* is seen in such a positive light as to be regarded as a stylesetter, capable in turn of generating 'sub-soaps' by slotting minor but 'strong' characters into stories that are perhaps more realistic but less successful than the original soap. (For example Ray and Donna, formerly in the parallel *Knot's Landing,* feature in a new programme, *Gary and Valene.* According to the critics writing in *Prime Time* ('California Dreaming', VI, no.3, March-May 1982), the decision to go for greater realism in examining 'the attitudes and perceptions of the average American', the 'absence of those "cult" and "glamor" trappings to be found in the richer Texan relation', meant that *Knot's Landing* did not really take off. Whereas *Dallas* can be regarded as a 'successful combination of both the sexual and the financial aspects of the beautiful life', *Knot's Landing* in the end is a 'cul-de-sac for the nuclear family'.

Horace Newcomb ventured an explanation of the '*Dallas* phenomenon' in terms of the 'nourishment that its creators are injecting into the veins of the public'. The average American does not want to see his or her 'contemporary image'. 'As a nation, we are actually growing older and developing the caution that comes with age. It is a time of decline, of recession and restriction, a time of real trouble. The grand old cities of the East and the Midwest are burdened with financial failure and bitter winters. Small wonder that the Sunbelt flourishes and *Dallas* leads the ratings.'[8] According to Newcomb, the really clever thing about *Dallas* is that it has transferred the old values of the Western to a new context of freeways and skyscrapers. The traditional fairytale has been dusted off and given a fresh coat of paint. It shows the family as a harmonious whole and Southfork ranch as a paradise to which everyone sooner or later, after a thousand complications, returns to sit down together for breakfast or dinner. This is how it is seen by S. Tee, writing in *Skrien* ('*Dallas*: het gezin van de week', no.118, May-June 1982). Also in *Skrien* (no.116, March 1982), in an interview with Stuart Hall by I. Ang and M. Simon, an attempt was made at a 'broader' reading of the popularity of *Dallas*, taking as the starting points those 'dusted off, painted up' traditional values. 'At a certain point,' says Hall, 'the programme attained a type of popularity that was not a popularity in terms of figures and ratings. I mean it had repercussions on culture as a whole. The viewers' involvement became something different. You couldn't help talking about the popularity of *Dallas*, because people were starting to refer to categories taken from the serial in interpreting their own experience. This type of "side-effect" popularity has now completely gone. People still watch *Dallas* today in the same numbers, but it is no longer a part of this collective cultural awareness. *Dallas* is now simply a popular programme.'

Among the many explanations of this popularity (and we shall be considering them in greater detail) is the explanation put forward in a report for the IBA (Independent Broadcasting Authority) by Mallory Wober in 1983.[9] It propounds two theories about *Dallas*, in relation to its British audience. The first is based on the socio-psychological aspect: *Dallas* transmits behavioural norms – rather than examples – to its fans. The characters' attitudes correspond to what viewers regard as 'normal' and 'appropriate'. The second theory asks us to consider the psychological connection between the thematic structure of *Dallas* and its attraction to the public. Although, as the IBA report seems to suggest, it may arouse 'positive' reactions in an audience, these two theories also explain why certain viewers reject its 'foreign-ness' and remain loyal to a more 'home-grown' product (*Broadcast*, 9 March 1984, 'Soaps Take the Ratings Cake'), and why it should trigger off negative reactions in those who are ideologically opposed to the 'Americanisation of tastes'. Jack Lang, for instance, the French Minister for Culture in the then Socialist Government of France, saw *Dallas* as the 'symbol of American imperialism', and Michèle Mattelart wrote that '*Dallas* casts tentacle-like shadows when the future of culture is being discussed: it has become the ideal Aunt Sally, the symbol of cultural impoverishment to be fought against.'[10]

The line taken by many Anglo-American researchers is outright rejection or, all too often, a view of *Dallas* as a text and a narrative structure surrounded by the various contexts in which it is placed. These researchers explain differing audience behaviours by interpreting the significance of *Dallas* to each one, certain premises remaining unchanged. According to Newcomb, on the other hand, many critics have seen *Dallas* as, at least potentially, subversive of established norms. In her book, *Loving with a Vengeance* (Methuen, 1982), the forerunner of many other works, Tania Modleski explains the essential function performed by the 'baddy' in the soap narrative. The baddy's role is to resist, not to submit or to acquiesce, and this resistance is charged with subversive significance. M. J. Arlen argues for the total instability of codes of behaviour, – 'a code whose specifics are in a state of flux or suspension – a code in which the rules have become destabilized and the players are making them up as they go along.'[11] While some people are disconcerted by this instability, to others it 'represents a potentially progressive form, enhanced by the serial, multi-plot structure, which does not allow of pre-packaged constructions or ideological stances.' According to Jane Feuer, 'The moral universe of the prime-time serials is one in which the good can never ultimately receive their just rewards, yet evil can never wholly triumph. Any ultimate resolution – for good or for ill – goes against the only moral imperative of the continuing serial form: the plot must go on.'[12]

Dallas is an 'incomplete text', affirms Gillian Swanson[13] (somewhat cautiously, given it would be hard in a partial analysis such as hers to pin down all the improbable endings of the various plots and their continual twists and turns in unforeseeable directions). But, she observes, the route towards the narrative core of the soap is interesting. 'The construction of the narrative is centred around the Ewing family, and it is their identity as a family which is the central standard around which relations are made and according to which characters are defined and events are constructed.' Going back to Lévi-Strauss and his study of myth, because – given 'the formation of themes in a non-linear way, referring both horizontally and through reflection in other thematics, vertically as well' – it would be too reductionistic to talk of 'neutral' television language, Swanson attempts to interpret 'the latent content through a model of binary oppositions and bundles of relations identifying conflict and opposition as the motivating elements underlying the narrative.' The family is central; there is:

> . . . a non-linear network of relations which cross-refer and form bundles of relations revealing a concealed and non-sequential deep structure, acting as a paradigm for other examples of the 'myth' or, in this case, acting as a base structure within which one can identify examples of correspondence and deviation between the episodes. It creates a two-dimensional time referent which is simultaneously diachronic and synchronic, relating backwards and forwards within the narrative flow and relating outwards to a context of alternative versions of the myth (episodes) in an attempt to formulate a structural law particular to the example involved and which would appear in variation within the system (serial).

Based on this assumption, according to Swanson, the relationships, characters and stereotypes – the details of which are filled out in the succession of episodes – are constantly dual: Ewing versus Barnes, positive versus negative. Unlike the Ewings, the Barnes are defined by what they do not have (Digger does not have Ellie and Southfork, Cliff does not have power, success and money, Pamela does not have a child of her own). The Barnes' family structure is a reversal of the natural hierarchical order: the son controls the father and the sister advises her brother. Quite the contrary is true of the Ewings, where, until his death, Ellie is subordinate to Jock and even JR has to obey his father! Each of the families, then, is subject in turn to dichotomous solidarity – unstable relationships which bind it to, and separate it from, the other family, as well as binding and separating its own members internally. The Ewing family is a unified structure, with firm rules by which all its members, original and acquired, have to abide but, at the same time, their compliance with stereotyped roles (the loving mother, the worthy son) represents a further source of conflict among them. The dangers of infiltration from outside by the rival family are reproduced internally by the threat to the codified roles from individual members. Sooner or later and in different ways, everyone tries to undermine family unity – from JR to Sue Ellen, from Bob to Pamela and so on. Each one is in search of personal happiness, but sooner or later each one has to submit to family conventions. As Laura Mulvey notes, the contradiction that is concealed in the melodrama is the impossibility of reconciling desire with reality. 'If the melodrama offers a fantasy escape for the identifying women in the audience, the illusion is so strongly marked by recognisable, real and familiar traps that the escape is closer to a daydream than a fairy story.'[14]

'Soap opera, melodrama and the "tragic structure" of feeling' is the heading of a section in a book by Ien Ang, *Watching 'Dallas'* (Methuen, 1985). This interesting, thoughtful work takes *Dallas* as a starting point for an analysis of the relations between popular culture and mass television. The author placed an advertisement in a magazine asking *Dallas* fans and detractors to write and tell her what they felt about it. Many of the people who replied were obviously aware of the thread linking the old melodrama to the present-day soap, 'a more or less conscious realisation of the tragic factor that exists in everyday life.' Recognition of the 'tragic structure' is the prerequisite for the 'cultural competence' to understand *Dallas*. Melodramatic imagination (in other words a refusal or an inability to accept everyday life as banal and meaningless, associated with a vague and inarticulate dissatisfaction with one's existence) is activated by *Dallas*, as in the past it was activated by other forms of culture. A sense of the 'tragic nature' of everyday life and a melodramatic imagination, according to Ang, have always been more highly developed in women but (as is apparent from some of the letters today), with less 'sex role stereotyping' and with many men's recent 'conquest' of the inability to show their own feelings, men too are able to express freely the 'pleasure' of melodrama. And since imagination is an essential component of our psychological world, the pleasure derived from *Dallas* – as a specific historical symbol of that imagination – is not that it compensates for the sameness of everyday life, nor that it is escapist, but that it is a *dimension* of that imagination. Because, as Ien Ang writes, it is only through imagination, which is always subjective, that 'objective reality' can be assimilated.

But while the definition of pleasure associated with the structural analysis of a text attempted by Ang is based on the way in which viewers subjectively 'read' the text, in the case of *Dallas* it is not quite like this. Viewers regard it not as a text but as a 'practice' – 'a cultural practice which is very much like a habit: accessible directly, casually and freely', just like looking at television. Many descriptions, sometimes combined with moralistic evaluations, have been given of this phenomenon, which is hard to explain in intellectual terms. According to the ideology of mass culture, most forms of culture derived from the American model, which attempts to align the contents of a product with 'universally consumable' motifs, are defined and denounced as 'bad mass culture'. It is a denigratory term, but it does not explain away the emotional attraction exercised by that culture, despite everything: critics start with open contempt, but move to irony and then self-mockery to neutralise the fascinating attraction of the genus. Now associated with everything that signifies a flattening out and the reduction to mass taste, this term is used by people who defend values and attitudes derived from different ethnic groups, histories and traditions.

In reaction to this, a counter-ideology came into being, the populist ideology to the effect that there must be total autonomy of taste – a useful argument for people who love *Dallas*, since it can be used against the norms of mass culture and since its ideas are based on common sense, the ideas that are acquired almost 'spontaneously' and unconsciously in everyday life. These ideas, however, can do little against an ideology – notes Ang – whose arguments 'possess great consistency and rationality' and are eminently intellectual. This explains why the ideology of mass culture is far more influential than populist ideology. The former has the advantage of being linked with people's cultural practices. Ang suggests that the normative predominance of mass culture ideology may also tend to provoke individual reactions in the practical form of preferences 'outside the norm'. This is, moreover, sustained by the populist position of rejecting any form of paternalism and aprioristic views as to the concepts of 'good' and 'bad' and eliminating any sense of guilt or shame over choosing one thing rather than another. The commercial culture industry has understood this very well and uses populist ideology as an argument for cultural eclecticism and for popularising the concept that it is impossible to express any opinion as to taste, any pre-set aesthetic judgement. But populist ideology can be applied not only for the purposes of commercial culture but also to what Bourdieu calls 'popular aesthetics' which, unlike bourgeois aesthetics, do not judge the artistic object according to 'universal' formal criteria but associate it with subjective passions and pleasures. This form of aesthetics is pluralist in nature and is fundamentally subject to conditioning, because it is based on the premise that the meaning of the cultural object differs from person to person and from situation to situation, on the affirmation of a continuity between cultural forms and everyday life, on a deep-rooted desire for participation and emotional involvement. What matters in popular aesthetics, in short, is recognition of pleasure, and the fact that pleasure is a personal matter. According to Bourdieu,[15] it is an aesthetics anchored in common sense, in ordinary people.

The ideology of mass culture ignores common sense and ordinary people and disregards the guiding criterion, that of pleasure – even in the little everyday things of life. The '*Dallas* phenomenon' thus becomes more understandable.

Among recent research on *Dallas*, of special interest is attempts to verify the various ways in which the story of JR and his family may be viewed in different national, social and cultural contexts. The aim is to highlight the active role of the audience and the process of mediation between the values encoded by the producers of *Dallas* and those decoded by the public. We refer, for example, to the field research carried out on broad audience samples by Tamar Liebes and Elihu Katz, to which we shall refer later.

On the theoretical level, there is an important study by our own Jean Bianchi, the author of research on the French serial, the 'feuilleton' (see Chapter 4). In his *Comment comprendre le succès international des séries de fiction à la télévision? – Le cas 'Dallas'*,[16] he gives an exhaustive, perceptive analysis of the various theories that have been put forward over the past few years in considering the internationalisation of television programmes. He proposes what he feels should be the guidelines for research on *Dallas* and similar programmes: the formal and structural aspects (the 'fiction-effect' as Bianchi calls it), and the function of cultural factors in the 'interpretation' of *Dallas*.

For reasons of space, we shall mention only briefly the first part of Bianchi's study, devoted to the international distribution of programmes, the internationalisation of television series and the various theoretical contexts against which the phenomenon is interpreted. There are basically three contextual theories: the Marxist-type theory of cultural imperialism (which has more recently given way to 'media imperialism'); the liberal-type theory of modernisation, to the effect that the current predominance of American programmes is simply due to market laws and is therefore bound to disappear; and the McLuhan-type theory of the homogenisation of television programmes[17] and the 'know-how of success'. According to the third theory, television now expresses a transnational culture which reinterprets and homogenises national cultures; the success of a programme depends on its following certain clear-cut production norms (with which the Americans are very familiar because of their many decades of experience), so that a programme can be shaped to suit an international audience. In the world today, it is argued, we have two televisions, one based on national culture, defined and confined by the particular nature of that culture, and an international television which packages international programmes. The fact that the latter is based in California does not necessarily mean it is American.

Cultural Codes and Modes of Decoding

As Bianchi observes, although the circumstances determining the relationship between the public and programmes are seen and assessed in different ways by the advocates of each theory, on taking a closer look one finds that the role attributed to the public in all three theories is the same: a passive role. The transmitter and the receiver are compared to communicating vessels positioned at different heights; in the process of communication, social values are seen as being transferred from the first to the second vessel without being modified in any way. This depiction of the popular consumption of cultural goods is unacceptable, as has been shown by Michel de Certeau[18] in the light of his analyses of elementary daily activities (reading, playing, talking, etc.). Although his analyses do not really constitute a theory in opposition to the theories we have described, they contribute a paradigm to the debate that directs research along other paths. It is what is known as the 'poaching' paradigm, as opposed to Lévi-Strauss's 'bricolage' paradigm which, although not elaborated with television as its starting point, sometimes alludes to television. Without retracing the debate on the degree of 'openness' of a work (the text of a book or a television programme),[19] let us say that it is nonetheless by definition an 'imposed' system, even when there is scope for interaction with the recipient (the recipient may assume an active role but will not be the one to create and activate the system). But the system is imposed in the sense that the physical structure of a city is imposed upon a person who happens to be walking through it, even though that person wandering within the system may trace his or her own route to fit in with their own interests and external conditions. The written and the television text are a reserve and a storehouse of forms waiting to be given a direction by the recipient. The poaching metaphor clearly expresses the margins of freedom established in an imposed system, the ability to go and hunt for food in other people's territory. It also highlights the set of behaviour patterns linked with the consumption of television. They are associated with space (the place in which television is consumed, the position of the television set in the room, the viewer's immobility and mobility, co-existence with other domestic activities), choice (switching over channels, pre-arranging one's evenings to fit in with a favourite programme, consulting television guides) and verbalisation (verbal underlining and spontaneous comments on what is happening on the screen, exchanging views about the programme with the others present when it is over, telling other people who did not see the programme what it was about). These practices are not simple peripheral residues of television consumption but expressions of operations forming an integral part of the reception process. To conclude, the poaching paradigm is an incentive, according to Bianchi, to rephrase the question of television consumption, releasing it from the constrictions of over-rigid and generalised theoretical parameters. This should be done by starting with three basic guidelines: 1) the form of programmes (in our case it is fiction, already to some extent determining the manner in which programmes are used); 2) the public's cultural codes, which act as a filter; and 3) the process of receiving programmes itself, something that is essential to an understanding of the type of consumption.

On the first point, Bianchi starts by criticising the traditional methods of content analysis which tend to identify certain contents, ideological themes and social values in a programme, viewing the programme as if it were a container, merely the outer peel that can be thrown away once the fruit has been squeezed to extract the themes and values. But a programme is not a simple vector of models; first comes a form that predetermines the contents being analysed. To disregard this fact entails a risk of misunderstanding the meaning and effects of television discourse, which can come into being only within a space structured in a given form. With regard to the programmes with which we are here concerned – serial fiction – it hardly needs to be pointed out that they trace their genealogy back to the radio serials of the 30s, 40s and 50s and that their forerunners include the serial stories published in magazines. But looking further back than those close relations, it is also clear that television fiction is a modern version of an age-old element of human society, the story and the story-teller. There is, then, a measure of continuity with the oral narrative tradition: the same management of social memory, the same art of telling a story, the same enunciative practice, the same manner of meeting the need for make-believe in which reality and make-believe are not in contradiction. Two approaches can be taken to the fiction-effect of television series: a) thought can be given to the way they are rooted in the mythical humus of society: and b) thought can be given to the way in which they are organised, according to a story-telling logic.

The analysis of the television message in the light of myth can illuminate – upstream – the genesis of forms of the message and – downstream – the manner in which that message is received. The myth can thus be seen as a mediator between the culture put into the programmes and the public's culture, in other words in the final analysis it can be seen as a potentially common language.[20]

Dallas draws on two rich veins of mythology. The popular tradition of the family saga is the source of many dramatic situations, and *Dallas* exploits them to the full: clan warfare extending from generation to generation; hostility between children (JR as Cain, Bobby as Abel, but also Kristin v. Sue Ellen and Pamela v Sue Ellen); every conceivable variation on the theme of conflict among heirs (legitimate children, bastards, adopted children); and the whole mythology of unknown origins, with sons and daughters in search of an unknown or vanished parent, and parents in search of lost children; and, in women, the contrast between motherhood and sterility, and so on. To this wealth of family mythology *Dallas* grafts elements of the American dream from the canonic Western genus, derived from a heroic mythology. The marriage between Jock Ewing and the old rancher's daughter is a mythical expression, set in a 'last-frontier' Texas, of the alliance between two generations of pioneers, the cattle farmers and the oilmen. The transition from one dominant class to another takes place within the family; in other words, there are no losers. The intrigues of big business are the contemporary versions of the duels between cowboys and oil prospectors. Here the violence characteristic of heroic mythology is expressed in a euphemistic code, confined to an exchange of telephone calls and cheques.

In a television series these mythical materials are expressed in the form of a fairly linear and obvious story, whereas in serials and soaps they are expressed in a more original and less easily decipherable manner. Continually slipping from one sub-plot to another, handling several story-lines at the same time, the soap is a pot-boiler in which the final ending to the drama is delayed as long as possible. It involves its audience not through the mechanism of high drama (quick-fire sequences of tension followed by crises followed by a *coup de théâtre*) which would fragment and disrupt the daily round of its audience, but by gently insinuating itself into the daily routine of millions of people. With its typical repetitive ritual, with stories designed to attract even people who are busy doing other things, the pleasure a soap conveys is the pleasure derived from habit, not from strong emotions, the pleasure that comes from a sense of familiarity, with the viewer identifying with the hero, the anticipation game promoted by situations that are a foregone conclusion. Although its structure is the same as that of a soap, however, *Dallas* does not seem like one of those 'gentle' narratives typical of the genre. It steps up the pace of the story, systematically and rapidly alternating characters and situations – humour and tears, plot-weaving and plot-dénouement, business and sentiment, etc.[21] The script is simple, veristic, stripped of metaphor and 'cultured' codes, so that it is as legible as possible. It is typical of the soap that sound should prevail over image, so that a whole episode can be followed without hardly ever looking at the screen (the names of the characters are frequently mentioned in the dialogue, to make it easier for the people listening to follow). There are many critics who perceive the characteristics of radio drama in *Dallas*. The subordinate role of the image and its 'visual poverty' (the absence of spectacle, strict rationing of location shots) is undoubtedly in part due to the need to produce cheaply, but in the end it fits in with the aesthetic and narrative codes of the soap genus.[22] It is sound more than image, Bianchi observes, that creates the emotional impact of the soap. While intensity of feeling is depicted in the facial acting shown in close-up, the quality of that feeling is expressed above all by voice-effects. It is the sound track that often conveys emotional colour, the tonality of the scene (including background noise and music), whereas the image merely expresses the gradation of sentiment. The concern for maximum legibility, for giving the viewer clear-cut points of reference, is also evident in the construction of the images.

At the beginning of each sequence, the camera unambiguously defines the time and place. The passage of time from one day to the next is indicated by night effects (often immediately preceding the break for advertising). A sequence ends with a close-up of the main character in the scene. Action is almost never depicted. The camera dwells endlessly, with long shots and reverse angles, on characters in conversation, who remain in clearly defined positions and rarely move from one place to another. There are no zoom shots, nor does the camera explore the space available. All it does is to record caricatural settings, through an accumulation of visual signs.[23] The same applies to the time factor: time is merely recorded, not speeded up or underlined by freeze-shots, and there are no flashbacks. The story unfolds according to the traditional popular logic of melodrama: happiness is intensely desired, comes almost within reach and is then frustrated by a series of misfortunes; social differences between characters persist even after they are married, because of family conflicts; heroes are undecided, torn by circumstances, often on the verge of a nervous breakdown, and so on. By this constant recourse in the story to the values of melodrama and by playing every possible variation on the theme that money does not bring happiness, *Dallas* exploits the unfailing secret of success and brings the fiction-effect to a point of high intensity.

Bianchi introduces his own analysis of the cultural codes of recipients and the concept of popular cultures when he refers to *Dallas* audience ratings in Algeria and Peru, two countries that are culturally far removed from the United States and from each other. The case of Algeria, where *Dallas* has proved very popular with the public (unlike Peru) is of particular interest. Algeria has a state television corporation, RTA, whose one channel beams its programmes throughout the country. One wonders why the television of an anti-imperialist, anti-capitalist state, the guardian of a social and family morality deeply marked by the Islamic religion, a pioneer of collective values (a single-party state with centralised economic planning), should wish to put out a programme so imbued with antagonistic, 'American' values. Moreover, the very authority that scheduled *Dallas* was simultaneously orchestrating protest at its ideological content in the Government-controlled press. It would seem that the state tried to exploit the message of *Dallas* (the criticisms were read by only a few but the programme was watched by a large majority of the population) to support changes in direction in Algerian policy in the 1980s: a slowing down of the nationalisation of the economy; diversification of the countries on which Algeria depends for its technology, with a more open attitude to the United States; an attempt to contain Muslim extremism without confronting it head-on. One reason for the success of *Dallas* was the connivance established between the Algerian public and the family clan as it is depicted in *Dallas*, with several generations living under the same roof, ruled according to the patriarchal ideal.[24] In Algeria, as in other Third World countries, the family group is a spontaneous form of unionisation to counteract the abuses and shortcomings of the state. There is no trace, moreover, of the state in the world of *Dallas*, whose ideology is Texan ideology and which rejects both the control and help of the Federal authorities.

Through *Dallas*, Algerians take a sort of revenge on the socialist, paternalistic state, which is represented in every public place by portraits of the president. *Dallas* makes up for the absence of a paternalistic state by proposing a very strong image: the image of Jock, a silver-haired but still vigorous *pater familias* whose sons obey him and who keeps his business affairs separate from his wife. It is a reassuring image, a patriarchal ideal close to the hearts of Algerians, especially now that it is under threat as a result of the destruction of rural society. With the security afforded by the presence of these old-fashioned models, the Algerian public can more easily cope with the new models of behaviour offered by *Dallas* and its divergence from the community tradition and the values of a socialist regime. The image of capitalism conveyed by the main character is seductive, a eulogy of risk, 'a dynamic vision of another future in contrast to the all too foreseeable future of planned socialism', an awareness of owing one's success to one's own and one's family's efforts rather than to the decisions of a remote bureaucracy. Pamela as she first appears is an acceptable model of female emancipation, combining traditional values (a sweet wife with a longing for motherhood, on good terms with her mother-in-law) and new aspirations (to be a career woman, to gain emotional independence, to develop the ability to take the initiative and to advise and help other people). This identification with family values mitigates the frustration of seeing this world of well-being and luxury. The sexual aspect is more ambiguous and controversial (although the explicit scenes are censored), as is the theme of illegitimate children in a society such as Algeria where the problem is widespread but not openly acknowledged.

In Peru, *Dallas* proved to be a losing card in the war between the two leading commercial networks.[25] It was scheduled on Channel 5 on Mondays from 9 to 10 in the evening (from May 1982 to March 1983), where it clashed with a comedy programme on Channel 4, *A cholo color*, built around the personality of Tulio Loza. In the role of a former lawyer of working-class origins, he poked gentle fun at Peruvian life and set himself up as an advocate of the little man under threat from the politicians. The programme was such a success that it sabotaged the launch of *Dallas* on Channel 5 (in 1984, Channel 5 took its revenge by 'poaching' Loza and his team from its rival – it is the same story the whole world over!). In Peru, then, when the public was offered a choice between an imported programme and a popular entertainment programme rooted in the country's own tradition, it opted for its own culture. Nevertheless the choice might have been different had the alternative to *Dallas* on the other channel been a programme less good than *A cholo color*. A comparison with Algeria is of only relative significance, since the audience had no alternative viewing in Algeria. But as we have seen, when faced with a programme offered/imposed by the sole television channel, the Algerians found it to their liking because it seemed to correspond to their own situation and their own culture. Are we to deduce, then, that in both countries the phenomenon of reception of television programmes is governed by dynamic processes which relate to the cultural identity of the respective audiences?

Nevertheless, notes Bianchi, cultural identity is a concept that is not easy to apply. It refers of course to the specific nature of a group, its history, its situation and its means of expression. But it also contains ambiguities possibly leading to sweeping generalisations that are only superficially true, and also leads to a dangerous ethnocentrism.

Taking this as his premise, Bianchi has tried to make it usable for analytical purposes by pursuing two lines of research: on the cultural codes of recipients, and on popular cultures. It is fairly common for one and the same television programme to give rise to a whole range of reactions, from enthusiastic acceptance to outright rejection, but this has not been studied in sufficient depth in contemporary communication theories. In Great Britain, drawing on Marxist and semiological sources, Stuart Hall has tried to elaborate a theoretical approach, starting with a definition of the television programme as discourse, as a syntagmatic form of meanings.[26] At one end are the programme production practices, the encoding practices. At the other end are the decoding practices, whereby the public reconstructs a meaning from the television discourse. All these practices do not just materialise out of thin air: their roots lie in the corpus of knowledge and structures of meanings within a given society, and they operate through the producers' social relations (in particular the rules of professional expertise) and the devices (audio-visual language) characteristic of the media. Even so, the encoding and decoding devices are not entirely symmetric. In encoding the programme, the producers supply the elements and map out the confines within which the message can be decoded. In other words, in practice they transmit one or more readings to the public from which others are free to choose. The public may adopt the readings suggested but it may also read the television message in other ways. There is thus scope in reception practices for an interplay between complicity with the codes incorporated in the message and resistance to those codes. This interplay will not be purely subjective and individual: because of their individual histories and ideologies, whole social groups will decode the messages in the light of one set of values rather than another. The public is not an indistinguishable mass of individuals, but a complex structure of many classes, groups and sub-cultures in which each group has its own identity and its own code. Referring to the work of Frank Parkin,[27] Hall identifies a typology of three positions that can be taken as a starting point for the work of decoding:

1) when the public adopts the same preferred meanings suggested by the producer, the situation is one of dominance or hegomony of the reception code suggested and shared;
2) when the public, without disputing the general meaning encoded in the message, relates it to its own situation and interests and in so doing interprets and adapts it in the light of those interests, we have what is called a *negotiated* position;
3) when the public, while recognising the code use to construct the message, interprets it according to an alternative set of values and uses a different logic in reconstructing its various elements, the reception code is called *opposition*.

Using this typology, Hall tries to contextualise the complex 'reading' practices; he argues that semiologists tend to relate those practices to simple linguistic competence and Marxists relate them to an abstract theory of ideology.

Hall's theoretical construct has been put to the test in field research by David Morley, based on the television news feature programme, *Nationwide*. It has confirmed the validity of Parkin and Hall's typology as a research instrument[28] and at the same time has shown the need for its refinement, for example by creating certain sub-divisions within the 'negotiated' reception category. This explains Morley's caution in arriving at generalisations from the findings of the '*Nationwide* project'. One of the reasons he advances to justify this caution is the observation that the recipient's cultural code is an inadequate key: the code has no validity in itself but refers to the cultural 'repertoires' and 'symbolic resources' of the various sub-groups making up the public. In other words, observes Bianchi, not everthing can be reduced to a simple algebraic encoding-decoding formula, without reference to the sedimentation of other social practices.

Popular cultures form a line of research which, according to Bianchi, will help us to allow for this sedimentation when considering the position of the recipients of the television message. It may illuminate reception practices from more than one angle. It can relate those practices to leisure activities, which television may prolong or replace (going to a match/watching the match on television), to the space in which those activities occur (with television part of 'domestic culture' rather than 'work culture' or 'street culture'), to the genesis of collective taste (television as a repository of traditional tastes but also as an effective vehicle for new, imported tastes) and finally to the consumption of other cultural products. After reviewing [29] the various schools of thought, both ethnological and sociological, which have contributed towards the sociology of popular cultures, and the schools that have propounded theories on the relationship between mass culture and popular culture – from the elitist pessimism of the first Frankfurt School to more recent theories in the 1970s legitimising popular cultures by acknowledging the autonomy denied to them when they are assimilated with standardised mass culture – Bianchi arrives at the conclusion that to understand the television phenomenon not only must a distinction be made between mass culture and popular culture but their likeness must also be highlighted.

Originally – in other words at the time of transmission – television is mass culture, manifestly standardised and industrial, but at the time of reception it acquires more of the distinctive traits of popular culture. There are then, it is argued, dual controls for the television phenomenon: mass culture on the whole controls production but does not always control reception, and when it does, that control is imperfect; whereas popular culture is almost non-existent in the production phase but is a strong force in reception.

The final part of Bianchi's study examines the third factor (the first two being the form of programmes and the public's cultural codes), as he believes it may help us to understand the international success of television series: the *process of reception* itself, defined as appropriation by a subterraneous, mute transaction – the most enigmatic facet of television communication. His analysis is set out in three short chapters under the headings of 'the aesthetics of reception'. 'the work of reception' and 'the ludic register of reception'. Here we shall confine ourselves to the second and in our opinion most interesting chapter. The term 'spectator's work' was used by Anne Ubersfeld in her studies on theatrical performance.[30] In the language of psychoanalysts, it means a deeply felt intra-psychic process of individual evolution, activated by specific circumstances (for example the work of mourning) and/or the elaboration of a mental state from pre-existing materials combined with precise mechanisms (for example the work of dreaming). This accepted meaning of 'work' could also be used to promote an understanding of the activity of receiving television, where the interaction between a programme and the audience receiving it takes the form of that audience's internal process of mental transformation and at the same time is an operation of elaborating a state and a meaning. To say that this process is internal is inadequate. It is subterraneous, largely unconscious and only rarely, and to a partial extent, brought to the surface by verbalisation after the event: in other words, it evades direct observation and can be treated only by means of interpretational techniques. We do not mean that it is fundamentally enigmatic. It is safe to assume that in receiving a programme the audience's reaction is of a transactional nature.[31] Each of the two parties to a transaction may choose what facet of its own identity is foremost in the process of communication. Nevertheless the receiver, the party not originating the transaction, is able to choose (and change) the modes of communication, depending on which of the three positions it is in (defined in transactional analysis diagrams as the three possible types of transaction: 'complementary', 'crossover' and 'two-way'). The control room for communication, what decides the choice of transaction procedure, is to be found in the recipient's 'ego'.

On what contents is the transaction based? In the field of television, where the receiving public can take its pick of what is on offer, the transaction takes on the significance of cultural appropriation. Basically television also has the social function of providing the public with constant reassurance as to the existence of practical values in a given society. The hypothesis advanced by Bianchi is that television offers day-to-day re-accreditation for the models used in everyday exchanges, it updates the rules of the collective game and it makes the borderlines of the credible and acceptable visible to more people. Faced with the small screen, the general public is engaged in a continuous transaction in the course of which the ways in which it senses its own identity, experiences its relationships, expresses its desires and frustrations, formulates its strategies, etc., are continuously being bolstered, re-adapted and re-appropriated by the comparison with the television message. The public's investment of imagination cannot be explained away as evading reality: it has a very direct function in that it serves as a cultural matrix.

An attempt to identify how this matrix works and how popular television series affect the public's values and models was made by the American, James W. Chesebro.[32] His typology of five systems of communication between programmes and the audience is constructed around the main character (in a soap) and his or her intelligence and ability to master situations, compared with the intelligence and ability of the public. For example, we have a system of 'ironic' communication when the main character's intellectual level and ability to steer a course through the obtacles and vicissitudes of everyday life are spontaneously perceived by the audience as inferior to its own. When the main character is an 'ordinary little man' like the viewer, the system is called 'mimetic'. When the main character is placed in a position superior to that of the audience, but merely because he or she has had the benefit of favourable circumstances, in situations not unlike those many people enjoy, the system is called 'leader-centred'. When the intellectual and moral stature of the key character is on an exemplary or heroic scale under exceptional circumstances, the sytem is called 'romantic'. Finally, the system is 'mythical' when the hero floats aloft in a decidedly higher sphere. Cheseboro grouped the series transmitted by networks in the 1974-75 and 1977-78 seasons in these five classes[33] and noted a steady increase in series following the 'mimetic' model and a drop in 'leader' and 'romantic' series; he found that the series – in the minority, moreover – based on the 'ironic' and 'mythical' models have remained more or less at a constant level. He then went on to compare these trends with figures on the American public's state of mind as revealed by opinion polls and arrived at certain conclusions. For example, the growth in the 'mimetic' model was linked with an increase in the number of Americans who were satisfied with their own lives and a decline in the public's confidence in its leaders. Cheseboro would undoubtedly have classified *Dallas* (which was not yet on the air at the time of his survey) in the 'leader' group, and he would also have noted, had he extended his research to the years thereafter, a 'Reagan-effect' in the form of a return to the values of power and authority.

Unfortunately Cheseboro did not go into sufficient detail in his analysis of the values and mechanisms of recognition/identification that determine the differences between his models of reception. According to Bianchi, who takes his own analyses of *Dallas* and other programmes as his point of departure, the processes of receiving fiction programmes can essentially be grouped under three headings. In the first category, reception may be direct, familiar and mimetic, in which case we find a connivance between the values conveyed by the programme and the audience's own values. Reception is an operation confirming, supporting and reinforcing the public's models of cultural identity. In the second category, the reception process/work often takes a less rectilinear and more dialectical course, in the sense that a distance is sometimes created between the content of the programme and the recipient's cultural identity by irony, diversity, etc. This occurs at the nerve endings, in other words the points at which the public's models are in a state of crisis or its values have not been fully consolidated. Appropriation is then not an operation entailing shifts and resistance, a partial redistribution of points of reference, a return to initial values or an exorcism. In the first category of reception, the television viewer is like a person listening to a story being told. In the second, he or she is like a person watching a theatrical performance. But these two forms, in their typical or ideal simplicity, are not the ones that occur most frequently.

The most common form of reception is a method of appropriating the television programme that functions on two levels, so to speak: faced with the wealth and variety of subjects and characters offered by the programme, the recipients carry out a stringent, continuous piece of editing, cutting out everything that does not interest them or that might threaten them while at the same time selecting and retaining the things they like – a character, an atmosphere, a special twist or turn of the plot, a setting, etc.

In the final analysis, therefore, the process of receiving a fiction programme consists of filtering its various elements and erecting a barrier behind whose shelter the viewer can consume whatever he or she wants to consume, and nothing else.

Dallas' 'American Message'

American television programmes readily manage to cross cultural and linguistic frontiers. It is a phenomenon so much taken for granted that there has been practically no systematic research to clarify the reasons for the success of these programmes and understand whether and how products so quintessentially American are understood. The statement that this phenomenon is part of a process of cultural imperialism presupposes: 1) that there exists an 'American message' in the content and form of those programmes; 2) that the message is perceived by the viewers; and 3) that it is perceived in the same way by viewers in different countries. But other hypotheses can be advanced as well. Many of these programmes are readily comprehensible more or less everywhere because of certain features: they tell superficial stories with stereotyped characters, they offer images of what are often very violent conflicts, and finally they are highly repetitive. This is partly true but it is not enough to explain the phenomenon. To begin with, *Dallas* can hardly be dismissed as merely superficial or action-filled. In fact *Dallas* is a fairly complex story, at least as far as family relationships and structures are concerned. It is a story that cannot be understood without its dialogues. But why then is it understood by viewers from other cultures?

This quotation is the introduction by Elihu Katz and Tamar Liebes to their research paper on *Dallas* presented to Teleconfronto 1983. Their final research findings have not yet been published, but sufficient material has been presented to conferences[34] for the novelty and importance of their work to be apparent. The reading of television programmes, declare Liebes and Katz, is a process of negotiation between what is happening on the screen on the one hand, and on the other, viewers' personal experience and culture, and it is also the outcome of an *interaction among viewers themselves*. This is undoubtedly the most novel factor by comparison with other research hypotheses and theories. In almost every country, programmes scheduled in prime time are viewed as a family or in company with friends. During and after the programme, people discuss what they have seen and thus build up a collective interpretation and opinon. *Dallas*, say Liebes and Katz, is a programme that provokes conversation and discussion.

In Israel to observe this interaction process 40 groups, each consisting of three couples, were formed (one couple was selected first and asked to invite two other couples from among their friends to join them) to view an episode from the second series of *Dallas*. They watched under real-life conditions: in other words the programme was viewed on the evenings on which it was shown on television rather than in the form of pre-recorded video cassettes shown to a sample audience, as is usually the case with this kind of research.[35] The people in all groups were of working- and middle-class origin and each group was ethnically homogeneous: Israeli Arabs, Russian Jews who were recent immigrants, immigrants of Moroccan origin and kibbutz members (10 groups per ethnic unit). Taken as a whole, they were regarded as a microcosm of the world audience for *Dallas*. The 'readings' that these groups gave of *Dallas* were compared with the reading given by ten groups of American viewers in the Los Angeles area. The discussion that followed the programme was informally guided by a moderator and recorded. It was followed by individual questionnaire-based interviews that included questions on the people with whom the interviewees normally watched and discussed the programme. The group discussions, according to Liebes and Katz, could be analysed as ethno-semiological data. Since the effects of a television programme are often inferred solely from an analysis of its content, they were interested in verifying the extent to which the audience was in fact aware of the messages which, according to critics and researchers, were being conveyed by the programme.[36]

Do viewers understand *Dallas*? What is the meaning of *Dallas* in the minds of the public, and does the meaning vary according to cultural context? To translate these questions into research operations, the first step was to ask the members of the viewing groups to give their own description of the narrative structure and the issues presented by the programmes. Of special interest were the relative emphases placed on the various issues (such as family or business), the way in which these were compared and discussed within each group, and the conceptual classifications used in the discussion. Would these classifications be universal models? Tradition? Personal experience? Television genres? The researchers were interested in how the viewers perceived the programme's 'message', in verifying whether the viewers had perceived any (positive or negative) correlation between such things as money and happiness, business and the family, in seeing whether *Dallas* was viewed as depicting the decadence of America or its supremacy. It was hoped that this type of analysis would, among other things, support one or other of two conflicting arguments: that popular culture is a hymn to the status quo, imposed (more or less deliberately) on the inert masses by the dominating classes (Frankfurt School, Schiller), or that it always has, by its nature, a subversive function with regard to those who hold the reins of power (Fiedler).[37] The researchers were also interested in raising another issue: what degree of identification or, on the contrary, of 'critical distance' may be discerned between the group discussions and the television screen?

Some of the groups might talk about the characters almost in the form of gossip, as if they were real people, analysing their motivations in everyday terms. Others might see their actions and attributes as symbolic functions and be more likely to resort to psychoanalytical labels in describing their motivations. There might also be a third level of analysis in the dynamics of group discussion: would there be an identifiable interaction among members of a group directed towards achieving a shared reading of the episode and characters, a collective judgement as to the extent to which an action was justified or realistic? And, if so, what routes would be taken in these consensus-forming and meaning-seeking processes?

It is obvious, observe Liebes and Katz, that the methodology thus described cannot offer a conclusive explanation of why American television programmes are so successful in other countries. 'We have chosen to study one of those programmes,' they say, 'as a starting point, to observe the mechanisms through which people understand, interpret and evaluate a programme, and to verify how these mechanisms operate in different cultures.' But in stating this premise the researchers may be erring on the side of modesty. *Dallas* is arguably a special case of its own and Liebes-Katz's research findings are not generally applicable to other programmes; even so, we feel it could legitimately be assumed that, were the same methodology to be applied to other programmes, the findings might not be altogether dissimilar.[38]

It is above all true that, in analysing the mechanisms of interaction between an audience and a television programme, Liebes and Katz have at the same time offered a convincing explanation for *Dallas*' international success. We do not know whether the four ethnic groups (five, if we include the Los Angeles sample) can truly be said to be a microcosm of the world audience, since they make up a standardised, if not homogenised, microcosm of ordinary Israeli citizens. This would be the only reservation regarding the Liebes-Katz research (but what about the replies given by the groups of Russian immigrants, deeply imbued with anti-capitalist ideology and class awareness?). The research data can be aggregated and analysed in several ways. In the preliminary reports presented up to this time (see note 37), Liebes and Katz have above all attempted to show how these findings might help us to consider two issues in particular in greater depth: 1) the use the viewer makes of the programme in thinking about his or her own life; and 2) the different types of reading and involvement.

In considering the first issue, three interpretative mechanisms and keys are identified. The first, termed '*moralistic*', consists of abstracting and generalising the supposed moral and supposed messages from the story. The second is '*pragmatic*': through what may be purely random mental associations, the viewer links events in the story being narrated to events in his or her own life. The third is defined as '*ludic*'.

The *moralistic mechanism* operates when the viewer assumes the role of a moral critic and, as such, identifies what he or she regards as an important issue in the programme and then analyses the stance taken by the programme-makers towards that issue. In accepting or rejecting the programme-makers' values, his or her own values are confirmed and reinforced. In the group discussions, the replies to questions about 'what is the message of *Dallas*?' and 'What does *Dallas* tell us about America?' essentially pointed up two themes, immorality and unhappiness, referring solely to two subjects – the rich and the Americans (are they synonymous?). This means that the messages generally perceived are that 'the rich are unhappy', 'Americans are unhappy' and 'Americans are immoral', often accompanied by the consoling comment that 'we are more happy' and 'we are more moral'.[39] The perception of those messages (an awareness of having been able to perceive them) may serve as an ideological alibi in the sense that not only does it offer consolation to those who can never hope to acquire certain things, but it also gives the viewer a licence to relish stories about luxury and betrayal, just as the message 'crime doesn't pay' permits a crime story reader to enjoy everything that happens without a pang of guilt. The replies given by the American and the Russian viewers are the exception to the general rule. The American viewers do not see the immorality or unhappiness of the characters in *Dallas* as conflicting with the message as to the pleasures and riches of American life, and they tend to reject the idea that *Dallas* contains messages of any kind. The Russians see the message and define it as a manipulation, although they regard themselves as immune by virtue of the fact that they have identified it as such (but, they say, the message will reap its victims among viewers less aware than themselves). In this way they find consolation not so much in the message being put out by the makers of *Dallas* as in the discrepancy between that message and the programme-makers' actual beliefs. In other words, the Russian viewer is equally critical of both the opinion that the rich are happy (and, in his or her opinion, the makers of *Dallas* are entirely convinced of this) and of the immoral logic on the part of the programme-makers in wanting us to believe the contrary.

The *pragmatic mechanism*, on the other hand (and it should be noted that the various keys may – and indeed generally do – co-exist within any one group and any one person), operates when the viewer identifies with certain aspects of a character's personality, interacts with the characters (through identification or by placing himself or herself in the opposite role or by recognising someone he or she knows well in a character) and explores the emotional and other implications of certain behaviour in relation to real life. In other words, viewers refer to their own experience of life in interpreting and evaluating what is happening on the screen, and vice versa. The logic is that 'JR is an unscrupulous businessman – all businessmen are unscrupulous, they have to be – my uncle has a business and he is unscrupulous'. A discussion on judges appearing in *Dallas*, and on whether or not they are open to corruption, led naturally to the question of whether Israel's own political system is as corrupt. These pragmatic/referential judgements are more open-minded than moralistic, more prepared to accept that the values that obtain in real life (and in the television programme) are many, varied and often conflicting. While the moralistic code suggests a hegemonic reading, according to Stuart Hall's typology,[40] the pragmatic code leads to mediated readings. Viewers are invited to identify not so much with the programme-makers as with the characters. In every group, many of a person's pragmatic judgements appeared to contradict the same person's moralistic reading of the programme. On the one hand the message was seen as 'the rich are immoral', while on the other the comments were made that 'you have to behave immorally to be successful' and 'success is something worth pursuing'.

With the *ludic mechanism* the viewer also identifies with certain aspects of the personality or problems of a character through lighthearted (but revealing) comments, which normally spark off joking replies from one or more of the other participants. It is at this level that the personal problems which sometimes colour an interpretation of the programme may come to the surface. Above all, it enables the viewer to identify with characters (such as JR) and situations for whom or which it might otherwise have been hard to display understanding or sympathy. It also enables people to face up to what may be difficult or at least highly emotional problems in relationships between the members of a group (as instanced by arguments about marriage and the respective roles of man and wife generated among some of the Moroccan couples by comments on JR and his women).

In their research, Liebes and Katz have been able to establish that the activation of one mechanism rather than another, the predominance of one key to the reading of *Dallas* rather than others, depend on the culture of an ethnic group, so that the prime and universal key may be defined as culture.[41] The data compiled suggest that whereas all groups give a referential judgment or reading of *Dallas* (the pragmatic mechanism), it is in the traditional groups (Moroccan Jews, Arabs) that such a judgment or reading clearly predominates. Readings of a metalinguistic type are relatively uncommon even among the more educated viewers in these groups, whereas they are considerably more frequent in the more westernised groups, the Americans, Russians and kibbutz members. Arabs in particular demonstrated a tendency to discuss the programme in moralistic terms and to take up what is simultaneously a defensive and participatory position on the programme. They discuss it pragmatically and seriously, but at the same time they reject it as a message in its substance, although they believe the apparent message that the rich are unhappy. It is this very type of decoding that the Russians, for their part, condemn as the most dangerous. While the Arabs defend and distance themselves from the programme in normative terms, the Russians distance themselves ideologically and reject the manipulation. Be warned, they say, they are telling us that the rich are unhappy because this is just what they want us to believe! The Russians also criticise the programme in aesthetic terms, comparing it with Tolstoy and other family sagas in their own country of origin. In group discussions they consistently view *Dallas* (and perhaps television in general) from a position of superiority, proving reluctant to talk about the programme in public out of a fear that their analytical comments might be misunderstood and interpreted as interest and approval. It is significant that only in the Russian groups did the researchers encounter suspicion and strong resistance to the use of a tape recorder, with many participants doubting the researchers' motivations and objectives.

Of an entirely different kind were interactions with the programme among the American and kibbutz groups, where there was a high rate of metalinguistic comment and where the viewers distanced themselves from the programme by tending to resort to the ludic mechanism. The moralistic mechanism was infrequent, and was not resorted to at all in the American groups. According to the Americans, *Dallas* probably does not contain 'messages'. Liebes and Katz suggest that the reason why Americans manage not to take *Dallas* too seriously is attributable not so much to a specific judgement on this programme as to the more critical detachment with which television is viewed in general, their familiarity with this medium being so much more intensive and long-established. This familiarity has not only created satiety but has generated a measure of sophistication in judging many television genres and their lightweight, transitory nature, combined with a certain cynicism as to their alleged realism.

Leaving aside the exceptional case of the Russians, perhaps the most interesting finding emerging from the group discussions is that non-Americans become far more involved in the programme than do Americans. In turn, this would paradoxically seem to suggest that closeness to a vehicle for culture and its makers generates less identification rather than more.[42] It may also explain the 'exportability' of *Dallas*. As others have pointed out,[43] *Dallas* surprisingly contains no specific cultural markers or indicators, so that it is all the easier for other cultures to read. Furthermore, it has been observed that television programmes with a precise cultural connotation are more successful in involving the audience, even a foreign audience, than in alienating them, and this is apparently the case with *Dallas*.[44] In consequence, the statement above about cultural proximity should be also tempered by consideration of the authenticity of the product. It is certainly ironic that *Dallas*, cited as an example of the worldwide success of American cultural imperialism, is a product that Americans themselves do not recognise as American in substance, although in form it is very familiar.

There remains the fact that *Dallas* has been a major success in almost every country in which it has been shown (the most significant exception being Japan).[45] Liebes and Katz have, in the course of their analysis of the mechanisms for reading *Dallas*, identified two elements in the programme which more than any others have helped to bring about this high degree of audience involvement: primordiality, and seriality. *Dallas* is a primordial fable, echoing vital mythologies in the history of 'mankind'. Take the Book of Genesis and look at the parallels between the Ewing brothers and Jacob and Esau in Canaan, each one competing with the other to demonstrate his superiority and win his parents' favour and the title of heir, while their parents conspire on their behalf. In Canaan as in Southfork, what matters is securing the continuity of one's line. In Canaan, this is done by seeking alliances with distant relations so as not to weaken oneself by assimilating everything that Canaan offers. In *Dallas* it is done by forming an alliance with rival dynasties, so that they can then be subverted from within. In the land of Canaan as in Southfork, women have problems with child-bearing; they fail several times in their mission of producing an heir, and are forced to give their consent to co-opting the children of others. They experience the tensions created by these other women – quite often their own sisters – living in the same house. There is one striking difference, however, between the women of Canaan and the women of *Dallas*: the former have far more influence over their husbands; between the two texts: the Bible favours the sedentary characters, the dreamers and the scholars, while *Dallas* favours the hunters and those who drink the cup of life to the dregs. We shall, murmur Liebes and Katz, refrain from saying that *Dallas* is more archaic than Genesis, even though this would appear to be the case . . . [46] The viewer has no difficulty in entering this mythical world and in drawing certain parallels, as evidenced by the way in which many members of the groups described the story of *Dallas*. Cain and Abel were sometimes mentioned by name. This acknowledgement of the mythical may be more or less sophisticated, more or less conscious, or may not be displayed in any way. What counts is the universality of the story. All the viewers, each one in his or her own cultural context and at his or her own level of sophistication, will discern in these family fortunes and intrigues an imprint of characters and events with which he or she is familiar because directly or indirectly they have experienced them. It is possible and at times probable that the viewer is so absorbed by these family histories as to block out all the other social and political realities, not even noticing their absence. It is at this point, obviously, that the phenomenon assumes a political significance as well.

The other element besides primordiality that secures audience involvement is seriality. We shall not go over everything that has already been written by others, especially regarding the complexity and ambiguity of the events and characters made possible by the 'open-ended' and potentially 'infinite' structure of the soap. We shall merely record some of the points made by Liebes and Katz, more directly derived from their theoretical approach and their fieldwork on the project. Unless we have misinterpreted them, Liebes and Katz suggest that seriality promotes a referential reading *within* the programme as well. The familiarity with the situations and characters created by seeing them week in week out leads to what has been described as a 'para-social interaction' – the viewer converses with the characters with approval or disapproval, wishing them well or ill, warning them of dangers, worrying about the shame or defeat to which they may be laying themselves open, etc. At the referential level, seriality often places the viewer in the position of knowing a character better than the character knows him or herself, thus reinforcing the viewer's urge to communicate with the character. The 'cliff-hanger' ending to each episode is reminiscent of the effect described by Zeigarnic, who argues that work broken off is remembered more than work that has been completed.

The involvement function of seriality also operates at the meta-linguistic level. Well-informed viewers may attach a label to the type of programme they are watching, define its attributes and dramatic conventions and compare them with others, recognise the constraints within which the programme-maker has had to operate, and identify the factors used in creating the story and characters. In short, when the viewers place themselves in a metalinguistic context they can do what they do not do at the referential level, i.e. fit all the various pieces together in a range of possible combinations. Involvement arises from realising that a story is like a competition whose result may vary, the pieces of which could be fitted together in various ways and whose characters may experience elementary sets of problems and changing relationships in rotation, all of which serve to keep the story going. In the long run, the characters themselves change and the viewer realises that the true pieces of the puzzle are not the characters (because they are never established and defined once and for all) but structural attributes, which may be redistributed among the various characters. For example, the goodies and baddies may not be restricted to battling against and overcoming each other but may exchange roles. This sort of puzzle or computer game calls on the metalinguistic viewer to predict the various possible combinations and follow the programme, if only to prove to him or herself that the combinations he or she predicted were right. All this is obviously very far from the linear narrative model as defined by Propp.[47]

Notes

1. 'The Rhythms of Reception: Daytime Television and Women's Work', in E. Ann Kaplan (ed.), *Regarding Television* (Frederick, MD: AFI, 1983).
2. *Silences* (New York: Dell Publishing, 1979).
3. American television networks divide their programmes into two main time bands, each with its own production policy, specific types of programmes and advertising policy. 'Daytime television' runs from about 10 a.m. to 4 p.m. and is the time band for soap operas, quiz programmes and talk shows. 'Prime-time' runs from 8 to 11 in the evening, and is the time for series, situation comedies and made-for-TV action films. *Dallas* has disrupted this schedule, being the first soap or serial to go on air in prime-time.
4. *Television: Technology and Cultural Form* (London: Fontana, 1974).
5. Muriel G. Cantor, Suzanne Pingree, *The Soap Opera* (Beverly Hills: Sage, 1983); Mary Cassata, Thomas Skill, *Life on Daytime Television: Tuning-in American Serial Drama* (Norwood, N. J.: Ablex, 1983).
6. *Crossroads – The Drama of a Soap Opera* (London: Methuen, 1982).
7. 'A Typology of the Viewing Public', in Richard Hoggart, Janet Morgan (eds.), *The Future of Broadcasting* (London: Macmillan, 1982).
8. Horace Newcomb, 'Texas: A Giant State of Mind', *Channels of Communication* vol.1 no.1, April-May 1981.
9. 'A Twisted Yarn: some psychological aspects of viewing soap operas', IBA Report.
10. A. Mattelart, X. Delcourt, M. Mattelart, *International Image Markets* (London: Comedia, 1984).
11. 'Smooth pebbles at Southfork', in Michael J. Arlen, *The Camera Age* (New York: Farrar, Straus & Giroux, 1981).
12. 'Melodrama, Serial Form and Television Today', Screen vol.25, no.1, 1984.
13. Gillian Swanson, '*Dallas*', Framework nos.14-17, 1981.
14. 'Notes on Sirk and Melodrama', *Movie* no.25, Winter 1977-8.

15. 'The aristocracy and culture', *Media, Culture and Society* vol.2 no.3, 1980.
16. Published in France by Laboratoire CNRS/IRPEACS of Lyons.
17. See Chin-Chuan Lee, *Media Imperialism Reconsidered: the Homogenizing of Television Culture* (London: Sage, 1980).
18. *L'invention du quotidien: 1. les arts de faire* (Paris: 10/18).
19. See in particular Umberto Eco, *The Theory of Semiotics* (Bloomington: Indiana University Press, 1976); Umberto Eco, *The Role of the Reader* (Bloomington: Indiana University Press, 1979); Hans-Robert Jauss, *Aesthetische Erfahrung und Literatische Hermeneutik I* (Fink Verlag, 1977).
20. See Gilbert Durand, *Figures mythiques et visages de l'oeuvre. De la mythocritique à la mythanalyse,* in 'Le social et le mythique. Pour une topique sociologique', *Cahiers internationaux de sociologie,* 1981, no.2; André Green, 'Le mythe, un objet transitionnel collectif', in *Le Temps de la réflexion* (Paris: Gallimard, 1980); Edgar Morin, *Le Cinéma ou l'homme imaginaire* (Paris: Editions de Minuit, 1956); Roger Silverstone, *The Message of Television: Myth and narrative in contemporary culture* (London: Heinemann Educational Books, 1981); François Pelletier, *Imaginaires du cinématographe* (Paris: Librairie des Méridiens, 1983).
21. But what precisely is the rhythm of *Dallas*? Giovanna Grignaffini, in 'JR: Vi presento il racconto' (*Cinema & Cinema*, nos.35-36, 1983, a special issue on 'the electronic story'), observes that 'the very short duration of each individual piece of action, the continuous changes of setting for scenes, the constant fragmentation of action and the proliferation of new cores of attraction' create an *impression* of great movement without any changes of note actually taking place in visual terms. Grignaffini concludes by wondering whether JR's mischief-making powers do not in fact consist of the fact that we are forewarned of each appearance he makes and we are presented with no more than a *promise* of a story.
22. From this viewpoint, it is not entirely correct to say that *Dallas* is 'forced' by the poverty of scenic resources to make prevalent use of dialogue (Giovanna Grignaffini, op. cit.). It is true that in *Dallas* 'people get married, break up, remarry, produce children, lose each other, find each other again, weave intrigues, get rich, die and so on without us ever really seeing these events acted out – we are informed of them, mainly through the dialogue.' But this narrative style in *Dallas* certainly does not give the impression of something put there *instead* of other approaches which would have been preferred had the budget permitted. It is a style legitimised not only by its success but by the professionalism that has gone into its creation.
23. See in Chapter 5 Bianchi's analysis of the use of close-ups, long shots and

shot-reverse-shots, and how these are integrated with the surrounding space in French films.

24. Jean Bianchi here cites the findings of a journalistic investigation by Joelle Stolz, 'Les algériens regardent *Dallas*', *Les nouvelles chaînes*, Geneva, IUED, pp.223-246.
25. Channel 5 is owned by Panamericana Television in the Delgado Parker Group, and is regarded as fairly close to Government circles. Channel 4 belongs to Compania Peruana de Radiodiffusion and is decentralised and regional in structure, being pluralist in nature. Its news programmes have the reputation of being more independent of the Government.
26. 'Encoding/decoding' in *Culture, Media, Language* (London: Hutchinson University Library, 1980). Stuart Hall is also the author of a famous piece of research on expressions of adolescent sub-culture within the British working class in the 1970s, in Stuart Hall and Tony Jefferson (eds.), *Resistance Through Rituals* (London: Hutchinson University Library, 1978).
27. *Class Inequality and Political Order* (London: Paladin, 1973).
28. This has proved workable in the sense that, in contrast to a Marxist summary reductionism whereby social class is assumed to be the essential discriminating factor, it has revealed other and not readily predictable correlations . . . See David Morley, *The 'Nationwide' Audience* (London: British Film Institute, 1980) and David Morley, 'Cultural transformations: the politics of resistance', in H. Davis and P. Walton (eds.), *Language, Image, Media* (Oxford: Basil Blackwell, 1983).
29. Bianchi, 'Le cas *Dallas*'.
30. Anne Ubersfeld, *Lire le théâtre* (Editrice Universitaria Romana, La Goliardica, 1984).
31. Bianchi considers it would be superfluous to verify the validity of this assumption in the specific case of the transaction concept as elaborated by the founders of transactional analysis. (Eric Berne, *Games People Play* (Harmondsworth: Penguin, 1971); Eric Berne, *Transactional Analysis in Psychotherapy* (London: Souvenir Press, 1975). He believes that a purely heuristic value is sufficient for the purposes of his argument.
32. 'Communication, values and popular television series. A four year assessment', in Gary Gumpert and Robert Cathcart (eds.), *Inter/media: interpersonal communication in a media world* (London: Oxford University Press, 1986, 3rd ed.).
33. Examples of the series classified by Cheseboro are: *All in the Family* (ironic); *Happy Days* (mimetic); *Maude*, *M*A*S*H* (leader); *Starsky and Hutch* and *Charlie's Angels* (romantic); *Planet of the Apes* and *The Bionic Woman* (mythical).

34. See the items listed under footnote 2 of the Introduction.
35. This makes for greater spontaneity of reaction, 'uncontaminated' by previously formed impressions or judgements if the episode has already been watched 'live'.
36. Our starting point, explain the authors, is not an analysis of the content of the text conveyed to an imaginary reader constructed by the text; we have proceeded inductively from real readers – and from a variation in their readings – to those aspects of the text that suggest various decoding levels and various forms of involvement. We can thus show how the two readers, the Ingenuous reader and the Critical reader, who clearly correspond to semantic and syntactic decodings, may in fact be one and the same person.
37. Leslie Fiedler, *What Was Literature? Mass Culture and Mass Society* (New York: Simon and Schuster, 1982).
38. The point must be here that Tamar Liebes and Elihu Katz's statement that 'the prime secret of the popularity of *Dallas* lies in its ability to activate many different types of viewers, unlike what apparently happens with other programmes' is belied by the researchers' own premise: they point out that for the time being they have confined themselves to analysing *Dallas*, with the warning that their analytical findings cannot be extended to other programmes.
39. These findings contradict other analyses of *Dallas* to the effect that the immorality in the programme is attractive for the very reason that it furnishes a pretext for discarding traditional moral codes. See Michael Arlen, 'Smooth Pebbles at Southfork', and Mary Mander, '*Dallas*: The Mythology of Crime and the Moral Occult', *Journal of Popular Culture*, no.17.
40. See above.
41 This may be an appropriate point to say that our presentation is based on our own independent summary and merging of various working papers, all of them interim documents as of this date. We would apologise to the researchers for any omission or inaccuracy on our part.
42. Liebes and Katz themselves, however, although more tentatively, express a reservation, wondering whether it is in fact the greater detachment of Americans from the medium, implying fewer defences, that may render them more vulnerable to ideological messages.
43. See Michael Arlen, 'Smooth Pebbles at Southfork'.
44. See the interesting study by Anne Hjort, 'When Women Watch TV. How the Danish female public sees *Dallas* and the Danish serial *The Daughters of War*' (Medieforskning, Denmark Radio, 1985).
45. Peru, as already discussed, and Brazil are the other exceptions.

46. Regarding the relevance of the mythical, see also the study by Jean Bianchi discussed above.
47. Vladimir Propp, *Morphology of the Folk Tale* (Austin: University of Texas Press, 1968).

3
Dallas in Europe

Many of the observations set out above on the mechanisms of interaction between audiences and programmes obviously apply to the European public as well. The microcosmic sample in the Liebes-Katz research project, by far the broadest and most systematic to have been conducted to date, does not of course include Europe in the geographical sense, but European culture is well represented (with kibbutz and Russian ethnic groups), even though – to repeat a reservation already expressed – it would be hard to gauge the shifts brought about by the values activated by their shared Jewish religion and their shared Israeli citizenship. Apart from that, however, bearing our research objectives in mind, what we were particularly interested in was the comparison between the reading and appreciation of *Dallas* on the one hand and the reading and enjoyment of domestic programmes on the other. In three of the countries covered by our research (Italy, Ireland and France), we set up viewing groups to which we showed, in each case, an episode of *Dallas* (the same in all three cases, the episode in which Bobby dies) and an episode from a successful homegrown serial. In the light of events, the methodology did not prove to be entirely adequate. The findings should be treated with some caution, since the samples were small: generalisations based on the data collected should be regarded in many cases as merely indicative. Even so, many of the findings are not without interest and at least have the merit of being the only ones available. In the case of Denmark, we had the good fortune to be able to link our project with research by Anne Hjort (*op. cit.*), although progress with the work – both ours and Hjort – was too far advanced for us to use the same methodology (for example, the Danish research had been conducted solely on a female audience).

In Great Britain, the data cited have been taken from an extensive piece of research by Geoffrey Lealand, published by the Broadcast Research Unit.[1] The British case is of special interest in that potentially the country is more open to American programmes (if only because the two countries speak the same language) but at the same time there is a good deal of hostility to imports from the USA at least among the critics. On the whole this hostility is based on preconceptions (i.e. that British television programmes are the best in the world while American programmes are bad, stupid and boring) and a reluctance to admit that these preconceptions may be misguided.[2] This may explain why, in the introduction to Lealand's report (and it may be no coincidence that Lealand is not a British citizen and does not have to respect the judgements or share the prejudices of British critics), the Broadcast Research Unit disowns the author's conclusions, although it acknowledges that they are stimulating and controversial. In considering the findings as they relate to Great Britain it should be borne in mind that foreign programmes may not be scheduled for more than about 14% of the total number of hours of television time and that they may not take up more than a given quota of peak viewing times.[3] This means that British audiences are not exposed to massive doses of American programmes, unlike the Italian public, for example – Italy being the country at the other end of the scale, with the highest exposure in Europe.

It might be considered logical to suggest a correlation between intensity of exposure, competence/knowledge and viewing and popularity ratings, particularly in the case of the first two factors cited, but from the little information in fact available the contrary would seem to be true. For instance, whereas Japan devotes less that 5% of its total broadcasting time to imported American programmes[4] and New Zealand over 40%, the viewing and popularity ratings for those programmes are more or less the same in the two countries.

The comments and observations emerging from interviews and group discussions in the four countries (Italy, France, Ireland and Denmark), following the showing of an episode of *Dallas* and an episode of a domestic serial to sample audiences, build up a fairly standardised picture of viewers' readings, as well as coinciding with many of the reactions to *Dallas* recorded in the Lealand survey in Great Britain. The variations among countries are matters of stress rather than content. The only substantial and noteworthy difference lies in the greater detachment or lesser degree of identification among the French and Italian groups, whose reactions to *Dallas* appeared to be both more superficial and more critical than those in the three other countries.

Among the reactions common to all groups in all countries, those arising most frequently are the 'aesthetic pleasure' derived by the viewer from *Dallas*, the function of *Dallas* as an escapist programme, and the character of JR. In most cases the reactions and observations are fairly general in the sense that they express the most obvious and immediate things that spring to mind when someone is asked to explain in a few words what most struck them about, and attracted them to, a programme. Many viewers mentioned the combination of 'beauty and wealth' and the glamour of *Dallas*:

> But apart from the plot, what is always nice is that you are looking at beautiful pictures, beautiful women, beautiful clothes, beautiful settings, stupendous houses – it's a feast for the eyes . . . (Italy)

> In programmes like *Dallas* and *Dynasty* I like to see how the other half lives . . . I like the glossy fantasy of some of the programmes. In England we go too much for kitchen sink dramas – sometimes we have to live through them in real life and on top of that we have to look at them on TV when we want to enjoy ourselves . . . (Great Britain)

> There's no way in the world that I'd be able to afford anything that's in it, it's a waste of time looking at it, do you know. But it's like looking at a painting or looking at anything like that, it looks attractive . . . (Ireland)

It *looks* so beautiful. Perhaps it really is beautiful. But this is irrelevant for any practical purposes, because the audience knows that, true or untrue, it is a far-off world, like the worlds described in fairy tales. And the public accepts it and enjoys it as it stands because:

> We really need this form of escape, the times being what they are . . . (Great Britain)
>
> I normally enjoy *Dallas* as light, unrealistic entertainment, very unrealistic . . . (Ireland)
>
> You escape from a boring existence for a couple of hours . . . When you watch *Dallas* there's always something happening. Everyday life is nothing like that, is it? . . . (Denmark)
>
> I sit down in front of the TV and I don't think about anything. At most I go for a character, I think 'let's hope this or this happens to him'. Like children with cartoons . . . it's a cartoon for adults, a big photo romance story which sets you dreaming for a moment. Then you came back down to earth . . . (Italy)
>
> It's fine for the very reason that it doesn't make demands on you, it shows a world far removed from our own, a very wealthy world, so that it has those aspects . . . of the exceptional which grab you. It's nice to dream that you're swimming in champagne for half an hour . . . (Italy)
>
> It's a fairy story. Even though unpleasant things happen you take them light heartedly . . . they have problems but you don't agonise over them. I just watch like that, as I watch the ads . . . (Italy)

Dallas is a 'fairy story' above all for lower to lower-middle class viewers, whereas the more educated viewer is less likely to take it too seriously, basically because it is seen as an artistically inferior product. For the educated viewer, the characters are stereotypes with whom it is hard to identify. For less educated viewers this obstacle does not exist; indeed they prove to be more 'competent', in the sense that they see the stereotype as an inseparable and necessary part of the fiction. This is, we feel, one of the most interesting findings revealed by Anne Hjort's research in Denmark. In other words, if our interpretation is correct, a working-class viewer, who is not highly educated or conditioned by such education, may prove to be a more perceptive and pertinent critic of television than others.

The world of *Dallas* is one where daily life is action-packed but at the same time burdened by problems; by comparison, a housewife's life may, it is true, seem dull, but not beset by such major problems. But *Dallas* is also a dramatisation of daily life in the world of the rich and powerful. According to Äse, a 50-year-old working-class woman:

> It is like real life, but life in the upper classes. But the same things can happen among less wealthy people, they can really happen. I mean, a man with lots of women . . . there are wives who stay at home because it is the husband, a plumber for example, who works to earn a living, but wives like this still have to solve the problem of how to fill the time. They can't always go on expeditions to the supermarket or have a cup of tea or whatever. In fact, the problems are exactly the same . . .

What Äse is doing is reinterpreting *Dallas* in terms of everyday life as she sees it: a bored wife, a husband who has little affairs on the side in his odd moments. So *Dallas* is not regarded as 'unrealistic' but as *something that might be real*, perhaps not in one's own case but in others.

In almost all the discussion groups, observations on the fairy-story and escapist dimension of *Dallas* are always accompanied by positive views as to the professionalism of the programme ('it's well made'). These views are almost always of a general nature, except for a few references to 'pace', staging and camerawork. In some of the replies given in Britain, professionalism is seen as a result of the high budgets invested in programmes by Americans. The British are also the most critical, in that some people define as 'excessive' the glamour, the elegance of the clothes ('They all look so elegant and well dressed, like tailors' dummies') and more or less everything else. The criticisms sometimes refer to the 'technical' aspects of production as well, from the sound track ('too noisy') to the editing, and even details such as the credit titles at the beginning and end, 'which go on and on for ever'.[6]

In all discussion groups, the negative comments made by those who do not like *Dallas* are often the mirror image of the approving comments, as in the case of the British comments on glamour cited above. But there are people who condemn *Dallas* wholesale, in a few (but isolated) cases from the moral viewpoint (wealth is regarded as a negative value), in other cases with regard to the narrative structure and credibility of the characters:

> The characters seem to move in a sort of Olympus . . . they are completely abstract, in a rarefied atmosphere . . . (Italy)

> It is too superficial . . . otherwise they would have had to extend each episode over longer periods and change the dialogues completely . . . All they ever do is to outline things . . . they don't go into detail . . . something is always missing . . . But in a way it works . . . (Denmark)

The group discussions confirmed the absolutely central role of the JR character, which often seems to be a decisive factor in determining the relationship between the audience and the programme, without in any way detracting from the importance of the Bobby character. The two characters, moreover, define and reinforce each other (what would the 'baddy' do without the 'goody' and vice versa?) in a story which authoritative scholars have acknowledged as biblical:

> JR has an evil look, when I saw his look I used to feel all funny inside . . . (Italy)

> I hate JR, he's a scoundrel . . . (Italy)

> But now that Bobby is dead I feel all knotted up inside . . . (Italy)[7]

> [Bobby is] lovely, very kind and considerate and never hurts anybody and he's handsome and he's romantic and he's a very good swimmer(!) . . . (Italy)

> I could actually actively dislike him [JR], you know, any time I hear his voice or even see him on an ad, I just want to remove myself from him. His presence just offends me . . . he would walk over anyone to

get where he's going and nothing or nobody's going to stop him . . . (Ireland)

> I mean, seeing JR in bed with all the women is the most off-putting thing . . . it happens so glibly I mean, it's the using of a woman all the time. He's taking her to bed to get some inside information from her. . . (Ireland)

> That bastard . . . (Denmark)

> He is so popular because he's so unpleasant, because he makes us feel so many different things . . . (Denmark)

> Well, everyone doesn't like JR, still they love him . . . he's just a person that you hate and you love at the same time . . . (Ireland)

As is evident from these examples, the opinions expressed are often more stereotyped and banal than the characters. Even so, there are more analytical and perceptive comments. For example, an Irish woman viewer 'read' Bobby as follows:

> I didn't like him because of the way, I mean he has left a trail of women because he didn't have the courage and the guts to stay with any one of them . . . there was Pam, if he had been a stronger character she wouldn't have had to leave . . . she was strong to go off and do that, but he wasn't . . . I mean his treatment of women, inevitably he doesn't have the courage to be one thing or the other and he's been led constantly by whatever is easiest to benefit out of . . .

A Danish woman viewer, already cited by Äse herself, distinguishes between JR as a person and JR as a character:

> He has a good part, he brings in colour . . . not because you can like him as a person, but without him the serial would be worthless . . . it's because of him, JR, that everything happens . . . .[8]

As may already be apparent from the comments cited, our research findings on the European public unequivocally show that *Dallas* has gained a hold mainly over female audiences; however that may be, the most significant comments have come from women, which is hardly surprising. In *Dallas* women do not have a say in things and are continually being humiliated by their husbands and lovers. It is only natural that the way they are treated should spark off reactions of anger and solidarity in women. The male characters in *Dallas*, observes Hjort, thus become targets against which women can project their suppressed aggression. 'This is why so many people like *Dallas*, it makes you so furious!' (Bente, housewife, 25). Most women, notes Barbara O'Connor in commenting on the findings from the Irish discussion groups, expressed critical views as to the episode of *Dallas*,[9] but at the same time they said they had been emotionally involved. The most significant differences encountered in the reactions of the Irish groups to the American series were gender-based: women reacted ambivalently, while the men reacted by almost total rejection. In the men's discussions, no reference at all was made to specific characters or situations: the tone of the discussion differed from the women's mainly in that they distanced themselves more through jokes and heavy irony:

> I watch it sometimes . . . for a good laugh . . . there is that element of knocking it for some reason . . . and just an incredulity that the producers of it, I mean, maybe I watch it again and again to see are they really serious. Do they expect me to get involved in this? Or are they seeing it as all a big leg pull?

> I found it was the most boring thing to go through that . . . for me, eh, it was funny in the places where I don't suppose it was intended to be funny . . . In the early stages, maybe, you would be inclined to believe some of it but now that it's entered into the realm of make-believe, the total make-believe, then well, it's actually got better for the wrong reasons. I found it much more enjoyable, I mean I recognised that I wasn't meant to find Bobby's dying enjoyable . . .

This is a type of involvement that could in short be defined as 'subversive'. It is interesting to note that many men, while saying that only rarely have they watched *Dallas*, seemed to be very familiar with the characters. When asked to explain this apparent contradiction they replied (a striking example of the concept of 'centrality' in popular culture)[10] that it would have been difficult not to know about *Dallas* since 'everyone was talking about it':

> ... it's sunk into the whole culture in many ways. Like you go out for a few drinks or something and, you know, *Dallas* is quite likely to crop up as a legitimate subject of conversation ... and people will talk and talk and talk about it and 'do you remember this happened and do you remember that happened?' ... everybody knows that JR is the bad guy ... you just need to say JR and everybody knows what you mean ...

Many members of the men's discussion groups expressed the opinion that *Dallas* is a programme that women like because it tells what is both a romantic and a tragic story,[11] and almost all the men said they were unable to identify with the characters emotionally, not only because – as some of them observed – those characters' emotional world was very far removed from their own ('it goes over our heads') but also and above all because of the sense of boredom generated by what they saw as very unrealistic events:

> I was just bored right through the whole thing ... there is no plot of any significance in it, they are all trivialities around romantic relationships ... they get divorced today and the same couple get married again tomorrow, that doesn't happen in Ireland[12] ... at least if you do get divorced you can get married to somebody else but not marry the same person again and, eh, the whole plot is romance, romance, romance ... it's all romance and that to me is not a plot.

Nor does the male Irish viewer manage to identify with, or even merely be interested in, the power struggles among the characters in *Dallas*. From this viewpoint, the replies given to the interviewers (whose questions were designed to elicit why, despite all this, there are more male viewers of *Dallas* than of any other soap or serial) were all negative. Their lack of interest was explained by the fact that the male viewer sees it as impossible that he might ever be placed in similar situations.

> It's hard to visualise yourself being in a position of power to that extent. You might get promoted, you might become ambitious and your job, say, getting yourself up to a position . . . never to be talking in millions and millions . . .

or by the fact that the resolution of the conflict is too predictable:

> You know that JR in the end is going to come out on top and Cliff Barnes is going to be the loser again . . .

The fact that these gender-based differences in assessment emerged far more clearly in the Irish discussion groups than elsewhere is undoubtedly attributable to the different ways in which the groups were made up in Ireland; two of the four groups of ten people each consisted entirely of men and two entirely of women.[13] This presumably meant that discussions flowed more freely within each group, without the inhibitions created by the critical presence of people of the other sex who might have expressed diametrically opposing views. Even so, the same differences in involvement were encountered to a less marked degree in discussion groups in other countries. In the Italian sample, for example (consisting of 80 people as compared to 40 in other countries), women became far more caught up in the plot and characters than did men, expressing a more varied range of views. In the British audience, according to the Lealand survey, the popularity of American programmes was greater among the women.[14] In France too, the findings from our discussion groups confirm that female audiences are more involved, although this is manifested in less direct, less obvious and perhaps less personal but no less 'feminine' forms. For example, fewer women than men called the *Dallas* and *Chateauvallon* stories 'modern'. Our analysts have suggested, in the light of comments made within the groups, that this might be due to an awareness among women that the female characters in these stories are never in fashion or out of fashion in their way of dressing but are in a sense outside fashion.

One might be tempted to infer that the points made and theories advanced elsewhere regarding the success among women of a genre originally created for and directed towards a female audience have been shown by our research as equally applicable to Europe. For the purpose of our research, however, the question of whether or not *Dallas* belongs to the 'soap' genre is pointless.[15] We should merely note two points: the involvement of a good deal of the female audience has been 'guided' by a critical sense, leading to a dissociation from the values proposed;[16] conversely – even in countries such as Ireland where male audiences have proved more critical and have given a more 'subversive' reading of *Dallas* by comparison with the values encoded by the programme-makers – male viewers are nonetheless involved, if only in terms of social television-linked practices (*Dallas* as a subject of conversation, as a 'cultural event').

Bearing this in mind, as we come to the end of these notes on audience readings, what we regard as a more interesting point is that it was the female audience who suggested a far more significant key to the reading of *Dallas*: we refer to that key that Ien Ang, in the study to which we have referred several times, has defined as 'emotional realism'.

In her chapter on '*Dallas* between reality and make-believe', Ang examines the reactions of viewers who identify or think they identify 'realism' or the 'absence of realism' as the factor they love or hate most in *Dallas*. *Dallas* is not realistic, its critics say, because its situations, characters and events do not coincide with 'reality'.[17] The only reality, some people feel, is the reality of ordinary people (and their 'real' problems: unemployment, housing, etc., which are not at all the same as the 'pretend' problems of the rich). Another set of people thinks that reality must be recognisable, in other words comparable to the viewer's own reality; and yet another group considers it should be 'probable', or 'normal'. Finally, there are the people who think a story is unrealistic if it simplifies reality through exaggeration or clichés. This view, based on a comparison between the internal and external realities of a text, may be defined as 'empirical realism'. But such a concept of reality raises not a few problems. First of all, it is based on the premise that a text can directly and immediately reflect the outside world, whereas we know that every text constructs its own version of reality and is the outcome of a process of selection and interpretation. Furthermore it offers no explanation as to why on earth so many viewers see *Dallas* as a realistic experience. Is their reading wrong? Does the viewer not know what reality is? The explanation cannot be so simple. Whereas, according to the empirical concept of realism, the thematic contents of a text form the basis for an assessment as to its realism, what is called the 'illusion of realism' is created by the way a story is told. The illusion that the text is a faithful reproduction of reality is achieved by suppressing the structure of the text.[18] The creator of a text must suppress all traces of their own creation in order to create an illusion of naturalness and spontaneity. The story must be told in such a way that the reader or viewer does not even notice the existence of a story-teller (this is the so-called 'classic realistic text').[19] This narrative style is common in the cinema and its rules and conventions have been developed and refined to the peak of perfection by the Hollywood school. The reason we no longer regard these rules as rules is merely that we have grown so accustomed to the language that we no longer recognise it as such. *Dallas* too abides by these rules to a great extent. The camera shows only what is essential to an understanding of the event taking place; one scene follows on another in natural sequence, with no 'time or space leaps' that might break down the illusion of narrative coherence and continuity. That illusion is reinforced by the strictly chronological order of the story line (even flashbacks are presented as an exercise in retrospection in such an explicit way as to rule out any possibility of misunderstanding). According to MacCabe[20] and others, it is this very artificial illusion of reality that is the source of pleasure. The viewer is enabled to forget that it is make-believe: he or she manages to feel a sense of intimate familiarity, and the apparent 'transparency' of the narration produces a sense of direct involvement so that the viewer can behave as if the story were really happening.[21] It is the *form* and not the content of the story that produces pleasure. And yet, observes Ang, this explanation of pleasure cannot be regarded as entirely satisfactory, because it does not take account of the content of the story being told. Not all texts that are transparent in narrative terms generate equal levels of pleasure, and it is unthinkable that *what* is being told in the story should not contribute towards producing pleasure.

Why then do so many viewers define *Dallas* as realistic? A text may be read at different levels. One is the literal, 'denotative' level of what the story is about (the obvious, literal content of the plot: the characters' actions, the ways they react to each other, etc.). At this level, Ang's research findings clearly show that the world of *Dallas* is not seen as realistic; on the contrary, it is viewed as remote from reality. But the text may also be read at the 'connotative' level, in other words for the meanings attributed by association to elements in the text. What is striking, notes Ang, is how the viewer defines situations and characters in *Dallas* as unrealistic at the denotative level but then 'recognises' them at the connotative level:

> What happens in this serial is something you would never, but never, come across in the course of your life or in your circle of acquaintances . . . A pleasant thing which has a semblance of humanity, is not so unreal as to prevent you from having a relationship with it. Inside there are recognisable things, recognisable people, recognisable relationships and situations.

> We are not rich like them. I too know, in real life, a monster like JR. Except that he is just an ordinary builder . . . Yes, these are really the ordinary everyday problems that you find in it, more than anything, and you recognise them there . . . Because those problems and intrigues, the major and minor pleasures and pains, they happen in our own lives as well.

In a sense, observes Ang, citing Roland Barthes, viewers of *Dallas* find the elements that for one reason or another are important to them and ignore the others. It is this 'rhythm' between what is read and what is not read that creates pleasure. In testing the realism of *Dallas*, for example, these viewers disregard the denotative level of the text. They do not know the practical circumstances of the characters' lives, but they pick up the situations which are symbolic of more general life experience: the quarrels, intrigues and problems. It is in this sense that *Dallas* is in fact defined as 'realistic' since, at the connotative level, the viewer mainly attributes emotional meanings to it. And it is also in this sense that the realism of *Dallas* may be defined as 'emotional realism'. This explains why the concepts of empirical realism and classic realism described above are not enough to understand the experience of realism described by *Dallas* audiences. In both, the cognitive-rationalistic idea predominates, both are based on the assumption that a realistic text offers knowledge of the 'objective' social reality. But the realism cited by *Dallas* viewers is altogether unrelated to cognitive perception: what is recognised is not knowledge of the world but a subjective experience of the world, in other words a 'structure of feeling':[22]

> Now I can tell you why I like watching *Dallas*:
> 1. There is suspense
> 2. It can also be romantic
> 3. There is sadness
> 4. And fear
> 5. And happiness
>
> In short, there is simply everything in that programme.

It is in this 'tragic structure of feeling' that many viewers seem to recognise themselves and therefore perceive *Dallas* as 'true', and it is precisely this that creates pleasure.[23] The realism of *Dallas*, then, is produced by a psychological reality and is not connected with its (illusory) reflection of external reality. One could go so far as to say that in *Dallas* 'internal realism' is combined with an 'external unrealism'. People naturally like the external manifestations of the imaginary world of *Dallas* as well, but it is because they are stylised: those beautiful women, those beautiful clothes, those beautiful houses and so on. It is this very glamour that makes the viewer aware that this is an imaginary world he or she is watching, so that the illusion of reality is not total. Furthermore, recognition that this is an imaginary world does not preclude criticism. The audience reactions analysed by Ien Ang reveal a distance between the 'real' world and the imaginary world, and Ang suggests that it is mainly because the viewers are aware of this that they can freely indulge themselves in the emotional world of *Dallas*.

The importance of 'emotional realism' in the processes of interaction between the audience and *Dallas* as recorded by Ang in her research in the Netherlands is reflected in significant ways in the research in Denmark and Ireland – more than in other countries. This cannot be regarded as accidental when one considers the audience samples analysed. Anne Hjort's research in Denmark placed the stress on female audiences, as did Ien Ang in the Netherlands,[24] whereas reactions that might be related to the concept of 'emotional realism' in the Irish research were recorded in the women's discussion groups in the Irish project.[25] As a Danish woman viewer comments:

> It plays on our feelings, of course it does; we can identify with whatever is happening. It's not just 'entertainment', as we say it is . . . I believe it is emotional – I only realised this when we were talking just now about why we like it . . . I believe that it has something to do with all this emotional coming and going.

So, comments Anne Hjort, the fascination of *Dallas* lies in the tension between security and insecurity, which means that those emotional states associated with the need for harmony, happiness and success are constantly under threat. When the viewers abandon themselves to the *Dallas* experience they abandon themselves to an emotional alternation, from one emotional extreme to another, from harmony and devotion to aggressiveness in quickfire succession. In the words of Gitte, aged 36, a slaughter-house employee:

> Look, as in this case. You see Miss Ellie on the stairs with Jock and she says 'Everything's OK, isn't it?' but you have just glimpsed JR up there, 'the bastard'. So you are absolutely lost, 'oh, it's so sad', and then you say 'bastard' again [laughs] and so forth . . .

One finding highlighted in the Danish project is worthy of note: while *Dallas* undoubtedly depicts many problems inherent in human relationships (loneliness and unfaithfulness in the episode analysed, 'Julie's return') so that the viewers can recognise themselves in it without having to refer directly to their own experience, making it easier for them to discuss those problems, *Dallas* also tackles those emotional problems in a superficial manner. The feeling of frustration to which this gives rise is clearly evidenced in some of the interviews, Hjort observes: obviously, it is not one of the purposes of *Dallas* to go into these problems in depth; they are used to attract the viewer and are then just dropped (and the viewer with them) as soon as the goal has been achieved. The purpose is to sell the product, not to share human experience. And yet the audience allows itself to be involved: 'It's superficial . . . but it works.'

But perhaps it works, one is tempted to suggest, *for the very reason* that even the superficiality, even what Hjort defines as a sense of frustration, are functional to the narrative mechanism which knows how to bait a trap to involve the viewer. Once the trap has worked, to dwell on psychological details might generate effects opposite to those being sought. Delving into things means defining, specifying, proceeding from the general to the particular. For every one viewer who might become even more closely involved as detail is added to detail, ten other viewers might be lost along the way. As one goes into greater and greater depth, the area of identification (with situations, the attributes of a character) might shrink correspondingly. In other words, can it be postulated that the size of the audience that may potentially be involved is proportional to the universality of the stereotype? The reply is probably 'yes' in the case of programmes aimed at the international market. This would obviously be a prerequisite, but it would not be enough on its own; the other conditions would be the quality of the product and the subject covered. A national (or regional) stereotype in a programme, for example an Italian stereotype, may and generally does trigger off *different* processes of identification and involvement, and may and generally does attract a broader audience than the audience for *Dallas*. But only in Italy. We should point out here, to avoid misunderstanding, that we do not consider the stereotyping of *La piovra* [*The Octopus*] to be 'national'. We shall return to this point.

As for 'emotional realism', it should be pointed out that, in the light of what has been said by the *Dallas* scriptwriters quoted at the beginning of this chapter, we could hardly define it as an original, still less a subversive, reading of *Dallas*. On the contrary, one is tempted to say (using Hall's typology) that here we have a reading corresponding to a 'hegemonic' situation (with the audience adopting the same preferential meanings as those proposed by the programme-maker) or at most – but only in a few cases – a 'negotiated' situation. According to the *Dallas* scriptwriters:

> Here in *Dallas* you can always find something of yourself. Everyone needs love and seeks it just as Sue Ellen seeks it, although perhaps not quite in the same way, everyone betrays people and is betrayed, and so you watch *Dallas* and you feel you're not so alone as you thought . . . People can imagine themselves . . . at Southfork, they can identify with that way of life, perhaps with a few more worries about money matters but with the same emotional problems as the Ewings . . . [26]

The research in Ireland has also shown that the critical attitude towards *Dallas* and soap opera in general does not inhibit emotional involvement:

> I watched it for Pam and Bobby to get back together again but sort of realised emotionally, those two, to get back together again . . . but realistically she's a selfish conceited little wagon and he's weak and he's a bloody heel and he never says what he means, he never seems to decide anything . . . I did watch it, yes, because emotionally it makes me want to watch it but logically it's just so stupid . . .

But this is mainly because, comments Barbara O'Connor, women showed themselves to be particularly aware of the romantic utopian element in the Bobby and Pamela love story:

> So Pam and Bobby . . . obviously . . . still love each other but they were the star-crossed lovers, you know, and it's really attractive, so from that point of view when I saw them getting back together again I bawled my eyes out, I thought it was beautiful . . .

Quoting and concurring with Ang, O'Connor points out that the women in the Irish groups were also aware of the lack of empirical realism but could identify with the 'emotional realism' of *Dallas*. While realising that the lifestyle portrayed in *Dallas* was totally unrealistic they saw the interpersonal aspects, the problems, traumas and so on as

Victoria Principal as Pam and Patrick Duffy as Bobby in Dallas

being similar to those in their own lives:

> In terms of reality that is extremely realistic. Not . . . the way that the plot was resolved, not that he'd walk outside the door and her sister would drive down and murder him, but in terms of love affairs, it constantly happens day in and day out that a couple would be separated for whatever reasons and they would get back together again and something happens and splits them up again . . .

The remarks quoted were all made by middle-class women. In the group made up of less well-off women, the absence of comments on the Bobby and Pamela love story is significant. What prevailed here were expressions of sympathy for the Sue Ellen character and even a degree of sympathy for the JR character, whereas the middle-class women's views of JR were embedded in a feminist discourse.

Although the samples were too small to warrant generalisations, we feel that sufficient information is provided by the research on viewing audiences in the various countries to arrive at certain conclusions, even if only for general guidance:

1) *Dallas* satisfies and arouses the 'emotional competence' of women viewers;
2) In general it is essentially an escapist programme, hardly ever being read from an ideological viewpoint;
3) The most critical audience is the group of younger viewers, irrespective of their social class;
4) Educated viewers, both young and not so young, are very critical;[27]
5) Men are less involved than women;
6) *When faced with a choice between 'Dallas' and a good quality domestic programme, a majority of the audience opts for the latter*, which consistently obtains higher audience ratings.

While audience viewing figures for *Dallas* peak at about 7 million in Italy, *La piovra* [*The Octopus*] never fell below 8 million and at times reached viewing figures of over 16 million.[28] These figures are all the more significant in that *Dallas* is easily the most popular American serial shown in Italy (*Capitol* has an audience of about 3 million, *FBI* about 4½). This is not confined to *La piovra*, a fairly exceptional case: other Italian serials are more popular with audiences than *Dallas*. To mention only those programmes covered by our research, we find that . . . *E la vita continua, Voglia di volare* and *Quei 36 gradini* all achieved audience ratings of 9 to 12 million (although the figures were lower at times for episodes shown on Wednesdays). Even the fairly modest *Casa Cecilia, un anno dopo* had an audience of 8 million for at least one episode. It is also significant that a series such as *Caccia al ladro d'autore*, clearly inspired by the American made-for-TV action film, had a relatively small audience (7 million).

In Great Britain, *Dallas* reached its peak viewing figures of almost 20 million (39% share) in November 1980 with the 'Who Shot JR?' episode. In the same year it featured twice in the 'Top Ten' programmes nationwide[29] (once in second and once in seventh place). Since then, although its audience is stable and fairly substantial, *Dallas* has never returned to its initial ratings but has in fact declined in popularity; the only exception occurred in the last week of October 1983, when it headed the top ten programmes shown on BBC1. It was still sixth in May 1986 but by December of that year it was no longer up among the first 20 (with a 25% share and just under 13 million). It has always been outrated by the more popular English programmes, *EastEnders* and *Coronation Street.*[30] In the ratings for mid-January 1987, *EastEnders* came top, *Coronation Street* second, *Crossroads* 19th, *Dallas* 22nd *Emmerdale Farm* 31st, *Dynasty* 58th and *Brookside* 83rd. Among American programmes, *The A-Team* has recently pulled ahead of *Dallas*.[31]

In Ireland too, although doing better than *Coronation Street*, *Dallas* has never outperformed the Irish serial, *Glenroe.*[32]

In West Germany, in the first week in which it was shown (exceptionally, no fewer than four episodes were broadcast in the first week), *Schwarzwaldklinik*, produced by ZDF, was competing with *The Thorn Birds*, scheduled by ARD. The German serial beat the American mini-serial by a wide margin, acquiring an audience of 24.6% million, i.e. a 62% share, compared with the 27% share achieved by *The Thorn Birds*. Barely two months later, in June 1986, the audience for *Schwarzwaldklinik* rose to over 28 million. Today close on 50 million Germans have seen at least one episode of the serial. At the height of its success, each episode of *Dallas* was watched by about 22 million people. It was the success of *Dallas* that persuaded ZDF to produce *Schwarzwaldklinik*. Although in content it is derivative of certain genres firmly rooted in Germany,[33] it is very 'American' in influence. This was not the first time that the Germans have 'copied' American programmes: it happened with *Traumschiff*, the German version of *Loveboat* (audience rating 25 million in January 1984, 58% share). *Heimat* too might not have come into being had it not been for the success of the American mini-serial *Holocaust*. Have the pupils outstripped their masters? The reply must be in the affirmative, but it should also be qualified. American television has not just offered models of production and content. Its influence, as we shall see, has been far more radical, since it has legitimised, even in West Germany, certain types of television that had previously always been viewed with a jaundiced eye on the grounds that they were too 'popular'. Not even *Schwarzwaldklinik* holds the record for audience ratings, although it has come very close. The most successful format in the whole of Germany's production of serials, one which constantly dominated the audience ratings, was the police series (*Der Kommissar*, 1969-76, over 30 million), well ahead of the most popular American series of this type like *Colombo* and *Kojak*.[34]

France is the only country among those covered by our research in which *Dallas* for a time topped the audience ratings, although at the time there was no French serial to compete with it and the finding is not significant. What is more significant is that our groups of viewers, on being shown an episode of *Dallas* and an episode of *Chateauvallon* ('*Dallas* à la française'), lumped the two programmes together in expressing a negative judgement, the differences between the two seemingly being matters of detail and nuance. The same adjectives were used to describe both stories: not interesting, superficial, banal, plodding . . . The French programme was liked more (or perhaps, more accurately, disliked less) than *Dallas*. But although the latter was regarded as 'boring' and 'slow', *Chateauvallon* in turn was defined as 'very boring' and 'very slow'. *Dallas*, according to our audience sample,[35] has more 'pace', it is more lively, it has more action, more care is devoted to the settings, its situations are more coherent, the acting is better and it is a more professional product. Feelings and emotions are put over more forcefully – perhaps, it was remarked, in terms that are too black-and-white. The characters in *Chateauvallon* are less stereotyped, closer to real life. Taken all in all, however, apart from these differences, the two programmes were regarded as essentially 'all the same thing', to a point at which criticisms often seemed to be directed more against the '*feuilleton*' (serial) format than at either of the programmes in particular. In France too, the strongest and most damning criticisms came from educated viewers (and from regular cinema-goers), who only occasionally watched fiction serials, whereas less educated viewers and people who watched television all the time were fairly indulgent and on occasions quite approving in their views. Bearing in mind that, in the scripting of *Chateauvallon*, recourse is made to cinematographic techniques not to be found in the highly standardised scripting of *Dallas*, it is hardly surprising that a viewer who is also a film buff should be more critical of *Dallas*.[36]

France is the only one of the countries in which no difference of note was found between the sample audience's liking of *Dallas* and its liking of a homegrown programme. This is certainly due in part to the fact that *Chateauvallon*, more than any of the other domestic programmes analysed in France and other countries, most closely follows the *Dallas* model. Other factors may well have had a bearing as well, although these cannot be inferred from our data.

In Italy, the national programme compared with *Dallas* was an episode of *La piovra*.[37] As was to be expected, viewers tended to prefer the latter. In the discussion groups, it was read in different ways, in some cases not very dissimilar to the same people's readings of *Dallas*. In fact, differences in views and appreciation of *La piovra* arise from the different ways in which the leading character is viewed, with opinion on the police superintendant, Cattani, being reflected in, or transformed into, views on the programme itself. According to most people, Cattani is a positive character, a 'hero', despite all his human weaknesses. Others, while not denying the character's good qualities, also mention his indecision and passivity when faced with events, a presage of the final 'loser' resolution of the plot. The first type of reading appeared to correspond to a strong liking for the programme, the second in most cases to a highly critical view. The programme was defined as 'sad' and 'depressing'. There was almost unanimous consensus as to the realism and social relevance of *La piovra*, but not everybody liked it:

> I prefer to watch *Capitol* or *Dallas* rather than something that I know is real . . . In fact I don't need a screenplay, I only have to open a newspaper if I want to find out about the mafia . . .

Realism, however, was seen as the main factor differentiating *La piovra* from *Dallas*. It is certainly the reason why most people saw the Italian production as 'involving you a good deal on the emotional level, with a wealth of human content . . . fascinating even though it is so sad'. It is obvious, however, that in the Italian case this audience participation is altogether different from the 'emotional realism' evidenced by readings of *Dallas* in other countries. In the referential readings of the viewer of *La piovra* it is not the private sphere, the affections and personal relationships that are involved but the viewer's social sphere. Emotional involvement here calls into question the viewer's status and conscience as a citizen, it acquires a moralistic connotation. In the case of *Dallas*, there are virtually no referential readings related to either the private or public sphere; there is no identification. It is pure escapism: 'you are caught up in it', but it does not involve you. Nevertheless, in some cases the pleasure of escapism may be undermined by something close to a feeling of guilt:

> *Capitol*, *Dallas* and *Dynasty*, the TV soaps, are not your problems, I want to know what is going to happen next, if there is a drama, I have a little laugh about it but at the same time you get caught up in it. The mafia is not part of everyday life . . . I need to dream. When it comes to the evening I'm dead beat. I might look at the programme on the mafia for information, but subconsciously I prefer something lighter. I have my own problems, I need to get away from things for a little while and to see something undemanding before I go off to sleep. Perhaps I agree that they are making these programmes because so many people don't read the newspapers, and so they're a little better informed . . .

On this subject, the researchers conducting the audience analysis[38] observe that 'the treatment of an "important" subject implies that *La piovra* should *also* be able to meet the viewer's needs for information, updating and "intellectual commitment", and above all gratify the viewer's self-image by conferring a social and cultural value on the act of watching. *Dallas*, on the other hand, is perceived as a programme for people who want "to get away from realities", "not to have to think". Watching *Dallas*, then, is accompanied by a slight dose of guilt. To be a fan of "*Dallas*-type things" is considered to be socially downmarket, although to a differing degree from one person to another.' (But, as we have seen, there are also people who regard the choice of an escapist programme to be perfectly legitimate and not downgrading).

There is, however, a key applicable to the reading of both programmes (and it is on this level that *La piovra* was most liked): the symbolic reading, the perception of both stories as a battle between good and evil, the good guy and the bad guy. There can be no doubt, we feel, that the secret, perhaps the main secret, of *La piovra* is to be sought in its judicious combination of the realistic with elements derived from the classic model of the Hero fighting against Evil.[39] Realism prevails, obviously, when the viewer is denied a happy ending, since such an ending would be essential in an unadulterated classic model. The classic model in turn prevails in that Superintendant Cattani is kept alive when he would certainly no longer be with us were the rules of (mafioso) realism observed. A 'serious' film and an escapist film are not necessarily mutually excluding definitions. To say that a film is escapist is not necessarily a negative connotation. Reading a good novel after a hard day's work may be escapist, but that novel is nonetheless a good book. Having stated this, as an escapist film *La piovra* functions better in other countries than in Italy, for obvious reasons. It was no coincidence that *La piovra* has been perceived, appreciated and hailed outside Italy also (sometimes above all) as a *detective story*. Take the comments of the German press on *Piovra 2*: 'Once again Superintendant Cattani's new advertures contain all the ingredients that go to make up a good crime story: excellent actors and gripping action'; 'with the links between the routine and the exceptional . . . maximum suspense from first to last'; 'an extraordinary detective story'; ' . . . up against the mafia, we have an orgy of tension, a thriller accompanied by outstanding dialogue.' This is not to say that the police genre obliterates everything else. For example: 'It is not just a political thriller showing the probable but also an Italian social psycho-drama, a daring unveiling of national shame and a very moving human story of a family.' In an Italian review of *La piovra* too, the thriller dimension of the programme did not go unobserved and was much appreciated. The discussion groups saw the pace of *La piovra* as tauter than that of *Dallas*. Even so, among both the reviewers and the viewers' groups, the stress was always on the topicality and realism of the story. Only one member of the 80 in the discussion groups confessed to liking *La piovra* because 'I like police stories.' One last comment: in Italy, the strongest reservations expressed on the subject of *La piovra* (and *Dallas*) came from young people.[40] This reflects a finding in other countries as well: younger audiences are more critical, and their criticism appears to be directed more against the serial genre as such than against specific programmes.

Notes

1. Geoffrey Lealand, *American Television Programmes on British Screens* (London: Broadcasting Research Unit, 1984). Lealand is a citizen of New Zealand.
2. See Chapter 4.
3. Quotas are not laid down by law. In the BBC's case this is a voluntary, self-imposed restriction. In the case of Independent Television (ITV), quotas are negotiated and agreed with the television companies and the Independent Broadcasting Authority.
4. It has been suggested that the very low percentage in Japan is due partly to the fact that Japanese television programmes are made along very much the same lines as American ones.
5. We shall return to the question of 'realism' in *Dallas* a little later when we discuss the findings of the Danish and Irish research projects and the interesting study by Ien Ang, *Watching Dallas: Soap Opera and the Melodramatic Imagination* (London: Methuen, 1985).
6. These British comments, however, relate to American serials in general, not exclusively or necessarily to *Dallas*.
7. This type of comment, together with the others quoted, reveals a high level

of audience participation/identification. In the audience survey people were also asked to identify the three main characters in *Dallas*. These were the Italian replies:

	1st character	2nd character	3rd character
JR	42	13	10
Bobby	33	34	10
Sue Ellen	5	14	36
Others	0	19	24

8. JR, it has been observed, reflects and fits in with the distinction women make between love and sex: 'As a man, he is very attractive, but if I were his wife I think I would kill him.' Thus JR is transformed into a sex object, but he is decidedly not the type of man a woman would want to marry.
9. The episode is the one showing the death of Bobby, the same as was used for the French and Italian discussion groups. In the Danish project, on the other hand, the episode came from a previous series, which was shown in the United States in 1981 ('Julie's Return').
10. In the sense described by Stuart Hall above.
11. See the 'tragic structure of feeling' in Ien Ang, *Watching Dallas*.
12. This is a very odd observation; it contrasts what is seen as unrealistic, over-the-top make-believe with what happens in real life, citing an example which appears to be altogether unrealistic since divorce does not exist in Ireland!
13. Our Irish colleagues justified this decision by the fact that it would have been impossible to ensure that all the desirable variables were included in each group because of the small size of the sample (40 people). They felt, therefore, that the priority should be sex and social/educational status, forming two women's groups (working-class and middle-class) and two men's groups (also working- and middle-class), making sure that all age groups were represented in each group (minimum age 20, maximum 60).
14. See some of the replies to the questionnaires:

	Men	Women
There are too many US programmes on the TV	43.3%	37.8%
I like US programmes very much	4.6%	4.7%
I like them	25.0%	28.1%
I don't like them	17.8%	13.5%
I don't like them at all	9.2%	5.6%

15. An analysis of audience reactions to *Dallas* has nevertheless confirmed that this programme cannot be grouped with the classic genres but may be regarded, as already pointed out, as the forerunner of a new genre,

diverging from the traditional soap in that it is shown at different viewing times (prime-time rather than in the afternoons), in its more complex context and narrative structure, and in its brisker pace.

16. In this respect it is interesting to compare these reactions with those of the Algerian women cited above.
17. One example of the lack of realism cited by the audience: when people are so rich, how on earth could three families find it convenient to live in the same house without any privacy except for their bedrooms (not even separate sitting rooms or studies)?
18. J-M. Piemme, *La propagande inavouée* (Paris: Union Générale, 1975).
19. Colin MacCabe, 'Theory and Film: Principles of Realism and Pleasure', *Screen* vol.17 no.3, 1976.
20. Colin MacCabe, 'Theory and Film', and 'Realism and the cinema: Notes on some Brechtian theses', *Screen* vol.15 no.2, 1974.
21. In this context, when a film or television narrative is said to be transparent, the adjective refers to the function of the screen: a transparent window on the events taking place in the story told by the film or television programme.
22. The concept of the 'structure of feeling' was evolved by Raymond Williams. See, for example, his *Marxism and Literature* (London: Oxford University Press, 1977).
23. On the concept of the 'tragic structure of feeling', see the discussion earlier in this chapter and in Chapter 2 of Ien Ang, *Watching Dallas*.
24. Where the universe from which the sample was drawn consisted of (women) readers of the magazine *Vivia*.
25. See Chapter 4.
26. Since the interview was conducted in 1983, when *Dallas* had been on the market for more than five years, these comments by the scriptwriters could be regarded as a rationalisation of their work after the event. The authors may have more or less consciously assimilated the reactions of viewers and critics to their work. It is an interesting hypothesis which might itself be worth researching. We merely put it forward for the sake of objectivity. Nevertheless, we feel that from the context of *Dallas*' narrative strategy, it is reasonable to infer that the observations quoted are perfectly consistent with that strategy and not a belated discovery by scriptwriters trying to explain to themselves the reasons for their success.
27. In many cases this is a 'blind' criticism, in that the person has not seen the programme but bases his or her view on a general prejudice against a certain type of American programme.
28. *Piovra 2*, 5th episode, 16½ million (46.7% share), *Piovra 1*, 1st episode, 8

million (last episode, 15 million).

29. These ratings were published by BBC Audience Research. Other listings were published by the IBA. The two bodies now produce a unified list under the auspices of the Broadcasters' Audience Research Board (BARB).
30. See Chapter 4.
31. The most popular American programmes over the past few years have come under the heading of mini-series. In January 1984 *The Thorn Birds* reached viewing figures of over 15 million, and its third and fourth episodes came fourth and fifth in the top ten list. *The Winds of War* had audiences of between 11 and 14 million.
32. See Chapter 4.
33. Among others, 'Heimatfilm' and 'Artzfilm'.
34. It is also likely that, at least at the beginning, German producers based their police serials on American models as well.
35. In France as in other countries, except for Italy, the sample consisted of four groups of ten people each.
36. As is obvious, since the sample was so small certain correlations must be treated as only indicative. Nevertheless, it should be pointed out that the statistics on the use of leisure seem to suggest a correlation between the consumption of television and cinema attendance figures, although it is not easy to decipher the figures. In Italy, 11.6% of people who watch television 5-6 hours a day go to the cinema. Among those who watch 3-4 hours of television a day, the percentage rises to 48.4%. Below a certain level of television consumption (2 hours or less a day), cinema-going also declines (37.7%). Unfortunately, the figures do not specify frequency (once a week, once a month, ten times?) and it is difficult to arrive at any significant conclusions (Source: ISTAT). According to research conducted in 1986 by InterMatrix Italia on behalf of AGIS (Associazione Generale Italiana dello Spettacolo), it is rare for a film-goer not to be a regular television viewer as well. Someone with an average-to-high rate of film-going tends to be a low-to-average television consumer. According to 1983 figures, 53% of cinema-goers watched 4 or more films a week on television as well; 39% watched 1-3, 8% watched less than 1. Over the past three years the rate at which films are watched on television has probably risen. The same InterMatrix survey showed that today's cinema-going audiences are very modern in their values and patterns of behaviour. The socio-cultural profile of this audience does not coincide with the profile of television audiences nationwide.
37. It is the episode in which Superintendant Cattani's wife decides to go back to France (after the break-up of the marriage), their daughter decides to

stay on in Sicily with her father, and a sentimental liaison starts up between Cattani and Titti.

38. Mesomark, with Luigi Pizzamiglio acting as consultant, on behalf of RAI's Audience Opinion Service.
39. On this point we do not agree with the observation by the Mesomark analysts, who think that there is a *limit* (to the power to satisfy audience expectations) for realistic portrayal in that, by confusing and blurring the 'good' and the 'bad', it would hamper the process of symbolisation and idealisation. Besides, we do not feel that this conclusion is justified by the replies from the audience sample.
40. The audience with which the programmes were most popular was the 45+ age group.

PART II

European Production

4
Ireland and Great Britain

Among the countries covered by our research, two seem to have been more resistant to the '*Dallas* model' despite the fact that they speak the same language: Ireland and Great Britain. The first chapter of this part offers a summary of research on television fiction in these two countries. In both places, we have found a strong sense of national identity together with, among other factors, a firm Celtic tradition of story-telling, traces of which are to be found in television programming.

We shall then go on to consider the French serial *Chateauvallon* and the German *Schwarzwaldklinik*, known in Britain as *Black Forest Clinic.* They represent the most determined efforts in Europe to imitate *Dallas* as of this date although, as we shall see, they cannot be regarded as typical of television fiction in the two countries, especially in France.

Ireland

Irish television – Radio Telefis Eireann[2] – has produced serials from its very earliest years, always in the naturalistic tradition and all of them set in rural communities. The sole exception was the first, *Tolka Row*, although this has rightly been called 'an urban residue of a peasant family structure' rather than a slice of urban proletariat life, as its makers perhaps intended. *Tolka Row* went on the air in 1963 and came to an end in 1968 with the defection of its actors (their replacements not proving popular with the viewing audience) but above all because RTE did not have the resources to sustain the effort of producing two

Moira Deady and John Cowley in The Riordans

serials at once. Its second serial, *The Riordans*, was introduced in 1965. Focusing on the lives of the Riordan family in a rural community, it was to last for 13 years and then be transferred from television to radio. The latest serial, which is still running, has been *Glenroe* (see below), introduced in 1983. The only interruption to the production and programming of serials was a brief period in the early 1980s, although *Bracken*, a drama mini-series in two parts (six episodes each), was produced at this time. *Bracken* and *Glenroe* are the two programmes analysed in the course of our research (although we have commented extensively on *The Riordans* as well – see 'Television, past and future').

Bracken

The series recounts the story of Pat Barry, handsome in a dark broody way, who comes back to his homeland to defend the farm he has inherited on his father's death against the predatory intentions of a neighbouring landowner, Ned Daly. The conflict between the two highlights the similarities in their characters, each one seeing a projection of himself, older or younger, in the other. There are veiled illusions to the lead character's desire to climb the social ladder. The camerawork emphasises the 'heroic' nature of the series, using techniques reminiscent of *Dallas* when, for example, portraying JR (zooming in upwards to a close-up). Miley, the good-natured neighbour, helps Pat, whereas Miley's father Dinny (combining shrewdness with dishonesty and deceit) is secretly in league with Ned to drive Pat from the farm, although when his son leaves him he repents bitterly. In *Bracken* women are not just marginal but are used as objects. While Ned Daly's wife Jilly is portrayed as a 'typical' middle-class English woman (cold and distant from her odious husband, but also unfortunately from her daughter), interested only in travelling abroad, her daughter Louise is the main pawn in the power game between the two men. She has a strong emotional relationship with her father and is very dependent upon him; when she is drawn to and courted by Pat, her jealous father is furiously angry. The affair between Louise and Pat is not profound love but rather a mutual sexual awakening which, by the end of the series, drives them apart. Is this only temporary? Who knows! The future is an open book. One character that is almost always a feature of melodrama, the mother figure, is not to be found in *Bracken*.

It is the melodramatic nature of this serial that is the reason for the lack of humour and irony about itself, qualities to be found in *Glenroe*. There is an overwhelming atmosphere of romanticism and nostalgia for the past. The issue of one's forefathers and land ownership harks back to rural values, that are brought home by the lush, improbable imagery. The zoom shots may be borrowed from *Dallas*, but the pace of *Bracken* is very different (with sequences up to 5 minutes long!). But viewers seem to like this slow-moving narrative pace. Perhaps it combines with the idealisation of the past – almost like watching a home movie – and serves to counterbalance the intensity of emotional conflict (love, hate, jealousy, power) that is portrayed without the ironic 'distancing' to be found in *Glenroe*.

Melodrama is the keynote, but it is often combined with the traditional, naturalistic aspects of an Irish serial. The stress placed on the conflict between the two main characters affects the portrayal of other aspects of social life. The community, for example is only peripherally present in the shape of silent, distant sheep-farmers. The visual imagery is one of rural romanticism. The opening sequence consists of aerial shots of sheep grazing on the hillside and there are numerous panoramic shots of the lush, green Wicklow countryside. The opening sequence includes a shot of Pat Barry wearing his cap, blackthorn stick in hand, striding through the heather, that would put *The Quiet Man* to shame! This imagery is underscored by the lyrical music. The central values (also expressed through camera movement and *mise en scène*) are individualism and 'man's' solitary relationship with nature. Among the other predominating values noted by the researchers are the ownership of land, ambition, ruthlessness, social status and well-being and the power of dead ancestors.

Glenroe

Broadcast on Sundays at 8.30 p.m. since 1984, *Glenroe* has consistently been the top-rated programme on RTE1. The plot and characters revolve around the axis of the traditional versus the modern, the rural versus the urban. The two characters most popular with viewers are Dinny Byrne and his son Miley. Dinny is country-cute, sly and scheming, while Miley is naive, good-natured and an excellent foil for his father's tricks. The Byrnes have a neighbour: Biddy McDermott, unaffected, practical and good-humoured, with a hint of tomboyishness. She operates a mushroom-growing business with Miley Byrne. By dint of chasing after him, she has persuaded him to marry her. It is not grand passion but rather a companionable relationship between two people who have grown up as neighbours and share the same interests.

The girl's mother, Mary McDermott, is quite a different personality. A widow in her late forties, she is far more sophisticated than her daughter. She likes fashionable clothes and is attracted by the lure of the city Dublin, which she visits often. She has a relationship with Dick Moran, a local businessman in the building industry who is divorced with two sons. The couple would like to keep their affair secret. Both of them like socialising and an urban lifestyle. Mary McDermott is an interesting character, very Irish but novel at the same time. Her 'modernness', the fact of having successfully escaped the frustrations of being a housewife, does not prevent her from trying to live up to the codes of behaviour, conventions and respectability of the local environment. When an acquaintance meets her one morning on the threshold of Dick's home where she has, presumably, spent the night (a presumption reinforced by the fact that Mary is wearing a dressing gown) she feels the need to explain her presence there by concocting an implausible story. In general, however, her behaviour is a departure from the stereotypes of women in Irish serials: Mary is a mother, but she is above all a woman, with all a woman's desires, including sensual desires. Mary can be said to be a new and interesting portrayal of an Irish mother figure.

The other characters that have gradually been introduced into the plot more recently mark a shift of focus towards urban, more 'modern' values. The garage mechanic Brennan has an emotional relationship with Nuala Maher (and also a working relationship, the source of some conflict). Nuala thinks she can reconcile her marriage to Brennan with her desire for emancipation and independence. Mary McDermott and Nuala Maher are not exceptions, for in *Glenroe* women are generally depicted in roles that break with tradition. All the women work or at

Mary McEvoy as Biddy and Mick Lally as Miley in Glenroe

least aspire to acquire independence. A female character such as Teresa Marshall who is not financially independent evokes very negative images of psychological dependence (Teresa, like Sue Ellen, drinks and is bullied and badly treated by her husband). The reference to Sue Ellen and *Dallas* is very evident: the characters that have joined the story most recently (but also those perceived by viewers as farthest away from the 'spirit' of the serial) are Teresa and her husband Oliver Marshall: she is described by other characters in the local pub as a 'a real kind of Sue Ellen type', and Oliver as 'just like Miss Ellie's husband but not as big'.

The 'traditional versus modern' conflict is the keynote not only for the setting and characters but for all the various sub-plots. These raise such issues as work and the division of labour, relationships between the sexes and sexuality, motherhood and experience of motherhood, a sense of community and the places where people meet (pub and church). The naturalistic descriptions are close to Irish popular culture, displaying an Irish sense of humour, especially in dialogues and the unfolding of the plot. The programme sends up stereotyped ideas, as normally shown on television, as to how the social classes behave. Dinny and Miley, for example, dress like small farmers in the good old days – or rather an exaggerated version of the clichés. George, a member of the dilapidated Anglo-Irish gentry, dresses like a typical country gentleman and behaves as people of his kind used to do in the past – the fairly recent past, moreover – when position in the social hierarchy was expressed in one's way of speaking, manners and clothes. The visual style of *Glenroe* is fairly static, most of the scenes being set pieces and the camera hardly ever moving. Screen time is not real time: for viewers it may be Christmas, but in *Glenroe* it may be harvest time. Most of the scenes are set in the summer, almost as if to suggest a greater sense of harmony in the life of the community.

The Past and the Future

The strong emphasis on Irish identity and the conflict between the traditional and the modern – so often only reflected and obliquely referred to, but always recognisable – in RTE programme production is hardly surprising. In few other countries has the decision to launch television programmes been so hotly debated and so controversial, so conscious of all the possible consequences and implications, as it was in Ireland. A quotation from a speech by President of the Republic Éamon De Valera, the hero and symbol of Irish independence, to mark the inauguration of RTE, will suffice to illustrate the nature and intensity of those concerns:

> I must admit that sometimes when I think of television and radio and their immense power, I feel somewhat afraid. Like atomic energy it can be used for incalculable good but it can also do irreparable harm . . . [It] can build up the character of the whole people, inducing sturdiness and vigour and confidence. On the other hand it can lead through demoralisation to decadence and disillusion . . . I am confident that those who are in charge will do everything in their power to make it useful for the nation, that they will bear in mind that we are an old nation and that we have our own distinctive characteristics and that it is desirable that these be preserved.[3]

Three factors played a dominant part in the preparation and launching of the national television network (in the late 1950s and early 1960s), and their traces were still apparent in subsequent phases of development and programming. First, through television, Ireland opened a door onto the rest of Europe after forty years of isolation – not just social and economic isolation, but cultural as well. It opened out to the unknown factors inherent in multi-communication and the risk of 'contaminating' its strongly conservative national culture. At the same time, it had to counteract (somewhat late in the day) the 'bombardment' from transmitters in neighbouring Great Britain (BBC television dates back to 1936, although with a long gap in the war, and ITV to 1955). The feared 'contamination' had already penetrated wide sectors of the public, introducing issues foreign to the Irish cultural hinterland, and these were viewed by some as endangering the continuance of traditional values (in Britain these were years of considerable social and economic change). And thirdly, desire and fear formed a dangerous combination for those who wanted to introduce something new. The debate that preceded the creation of RTE was full of expressions of concern and calls for prudence, ranging from the instinctive reaction of veiled authoritarianism in wanting to stop it, to the genuine concern in which priests and ministers addressed this unknown medium in speaking from their respective pulpits.

At the beginning, Irish television had by necessity to cope on only a small budget. The licence fees paid by the tiny group of television viewers were not enough to cover its expenses. The Telefis Eireann Authority was modelled along the lines of the BBC and had to comply with stringent rules as to the content and format of programmes; officially it was independent, but it was subject to government supervision. There was a ban on any form of advertising. Although things have been changing over the years, so that today RTE derives most of its revenue from advertising, competition with its better-off neighbours has been stepped up. Today over 70% of TV sets provide clear reception of BBC and ITV programmes. RTE has to compete not only technically and in the visual quality of the picture it provides but also in terms of content. It has to devote special efforts to the most popular genres, such as serials and soaps, which have always come top of audience ratings. Right from the start those serials and soaps were at the centre of debate on the national characteristics that should be incorporated in television output.

In the 1960s, soap operas reaching Ireland from Great Britain were viewed with suspicion and alarm: did 'kitchen-sink drama', as it was sarcastically called, depict 'the sordid and scandalous sides of reality as entertainment', as some of the clergy maintained, or a slice of everyday life and the contradictions endemic in a welfare state society (a point to which we shall return)? It was a climate in which appeals for 'specific' Irishness in plot and characters found a ready hearing. On the one hand, there was a fear of the visual impact of dramatically topical social realism; on the other, it was pointed out that Ireland's history of industrialisation and urbanisation differed in time and manner from that of the neighbouring island.

The traditional values at issue in the debate on conservation or progress are the family and the rural community. In practice, these may be combined in the concept of the small family-run farm, the production unit on which the Irish economy mainly depends even today. A focal point rather than a broader means of socialisation, it implies the day-to-day practice of solidarity and non-openness to the world outside and to diversity. The small farm is a way of managing a less traumatic exodus to the town. The family as the substitute for an absent welfare state, something that certain sociologists are rediscovering today, was selected by Irish television as one of its strengths right from the beginning. In a lecture on the 'Challenge of Television' given in 1961, explicit reference was made to the need for 'special attention to ensure that television programmes do not project desires solely modelled on town life. We must avoid any sorded depiction of life in the countryside'. These family-related concerns are constantly present in Irish society, and the advent of the new medium inevitably reinforced them. In 1952, a sociologist priest wrote that the individualism of town life destroys family unity and weakens the bond of matrimony, because the man works elsewhere, away from the domestic hearth, and also because a growing number of married women now join the labour force. This means that 'work, instead of bringing a couple together, is separating the two', whereas 'work on the land strengthens the relationship between man and wife, since they are bound together not just by a domestic tie but because they are also business partners'.[4]

This blending of the domestic and the work dimension has not been without its effect on the dramatic structure of serials. In *The Riordans*, for example, the purely private side of people's lives is not shown, but they are depicted as part of a network of community and economic relationships. And yet in other respects *The Riordans* is modern in that it rejects the idyllic view of Irish life that has traditionally prevailed when depicting the countryside. It is of interest that *The Riordans* was first regarded as an educational programme, in what its makers saw as an 'undercover' operation, in the sense that the aim was 'surreptitiously to convey concepts of good farm management . . . to make sure that equipment and machines would be properly used . . . the validity of the series, which is of course constructed around the closeness to real life, depends on the actors' ability to act like farmers down to the tiniest detail.' The serial was so successful in this respect that it later led to an explicitly educational programme, one not dressed up as fiction, *Telefis Feirme*, aimed at 'real' farmers; the 'pretend' farmers are still to be found in *Glenroe*, where they live side by side with townies although they themselves – the country folk – are at the heart of the stories and are more popular with viewers, as our audience research has shown.

Another interesting aspect of *The Riordans* is the fact that what might have been a technical constraint proved in the end to be one of the reasons for its success. Its makers did not want to confine the story to studio sets plus a few landscape shots, and they decided to make widespread use of location shots and real-life countryside settings. To do this they employed RTE's Outside Broadcasting Unit, whose more usual job was covering sporting fixtures and special events and which had no experience whatsoever of drama programmes. The working conditions that ensued were often eventful, and it was the actors in particular who bore the brunt, but those conditions in the long run produced acting that may have been less than perfect but was undoubtedly more spontaneous, and the audience liked it.

To return to the content of programmes, it is of interest that the production of television serials, originally regarded – like other programmes – as an opportunity to extol the distinctive traits of Irish society and culture or 'Irishness', has in fact led to unexpected developments.

In many of these stories the narrative key, and also the audience's reading key, has become an ironic look at oneself and to some extent a critical re-reading of one's own past. This too is very Irish, of course. Humour, playing with words, satirical jokes and merely good-humoured irony, depending on the context, are part of the heritage of Irish popular culture. It is a narrative key that may lead to enjoyable 'exaggeration' or to the caricaturing of personalities. The break with the stereotypes that tend to be featured in the soap genre has led to counter-stereotypes that are immediately perceived as such, to the viewer's amusement. It is almost a game. Nonetheless, it should be pointed out that our audience research has shown that the guying of people and situations never reaches a point at which it detracts from the realism of the story: one of the main sources of enjoyment is certainly the credibility of situations and events, the naturalism of relationships among characters and the simplicity of the dialogue, the kind that is spoken by ordinary people. Noteworthy perhaps among the points emerging from the audience analysis is a strong sense of identification with rural values and characters, accompanied by an opposition to urban values.

The comments on humour apply even more to *Glenroe* than they do to *The Riordans*. There are many and significant differences between the two serials, which undoubtedly reflect two different stages in the development of Irish society. We have already discussed the specifically educational intent underlying *The Riordans*, the results of which were not foreseen even by the makers. Quite apart from this, over the course of the years the serial has come to have an educational value in a much broader sense, going far beyond the bounds of the small farming world and the rules of good husbandry to touch on the whole social environment of Ireland. One of the reasons for the popularity of the serial lies in the fact that it has tackled controversial social issues such as the living conditions of farmworkers, the role of the Church in education, mental disability, alcoholism and the abuse of tranquillisers, not to speak of morals, sexuality, the use of contraceptives (whose open sale is banned in Ireland) and the problem of illegitimate children. As someone commented, the serial 'brought into the open, with an almost indefatigable zeal, all possible transgressions of the traditional Irish family as consecrated by the 1937 Constitution'.[5] This has not shielded *The Riordans* from criticism by liberal and left-wing opinion on the grounds that it continuously raises controversial questions and then neatly sidesteps their implications, so that many issues which might have been developed with all their social implications have been brought up, handed round like hot potatoes for a week or two and then discreetly dropped. This line of attack seems ungenerous, and probably is so when one considers that Ireland is a very Catholic country which lives under the guardianship of an all-invading church. Only very recently, in 1986, a solid majority of the electorate came out against divorce, and many subjects are still taboo. It is an achievement in itself for them to be freely discussed in popular television. Furthermore, the reason why *The Riordans* may not have proposed solutions or taken a very searching look at the implications of certain problems was due, as Martin McLoone has pointed out, *to the very fact that this was a serial*, in other words an open-ended and potentially infinite narrative form, one that was not required to offer 'solutions' or neat conclusions at the end of each episode. In short, it could exploit to the full the ambivalence implicit in the narrative structure of a serial.

This novelty is all the more significant when it is contrasted with Irish theatrical tradition. It is no coincidence that the Irish theatre, despite its wealth of tradition, has produced no television writers of note.

That the serial – especially in the case of *The Riordans* – has been put to this purpose is ironic when one thinks back to the controversy preceding and surrounding the birth of RTE, at a time when the point of reference could only be the British model. In the conference in 1961 on the 'challenge of television', some of the speakers pointed to the absence of 'positive models' for television programmes. They contrasted television to the classic model for story-telling in the theatre, where the starting point for the action is a disruption in the established order of things, the action develops within the situation of disorder created by that disruption and concludes with the restoration of the original order and with a solution to the problem or the mystery. Contrary to the classic dramatic representation, 'which raises a problem, defines a conflict and offers us all (hopefully) the excitement of cudgeling our brains to solve the problem', in television, the critics note, we find only 'uncertainties, fear, anxiety and of course no spiritual values, merely total materialism'. The serial format, in the eyes of those critics, is the vehicle whereby the corrosive effects of television are most clearly expressed. In a memorandum emerging from the conference, addressed to the Pilkington Committee on Broadcasting in Britain (RTE had not yet started broadcasting), one of the recommendations was that the Committee should give 'special consideration to the effects of drama programmes . . . particularly those in serial form . . . the main influence of television on values and behaviour is derived from those programmes.' The serial format, according to its critics, was ambiguous, it failed to offer reassuring or certain solutions, to create unequivocal heroes or offer clear-cut distinctions between good and evil. The British soap opera was viewed with suspicion because of the disquieting people it depicted. The working-class or middle-class women in the kitchen-sink stories conveyed a subversive image: rarely were they mothers, or if they were it was in a 'half-hearted' way – half-hearted because the role of mother was always combined with other roles. More often they were single, widowed or separated, or at any rate women used to managing on their own without a man's help. In the course of their endless affairs, any hopes they might have had of building a traditional home and family were bound to be shattered.

Retrospectively, these concerns and all the admonitions and cautions that accompanied the birth of RTE can be viewed with a somewhat ironic eye when we look at the programmes that were later to be put on the air by Irish Television: *The Riordans* in particular, but also *Bracken* and *Glenroe*.[6] While it is true that the creation of RTE was in line with a clear-cut ideological programme intended to propagate traditional values, it is also true that the years during which Irish television came into being and grew up were the years in which Irish society was going through rapid and innovatory processes of change, and RTE took part in this liberalisation. Furthermore, at the beginning RTE attracted particular types of people who, in the Irish context, could undoubtedly be defined as liberal or radical, and they certainly left their mark. The very fact that RTE's first twenty years coincided with these changes may be why the portrayal of the realities in Ireland through its programmes fluctuated, often in a contradictory manner, between the past and the present, or perhaps more accurately between the past and the future. Reading what Raymond Williams wrote in the early 1970s,[7] that in Ireland 'the current image of the countryside is today an image of the past, and the image of the city is an image of the future, which leaves us . . . with an indefinite present', we wonder whether it may not be that very indefinite present, still burdened by the past and opening out to an as yet unconquered future, which is the necessarily contradictory reality being portrayed in Irish television fiction. A more positive description is offered by Barbara O'Connor, who says that it is incorrect to talk of an 'indefinite' present: the present in Ireland today consists precisely of this tension/confrontation between images of the country and images of the city. And it is this tension that has been captured by televison.

The self-mockery in *Glenroe* is far more lighthearted and indulgent, with far more humour than is to be found in *The Riordans*. In other words, on the whole *Glenroe* is less committed. This is no coincidence. *Glenroe* is a product of the 1980s, when the initial anxiety and the pressure for liberalisation had to some extent faded. And it is no coincidence that our audience research has shown that the age groups with which this serial is least popular are the younger ones. Young people criticise the stress on humour, feeling that in the end this produces a lightweight programme, inferior to British serials, particularly *Brookside*, which is regarded as far more attentive to social problems.

It is curious and worthy of mention that the scriptwriter for all the Irish serials was the same person, Wesley Burrowes, and it is even more curious that RTE, whose intention was to uphold the more traditional values of a very Catholic Ireland through the channel of fiction, should have assigned this task to a man like Burrowes, born in Bangor (a suburb of Belfast), in other words a British citizen by birth and a Protestant by religion.

Great Britain

> I wonder, could it be true that people not only get the governments they deserve but also the drama they deserve? In which case, in my opinion, the Americans must have been very naughty indeed to have wound up with Ronald Reagan, *Dynasty* and a series about a 'talking car', in which the car appears to be not only more intelligent than the hulk who's driving it, but also more intelligent than the aforementioned Ronald Reagan

The scene is Teleconfronto 1984 and the speaker is Linda Agran, then of Euston Films (Thames Television), the producer of *Widows*. Of course, says Linda Agran, the English should be grateful to the Americans for the fact that British television has reached such a high standard, although she acknowledges that:

> . . . we produce a load of crap, but when it's good it's better than that produced anywhere in the world . . . Could we beat the Americans at their own game? . . . I suppose it's possible, but . . . I doubt they will ever beat us at ours.'

However exaggerated, this opinion is a fair encapsulation of the attitude of most British (producers and critics) on the alleged dangers of American competition, which may explain why *Dallas* and 'American cultural colonialism' have aroused less controversy in Great Britain than elsewhere. It is no coincidence, moreover, that even within our own research group the people least involved have been the British, who never seemed to believe that content analysis and other exercises would produce significant results. While argued from a methodological position, their criticisms revealed an unwavering inner conviction: that it is quite useless to waste any energy on proving something so obvious as that the homegrown (for 'homegrown' read 'British') product is far, far better than the American. In the chapter devoted to *Dallas*, we have already discussed the attitudes of some British critics and intellectuals towards American programmes, fluctuating from resignation to condescension with regard to that 'American stuff, glossy junk' (our own paraphrase, but it clearly sums up many people's views); but we have also seen that this opinion is not shared by the general public.

Nonetheless, there remains the fact that British-made soap opera is easily the most popular genre in Great Britain. This is demonstrated not only by the audience ratings (and no American serial has consistently been at the top of the ratings despite the great popularity of *Dallas*) but also by the *longevity* of British soaps, in particular the five serials considered here: *Coronation Street* (starting date 1960, ITV); *Crossroads* (1964, ITV); *Emmerdale Farm* (1972, ITV); *Brookside* (1982, Channel 4); *EastEnders* (1985, BBC). Since their respective starting dates, four of them have appeared on television screens without a break (*Coronation Street* for over 27 years!). Almost all the soap operas, except for BBC's *EastEnders* and *Compact*, a relatively short-lived BBC effort in 1962, are produced by the commercial networks, especially those in the Midland/Northern belt of the country, which has given them a marked regional feel. Their settings are lower middle class and the traditional working class. (A London-based experimental soap made by Thames TV in the late 1970s, *The Cres*, featuring stories of upper middle-class people, did not meet with much success.) Another feature is that there are no stars. All the characters are of equal weight, something that has a bearing on the narrative structure. In each half-hour episode various sub-plots are developed. Interwoven and then gradually phased out, these sub-plots help to show the slow passing of time, which sometimes corresponds to real time. There are usually two episodes a week (sometimes combined in a repeat shown at the weekend), scheduled in the early evening to capture the attention of the whole family gathered together.

Coronation Street

Coronation Street is produced by Granada Television Ltd., one of the first independant companies, founded by Sydney Bernstein, the owner of West End cinemas and theatres, a millionnaire and a Labourite. Granada covers the northwest of England and is based in Manchester, a city connected to another – Salford – which is the setting for this serial. Transmitted for the first time on 9 December 1960, but only in the northwest, it was to consist of 13 episodes but it proved so successful that the decision was taken to schedule it throughout the national commercial network, and it is still being shown today.

The serial is the story of a street and its residents, people who go out to work or who have small family businesses (managing a pub, a shop), or who are identified with the northern working class. The social environment has changed only superficially since 1960, perhaps

Margot Bryant, Violet Carson and Lynne Carol in Coronation Street

becoming a little more lower middle-class. Two meeting places for the local residents in addition to the pub have been introduced: a cafe and a factory. The main characters are female (single, separated and unhappily married women, with or without children.) It is impossible to summarise the thousands of events which have formed the plots down the years. The stories have been followed for almost 30 years by a viewing public that ranges in age from 16 to 70.

Over the years the serial has tried out radical technical changes. From low-quality 405-line black-and-white pictures shot in the studio, the production has progressed to sharp and clear 625-line colour pictures and to a specially built backlot to give a greater feeling of reality. The serial does not seem to have gained much by the change: the sparse black-and-white pictures had all the intensity of the social realism being evoked on the large screen in those same years by films set in the industrial north, such as *Saturday Night and Sunday Morning*, *A Taste of Honey* and *A Kind of Loving*. Colour has added to the sense of unreality and, oddly, so has the increase in the number of interiors and the breaking up of long scenes into shorter sequences. The stories show a Britain that no longer exists, a country where few people are unemployed, where people celebrate the marriage of Prince Charles and Lady Diana but hardly ever mention the fratricidal war in Northern Ireland, where there are apparently no ethnic minorities. This unreality is reinforced by the direction which, in placing the stories in contemporary settings and decors, makes them appear altogether alien. As we shall discuss, the alienness is one of the elements that has proved most popular with audiences.

Crossroads

First shown in 1964, *Crossroads* was produced by Central Television (formerly ATV). It is located in the Midlands (Birmingham) and is the story of a motel in that area and the various plots woven around it. Initially planned as a story of a conflict between two sisters (one good, the other bad), it later changed to show the advertures of only one of the two. The main groups to which the various characters belong are the motel people (the owners and their staff, the guests) and the folk from the village, King's Oak. The serial mainly takes place in the locations where people congregate socially, such as the market, an

Noele Gordon ('Meg'), Jane Rossington, Roger Tonge in Crossroads

outpatients' department, the post office, an antique shop, etc. There are frequent references to social realities and topical issues, something not always found in other soaps, especially the longer-standing ones. Social hierarchies and the respective financial relationships appear in the plot although – as is obvious in this genre – it is interpersonal relationships around which the various plots turn.

In certain respects *Crossroads* is not a typical British soap. The frequency of transmission is high, with up to four episodes a week (currently there are three). It is shown in the early evening and is scheduled at different times in various parts of the country, but always just before peak viewing times. *Crossroads* is also the only soap that features one character (Meg, the owner of the motel) more strongly than the others. Indeed, the decision to write the character out of the serial in the early 1980s caused a good deal of unhappiness among devotees of the show.

All this has created a story which accentuates and exaggerates the features typical of seriality; frequent repetitions and episodes broken up for dramatic effect. Cheaply made, in the early years it was also technically sloppy (with, for example, poor cutting of scenes at the time of editing, with actors fluffing or forgetting their lines). Despite this, *Crossroads* has always achieved high ratings (15th in the list in February 1986). [*Crossroads* was finally brought to an end in April 1988.]

John Abineri and Frederick Pyne in Emmerdale Farm

Emmerdale Farm

This programme was first produced in 1972 by Yorkshire Television (based in Leeds), which covers what is perhaps the most rural of the industrial areas of Great Britain. It seems appropriate, therefore, that the story should be about a farming community. Initially the programme was shown during the daytime, but was rescheduled to prime-time in order to compete directly with *EastEnders*. Its audience has increased considerably (it is 24th in the ratings), which is an interesting fact in itself as it shows how scheduling can damage or contribute towards the success of a programme. The world depicted in *Emmerdale Farm* is an old rural England, where nature is highlighted as the crucial factor in people's lives.

Brookside

In the 1980s – according to Phil Redmond, the creator of *Brookside* – there was a new audience in the country looking for a different kind of soap in which traditional characters are combined with topicality and awareness of social changes. In 1982, the newly created Channel Four

Simon O'Brien, Sue Johnston and Ricky Tomlinson in Brookside

commissioned a brand new soap, *Brookside,* from Mersey Television, a production company based in Liverpool, where the story of *Brookside* is set.

Out of a desire for realism the producers acquired a complete square of real houses in a new housing estate – Brookside, in Liverpool. The serial is filmed inside and outside these houses, furnished in the same way as those inhabited by working people, where – as Redmond points out – 'when you open the fridge the light comes on inside'. 'When on earth have people lived in a place where the whole street meets in the same pub every evening?' asks Redmond, referring to the *Coronation Street* and *Crossroads* type of serials. 'People want programmes that tell the truth and show society as it really is.' The style of filming also helps to increase the sense of naturalness: a single camera, with fairly static, lengthy dialogue sequences.

The characters appearing in *Brookside* differ from those in other soaps in that they do not congregate in certain places at certain times – a convention that is helpful to the viewer, because the exchange of information and gossip can be used 'to sum up the story so far'. Instead, they are observed in turn in their respective social environments and in the variety of relationships they establish. This perhaps creates a fragmented type of understanding but it is also a more realistic portrayal of atomised life as it is lived today, when there is less and less opportunity for social interaction.

The audience for *Brookside* is far larger than Channel Four's customary 10% (about 5 million, compared with the 16 million for *Coronation Street*, the 12 million for *Crossroads* and the 10 million for *Emmerdale Farm* and *Dallas*). Certainly audiences have been attracted by Channel Four's showing of an omnibus edition of the soap at the weekend, when the two weekday episodes are combined. This is of special benefit to all those people who have not had a chance to see it because it is transmitted during their working hours.

EastEnders

This began in February 1985 on BBC1. It was the first soap opera to be produced by the BBC for over 20 years. Going out twice weekly at 7.30 p.m., for the first time it recounts the everyday lives of a group of working-class people in London's East End, in interiors reconstructed in the BBC's luxury Elstree Studios. The centre-point is Albert Square, onto which face a cafe, a grocer's shop, a launderette, a fruit and vegetable stall, a pub and various flats. The cockney characters are fairly stereotyped but, although in some respects they seem to be based on the characters in *Coronation Street*, in fact they offer a far more realistic cross-section of the community. For instance, they acknowledge the existence of ethnic minorities. The dialogue is always explicit, even when it is about sex (other British soaps tend to be vague to the point of evasiveness about this subject).

EastEnders is the most costly of the soaps produced in Great Britain. By the end of its first year, it also reached the largest number of viewers: over 23 million, in other words 45% of homes in the United Kingdom. It has borrowed from *Brookside* the practice of showing an omnibus edition at the weekend – a practice that was, indeed, introduced by the BBC itself in the past with the successful and long-lived radio serial, *The Archers*.

The cast of EastEnders

Historical development and features of the soap genre

The Archers and *The Dales*, highly successful radio serials that began in the 1940s, can be regarded in some respects as the forerunners of present-day television soap operas. They portrayed a cross-section of everyday family life and complied with the BBC public service directive: to inform, entertain and educate. When television started up, the same directive applied.

The audience was always visualised in general terms, as a family nucleus, although within the family each member's role, tasks and interrelations were seen as shaping the course of the day differently, together with his or her potential access to television programmes. The members of a family were also regarded as having different preferences and interests, and the aim was to identify and satisfy them all without ever neglecting to 'educate'.

In the 1950s, one of the most attractive ways of educating people was the documentary drama which, with gradual changes and improvements, was to place its imprint on the whole line of serials (a heading that included the soap opera) and series. A hybrid format, the 'docu-drama', as it came to be known, came into being as a result of combining two genres: the television documentary and play, at a time when technical resources were in too short supply for live broadcasts and there was rarely an opportunity to film topical events on the spot. This meant that stories of ordinary people, very much like the viewers, were recreated in the studio through the construction of plausible dialogues and by setting the stories in the locations where the actual event had taken place. This documentary dramatisation featured facts that were not sensational but, however modest, were relevant to the social scene at the time. The style appeared to be naturalistic and informal but was in fact constructed in the studio with meticulous care. One of the most significant social phenomena in post-war Great Britain was the changing structure of the family, whose nature had been called into question by the prolonged absence of its menfolk at the 'front', the economic independence acquired by women who were now doing 'men's jobs', the loosening of ties with family and friends, partly because of the housing crisis and the desire to create one's own little niche at a time when the family had become more nuclear and precarious (because of the rising divorce rate). At the same time, however, there was an aspiration towards new values and ways of relating to others. The younger generation wanted to organise their lives in different ways as regards sex, the couple and family ties. BBC documentary dramas tended to tackle the issues associated with this new-style family in an open-minded and often progressive way.

The incentive for putting on television soap operas came from the commercial network, Independent Television, which was set up in 1954. The independent television system was established on a federal/regional basis, partly in reaction to the centralised London-based policy of the BBC and partly to capture the potentially vast audience which was put off by the high culture values of the programmes made by the Oxbridge graduates dear to the BBC. ITA networks covering the Midlands and the North aimed at programmes embodying the popular aspects of regional life and harking back to tradition. As Sydney Bernstein, the founder of Granada, reminded us, this is a Celtic area where people have always loved to tell and listen to stories, an area that has given us many of the great literary works of the past. And it is the birthplace of most of the writers (John Braine, Alan Sillitoe, Alun Owen, Shelagh Delaney, Elaine Morgan and others) who influenced the movies of the late 1950s that indirectly led to the soap programmes with which we are here concerned. From the 1960s on, these programmes unfurled their plots in 'real time' on the small screen. The events (especially events in the lives of the royal family) which captured the feelings and imagination of viewers were 'incorporated' in the serials, at the same time as they occurred. An archaeology was also cultivated by magazines that featured significant events in the various serials and contained gossip and inside information from the popular press about the characters, who by then had become 'real' figures – far more real to the public than the actors who played them. The fact that the stories were not vehicles for stars, and their downmarket settings and the ordinariness of their characters, undoubtedly shaped the dramatic imagination that went into them, so that they developed along very different lines from Hollywood-style soaps. Unlike *Dallas*, they did not feature heroes in desperate pursuit of success, battling against anyone who stood up to them, nor did the families live through events from the sublime to the sordid, often piled up in an ever more grotesque and unreal fashion. Here the serious and the comic were balanced one against the other with moderation. Of course, as we have already pointed out, certain conventions became 'dated'. Even so, the relationship between audiences and soaps continues to be an 'active' one. The discontinuous structure of the soap, an 'ongoing' serial without beginning or end, made up of a multitude of episodes and narrative links, presupposes special levels of competence in the audience. It is not so much a question of the imagination stepping in to fill in the time gaps between one segment of the story and the next (unlike series, episodes are usually related to the time-scale of the viewers), but rather that the audience has to interpret correctly certain events, the key to which is held by those who watch regularly. On the other hand, the slow and repetitive narrative style means that those who are at least minimally familiar with the serial can understand what is going on even though they may have missed something. Indeed, sporadic viewing is another characteristic of the relationship between the audience and the soap opera. For example:

> *Crossroads* cannot be said to have a stable audience of 15 million people. Its fans probably number more than 30 million a month, three quarters of whom watch less than half an episode at a time. This 'slippage' by comparison with the overall figure is indicative of the 'intermittent but continuous' thematic structure of the soap opera itself.[8]

Of course the type of viewer participation in the British soap is very much the same as for US or South American soaps, but characters like Sue Ellen or Isaura the slave girl certainly are not part of the audience's everyday experience and are far less realistic than Bet, Annie, Meg, Elsie and other characters in British soaps. The British style can justifiably be called 'soap-opera realism', a blend of two narrative genres.[9] On the one hand, it retains the conventions typical of the soap (the indefinite postponement of any final solution, the interweaving of many plots to suggest a multiplicity of experience, recourse to 'cliff-hanging', substantial and sometimes stereotyped roles for female characters). On the other it adopts certain conventions of social realism that lend themselves to the serial format. Life is presented as a 'story of personal events, each one with a beginning, a middle and an end, events that are important to the main characters but also affect the people around them.' Those events certainly touch on social problems, but on the whole they are the problems encountered by ordinary folk. The characters depicted are working-class or from sectors of society that are immediately identifiable and credible through the type of homes they live in, their families and their friends. The settings are characteristic of a socal category: a pub, the street, a factory, the home, the kitchen. Because of the immutability of situations and settings over the years, some soaps can of course no longer be said to be truly realistic. The characters and personalities featuring in the early days of social realism have also changed. For example, there are now substantial roles for men, who have come more to the fore. This is partly because of a conscious effort to build up a different type of audience, and partly because there has in fact been a considerable increase in younger viewers and the male audience (40-45% of the total in some cases). These variations and differentiations bring products such as *Brookside* and *EastEnders* closer to the conventions of television 'social drama' than of soap opera. Whereas the soap has rightly been defined in some quarters as 'drama of social harmony', in *Brookside* and *EastEnders* the disruption of balance, harmony and social consensus is the prevailing feature.

In actual fact the history and development of the British soap opera have not always kept pace with, and have sometimes lagged far behind, social change in the country. In the 1950s and the 1960s, television was seen as standing for, and the ideal vehicle for depicting, the good life – now within everyone's reach – and consumerism, by now a practice and an ideology. Between 1956 and 1958, there was a vast spread in the ownership of television sets. To satisfy this public, ranging socially from the middle- and lower-middle class to the industrial working class (further up the social ladder people turned up their noses at what they regarded as a 'vulgar' medium), television had to scale down its ambition of 'culture-raising'. It introduced dialects and voices different from those traditionally regarded as speaking with the right accent; it had to produce programmes that were within everyone's reach. In the soap, where the stress was on the sphere of feelings and private life, there were a few explicit references to the social changes through which the country passed in the years thereafter, but there were also events which were, incredibly, never mentioned.

The first great change was mass immigration by non-white British citizens from the various dominions during the economic boom years, drawn by the lure of employment and a higher standard of living. This transplant was not painless: the race riots that were sparked off in 1958 and resurfaced every now and then over the course of the years bore witness to the difficulty of grafting new cultures onto the old. The white population tended to retreat to a non-political stance, as expressed in *Crossroads*. The shop in *Crossroads* was never entered by a black customer years and years after the actual urban landscape had been totally changed by migration – indeed, years after the real-life equivalent shop had been taken over and was being run by a Pakistani family! Moreover (and we shall find out why later) it was the viewers themselves who wanted this 'parallel world' to remain unchanged, with all the network of nineteenth-century-style social relationships it depicted: the working-class neighbourhood, which wielded more influence than the family itself in that it highlighted individual identity, defined status and stood for class solidarity. The other major social changes in the 1960s were the gradual disappearance of the extended family (with several generations all living together) and the fact that the family was more inward-looking because of its acceptance of the middle-class values of career and success. The unchangeability of the 'parallel world' was welcomed because it conveyed a sense of security and also because it was an exercise in nostalgia.

The major regional cities – Manchester, Glasgow, Liverpool and Birmingham – had been the heart of the first industrial revolution in the 19th century. In the mid-20th century they became the theatre of a new industrial revolution, this time recorded by television. Social changes were wide-ranging: the gradual disappearance of the traditional working class (in the sense of 'craftsmen'), the levelling out of social strata and, with growing prosperity, the decline of the sense of solidarity that used to bring the working class and the village community together. The village itself, often structured around a mine, also disappeared. It was fragmented by the building of new factories and new housing estates. New trades came into being and more people were being educated. But it also led to isolation and loneliness, to people sitting alone in their freshly decorated living rooms in front of the television set. This was the reason for stories that recaptured a lost sense of social community, if only in the form of chat and gossip, stories taking people back to places where they used to gather – the street, a shop, the local pub. It was a visual illustration of the ambivalent process that Wells expressed as a paradox: 'For the working class the most important thing is to get out of it!'. In getting out of the working class, however, one is left with a sense of partial or substantial loss of a collective identity. This could be expressed 'visually' as the meeting places, including the places where people used to shop. Instead of the pub and the family-run corner shop we now have the impersonal amusement arcade and the supermarket, except in the soap opera. In our consumer society, retailing is being automated and impersonalised just as production has been automated in the large factory, but in the soap the shop is shown as a background setting for chat among workmates. From these viewpoints the soap opera represents resistance to change, a corner of survival in an ever more impersonal society. The persisting ideal of the village community is recreated by *EastEnders* even in a metropolis like present-day London, a place where meeting points are fragmented and used by groups defined by their sex, age, religous or other leanings, in an impossible quest for similarity with others and out of a sense of intolerance about anyone who is different.

For this reason, perhaps, the audience is a composite one in Britain, unlike other countries. For the British, the soap opera offers the opportunity for intercourse that, in other countries, arises when people meet while shopping at the stalls in the market place or chatting over a coffee in the bar. Such habits have vanished from the British dormitory suburbs and the pretentious residential areas where the good middle-class watchword is, as it always has been, 'keep yourself to yourself'. They are on the way out, even in the more socially compact industrial areas such as the northern mining towns, where recent union conflict has broken many ties of unity and understanding, setting members of the same family or neighbours who were formerly on good terms one against another.

The early soaps harked back to values dating from the 1930s, when a strong sense of class consciousness emerged and took deep root in the British working class, bringing a sense of solidarity with the weaker members of the community. It was a society extolled by George Orwell in his books, and it was a society resurrected in the 1960s (the years in which the first soap operas were being launched) by Richard Hoggart and Raymond Williams. Hoggart's definition of 'working-class culture' is interesting in the effects it exerted on soap operas and in the interpretation generally found in television. He took the essentially anthropological view of this culture, as a set of models for interaction, assumptions, common modes of conduct, under the banner of 'common sense' in 'everyday life'. This everyday life, he said, had become a lifestyle and a system of values based on clear-cut historical entities such as the home and the community.

All these value, the emphasis on common sense, the non-portrayal of work and politics, the importance of women as the cornerstone of family unity and village life, the nostalgia, were to feature in the first serial, *Coronation Street*. Who was it who promoted those values in the television of the 1960s? Young nonconformist graduates, fascinated by the infinite potential afforded by the new medium; other graduates, without the right connections to pull strings for them, who were excluded from the prestige realm of the printed word; pacifists belonging to the Campaign for Nuclear Disarmament, sympathisers with the New Left, people who had deserted the official Communist Party at the time of the Hungarian uprising, and the brigade of 'angry young men' who were joining television, especially commercial television, as scriptwriters, producers and directors. In many cases they also worked with the film producers who had given birth to 'Free Cinema', with all its variety of issues associated with social realism, echoes of which were to be found in the early soap operas. And, it should be added, another theme of much of the television, film and cultural output was a hankering after the past, reinforced by fear for the future, caught between the twin spectres of Europeanism and 'Americanisation'.

During and after World War II, Great Britain saw itself as being overrun by its ally, the United States. A common language may in some respects have made the colonialisation less evident than in other European countries, but in other respects it highlighted America's subtle, comprehensive penetration. United in their critical views, conservative intellectuals (Evelyn Waugh, T.S Eliot) and progressives (George Orwell, Richard Hoggart) associated American culture with images that were admittedly dazzling (the new fashions and the cult of youth, the streamlined design of mass-produced objects, works of art and music designed to amaze) but were also 'splendidly' empty. Young people immediately seized on to everything that was different in American fashion: the literary (science fiction), the musical (jazz and rock 'n' roll) and the visual (pop art). All these represented a departure from tradition, in that these fashions were created from the base and then filtered up. And there were also new narrative styles that bordered on journalism (Truman Capote, Norman Mailer, John Dos Passos) and documentaries that drew on small everyday stories. These are the aspects of American culture that tend to be undervalued when its products are discussed, but in a sense they can be linked with certain genres, both television and non-television, that are the foundation for British soap opera production.

There is also a tendency to undervalue the influence on ITV and BBC of those transatlantic personalities (Silvio Narizzano, Sydney Newman, etc.) who, at the head of various Drama Departments, fought to 'make the working class a suitable subject for drama rather than merely incidental characters used as a foil to show how well the middle class behave'. It may be true that British culture, and also British television, is less of a 'closed shop' today and has become more receptive to outside models. Under the influence of the Americanisation which Hoggart discerned, new fashions and lifestyles seeping upwards from the grass roots have changed the portrayal of the working class, making it appear less strange and less anachronistic.

Notes

1. The full reports in the original language may be obtained on application from the Consiglio Italiano per le Scienze Sociali.
2. RTE began broadcasting on 31 December 1961.
3. Éamon de Valera, 'Address on the Opening of Telefis Éirann, 31 December 1961', reprinted in Martin McLoone and John MacMahon (eds.), *Television*

and Irish Society; 21 Years of Irish Television (Dublin: RTE/IFI, 1984).

4. Rev. H. Murphy, 'The rural family: the principles', *Christus Rex* vol.VI no.1. The quotations and information are taken from McLoone and MacMahon, *Television and Irish Society*.
5. See *Television and Irish Society*.
6. Indeed, commenting on readers' complaints that programmes like *Dallas* 'break down the moral fibre of the country', an Irish television critic went so far as to write with ill-concealed repugnance that he failed to understand why people should complain about *Dallas* in particular, when, 'between *Glenroe*, *The Riordans* and *Bracken*, every possible form of vice that can reasonably be imagined has been shown on the screen: we have had sex outside marriage, adultery, drunkenness and pub brawls, certainly not the type of things which will improve our moral fibre.'
7. In *The Country and the City* (London: Chatto and Windus, 1973).
8. Mallory Wober, 'Cinderella comes out showing TV's hits are its myths', *Media, Culture and Society* vol.6 no.1, 1984.
9. Marion Jordan, 'Realism and Convention', in Richard Dyer (*et al.*), *Coronation Street*, Television Monograph 13 (London: British Film Institute, 1981).

5
France

France was the first European country to try to 'copy' *Dallas*, committing substantial resources to the attempt and imitating not only its content but also the production process. Thus was born *Chateauvallon*, of which 26 episodes have been made and transmitted. The second series that had been planned has not in fact been made due to outside circumstances: a car accident involving the death of the leading actress (this was the official reason given by the producers but probably it was not the only one). It should perhaps be pointed out that such a difficulty would have been far from insumountable for an American producer. Arrangements would have been made to replace the actress, and the audience would have accepted the replacement. With a French audience, however, a stratagem of this kind would probably not have worked. Over the past few years, the '*Dallas* model' has become so ever-present as to become a yardstick. When (a few months after *Chateauvallon*) the 'feuilleton' *Le Paria* came on the air, the critics exclaimed 'finally, a *Dallas* à la française!'. It is not clear whether this implied a judgment that *Chateauvallon*, although French, followed far too closely in the footsteps of its model (which, as we shall see, is untrue).

Our research group in France chose not only *Chateauvallon* (two episodes) and *Le Paria* but also *Allô Béatrice*, regarded as representing a new trend in the production of French serial fiction, and *Les Cinq dernières minutes*, an old police series (it started in 1958), with sociological and psychological implications. The analysts were interested in comparing the old production and the new '*Dallas*-style' line. The analogy with Italian production is worthy of note: the recent serials, with the exception of *Chateauvallon*, are all mini-series (in six episodes). For obvious reasons, in the summary that follows more space will be devoted to *Chateauvallon* than to the other productions. One reason is that the researchers not only considered its content and narrative structure but also took a closer look at the way the serial was produced.[1]

Chateauvallon

The first episode in the series went on the air on 4 January 1985; and the 26th and last episode was shown on 28th June 1985. The programme was scheduled once weekly (on Fridays in the early evening). The series was repeated in 1986. *Chateauvallon* is a family saga. In a small provincial town, the 'reigning' family are the powerful Bergs, who own the local newspaper among other property. On the death of the patriarch, the heirs vie for leadership of the family and in particular for control of the newspaper. Around the Berg family are woven alliances with local politicians and a conflict with another clan – an immigrant family, the Kovalics. There are threats to the independence of the newspaper from an unscrupulous press baron. Among all these intrigues, power struggles, love affairs, political compromises and financial scandals there emerges the figure of Florence Berg, the director of the newspaper and the true head of the family.

The moral space covered by *Chateauvallon* consists of four areas, four sets of values. First of all we have the values of the family and its heritage, the values of a clan rather than a family in a narrow sense. The clan has to defend its history and traditions, the material interests common to all its members, its status in local society. It therefore needs to close its ranks, to combine forces under the undisputed leadership of one person, not so much as a question of honour as for 'military' reasons, becaused it makes strategic sense. Other people's manoeuvres have to be warded off and the family's own operations have to be managed effectively. Clan solidarity is threatened by traitors and deserters from within (some of them only temporary, as they will later return to the nest), and is disputed by some of its members who refuse to identify totally with the clan (including Florence Berg's daughter, Alexandra, although the two women are reconciled in the final episode).

The second set of values is the professional: competition, success, professional excellence. Most of the characters are described as expert professionals, including the politician Quentin and the police officer Nicolo, not a very likeable character but a true professional in that he knows how to keep the notables at a proper distance.

The third set of values is the political and electoral battle. It is not so much political office that is the motivation as the urge to defeat and discomfort the adversary.

Finally, the fourth set of values, feelings and the private sphere, is not aligned with intra-clan relationships; indeed, sentiment may cut across them. Connivance or friendship between members of opposing clans, complicity arising from love and passions may, for example, distract the characters from their battle to uphold the clan's interests. At the end, the two clans – the Bergs and the Kovalics – will bring the hostilities to an end and form a united front against their common enemy, Boulard, the press magnate who fails in his attempt to take over the newspaper. Travers, the editor and Florence's colleague, will marry Catherine, a Kovalic. The characters in the soap embody various combinations of all these values, many of them contradictory. Armand, Florence's brother, for instance, is often defined by the values of his profession (he is a politician) and his feelings and loves: clan values and political values are not his own priorities. But at the end he will return to the fold, giving up his young mistress. For Florence there is also conflict between the values of the clan and her feelings: in her profession and as the leader of the clan she finally comes out on top, but on the sentimental level she is a loser . . .

Chateauvallon was the brainchild of Pierre Desgraupes, the president of Antenne 2, a former press journalist. From the start in 1983, when the project was first aired, it was presented as a '*Dallas* à la française'. Louis Harris was commissioned by Antenne 2 to conduct a survey pinpointing the successful ingredients in the major American and French serials. Among its findings was that the French public preferred stories about rich people with beautiful homes and luxury cars. This preference, it was pointed out, referred to contemporary stories, not to stories set in the past (as evidenced by the popularity of the 'feuilleton', *Jacqu le croquant*). Based on these premises, Desgraupes worked out the ingredients of 'his' *Dallas*: grand passions (love, the profit motive, hate) set in the provinces – because life is too dispersed in Paris.. Provincial life is represented by a town with a population of 350,000 people, and the inevitable backdrop for the raw elementary passions is the local newspaper.

Chateauvallon has many points in common with *Dallas*. They include:

– Dropping the conventional narrative structure, with its clearcut distinctions between good and evil, and the tradition of the French feuilleton in which the social norm is a strong factor. There are no 'heroes', there are no models. Modern life is presented in a falsely realistic and only a slightly romanticised way by depicting the day-to-day lives of a clan of wealthy people. It is a 'roman-fleuve', which often creates a feeling of *déjà vu* and enables the viewer to turn his or her attention elsewhere for a time and still follow the plot. The characters are stereotyped, corresponding to general categories. The location is a feature of the story. Members of the public are shown in the story as no more than onlookers and are not required to express any moral judgement on what is going on . . .
– The chosen genre is the serial, with a potentially infinite number of

Stacy Gregg and Chantal Nobel in Chateauvallon

episodes, each episode lasting 55 minutes. This is a novel format for French television, which has always tended to have long-lasting series made up of very short (13 minute) episodes (such as *Janique Aimée*, 1963) and, more recently, series consisting of six one-hour episodes.

– Episodes were still being scripted when filming was about to begin on previous episodes.

– Most of the programme was recorded in the studio or at a small number of outdoor locations, always the same ones and at a reasonable distance from the (Téléfrance) studios. However, unlike *Dallas*, lightweight (1″) video was used, the general idea being to increase the quantity of material recorded each day and to develop the plot along lines compatible with production conditions and the financial imperative of keeping production costs down. The result was that 7 minutes material was recorded per day, compared with an average of 4 in traditional productions. The maximum number of days taken to film each episode was 8.

– The cost was much less than an episode of *Dallas*, i.e. £200,000 per episode.

– Merchandising: products based on the programme, such as records and books, were marketed.

– The use of many writers to produce the script.

This last factor clearly showed the intention of following the American model of production and was a complete break with French tradition. It also demonstrated the difficulty in translating such aspirations into reality, since no allowance had been made for differences in attitude or mentality before even starting to think about differences in production methods. At first the scripting was entrusted to Jean-Pierre Pétrolacci, an experienced television author. He was given clear-cut terms of reference: the plots and the leading characters, the scenarios and other parameters had already been worked out by Desgraupes and the producer in charge, Roland Gritti (Telecip). Because the task was so great and time was so short, many people were attached to Gritti to help with the script and dialogues. Confusion reigned in the early stages, with more than 15 writers working on the project, many of whom paid scant attention to the previous episode scripted by their 'rivals'. Gradually a stable team was formed around Georges Conchon, a writer and a member of Antenne 2's programmes board. Everything was done in a great hurry. Barely a month before shooting was scheduled not a single episode had been fully scripted, and by the time filming in fact began only the first six episodes were complete. Some of the dialogues were dictated by their writers over the telephone just a few days before filming. The story is told that Desgraupes re-wrote some of the scenes without realising that they had already been shot. The history of the production of *Chateauvallon* is one of people being fired, scriptwriters going on strike, the 210 actors in hysterics because they did not recognise the characters they were supposed to be playing from one episode to the next. 'Depending on who had written the dialogue, suddenly we were no longer speaking the same language.' The work of collective scriptwriting, of which the producers were later to boast, was in fact done without any method, often quite haphazardly, with frequent switches in writers that had little or nothing to do with production requirements, still less with the logic of the script. As is evident, all this was far removed from the production methods traditionally employed in France.

The public, however, responded to the massive promotional campaign, and audiences reached an average 35%. The producers received an overwhelming volume of correspondence from viewers writing in to express their approval or disapproval. Despite the popularity of *Chateauvallon* in France, efforts to sell the production in other countries met with very little success. And yet when Desgraupes had dreamed up the action-packed plot of *Chateauvallon* with all its money scandals, power struggles, family conflict, intrigues and so on, together with the subject itself – essentially 'the whole of a small town's life miniaturised to the lives of a few powerful people', as it was to be described by a television critic – he aimed to make an exportable series, paced to satisfy the tastes of a public that had cut its teeth on American serials. Apart from the four European networks that had collaborated on the project right from the start, no other network offered to buy the finished product. In this respect *Chateauvallon* was almost a fiasco, for it did not prove to be competitive on the international market. The producers could console themselves with the thought that they had at least achieved their aim of making a popular serial (popular on the home market) at reasonable cost: 2.2 million francs an episode. This was higher than budgeted (1.9 million) but less than the cost of a traditional television fiction series, normally estimated at 2.5 to 3 million francs for an hour's programme.

Le Paria

This was made by FR3 and was a serial in six episodes, each lasting 50 to 55 minutes. It was shown in October and November 1985 and was reasonably popular with audiences (average share 13.1%) compared with FR3's usual audience ratings for fiction. It is a well-made production backed by a substantial budget, to judge from the many location shots (Camargue, Arles) and the number of extras used in some of the scenes, for example the wedding in the first episode. The attraction to the viewing public was undoubtedly that Charles Aznavour, in his first television role, played one of the main characters. The director, Denys de la Patellière, well known for his work in films, has already made many series for television.

Once again this is a family saga. It was presented – as we have mentioned – as a '*Dallas* à la française'. It tells the story of Julien Mauriès, who disappeared when he was accused of financial fraud but has decided to come back and fight for recognition of his innocence. He is a man transformed, compared with what he was twenty years ago when he fled the country, was tried in his absence and found guilty. He left defeated and financially ruined, but he returns a rich man, his head held high, determined after all these years of passive silence to regain the initiative. It is the story of a man regarded as a reprobate and pariah, and his long and painful return. At first he is welcomed by some, fought against by others, but finally he is recognised by everyone as innocent.

There are all the elements of melodrama, including physical attacks, violence and ambiguous relationships with women in the clan. When Julien reappears, there are people who at once welcome him with joy (the old couple who looked after his father's home, his aunt Marta), people who are not hostile but cannot easily forgive him for remaining silent for 20 years (the notary, Caterina), people who oppose Julien out of a sort of conditioned reflex of clan solidarity, and finally his true enemies (Jacques Mauriès, Senator Aramon), who were guilty of the financial irregularities which led to Julien's disgrace and who were very determined not to step in and save his name.

Three different sets of values are clearly recognisable in the first episode of the series analysed in the course of our research. In the first place, there is honour – honour lost and retrieved. Julien engages in a battle to restore his own image (in the clan, in society) and establish the truth which was trampled underfoot in the course of the unfair trial. From exile to a reconquered kingdom, the second set of values in this episode turns around the problem of one's roots, the places where one has grown up, and childhood memories. Julien wants to rediscover these places – not just his father's house but also nature, the Camargue plains with their horses, towers and the sea. The third set of values is that of loneliness and the leading character's affections. By nature a loner, Julien has become even more isolated through exile. On his return, the war he is waging to unmask his enemies and revenge himself is one he has to conduct on his own, without help from the police; indeed, he has to take over the role of the forces of justice in gathering the information needed to justify a retrial. Then over the course of time, emotional relationships gradually come to take up more and more space in his life, sometimes when he least expects it ('I did not think I would find a family again . . . '), sometimes despite his clumsiness, as when Julien tries to turn the relationship with the old couple who look after his home into friendship (when in fact the couple's feelings are essentially those of loyalty to the master who has returned, and Julien's attitude is above all paternalistic). Almost with amazement, Julien discovers that Catherine has always loved him passionately and has been faithful to him, often being despised because of it. In the same way, he finds it hard to understand why she has been so hurt by his prolonged silence. The hero is at his most vulnerable - and this is beautifully portrayed by Aznavour – in his relationships with women. Finally, his wealth and his success in the business world are shown in a fairly ambiguous way. Only after he has become rich again can Julien allow himself to try to restore his name. And the defence of his family heritage seems to have been fairly important when, 20 years earlier, his family abandoned him.

Allô Béatrice

This is a series consisting of six self-contained episodes, each lasting 55 minutes. It went on the air in the early evening in November-December 1984. It was a low-budget production by Antenne 2, although it was to prove very popular with the public (average share 37.7%). The leading character is Béatrice Roussel, the anchorwoman on a phone-in radio programme which is special in that it is only men who are allowed to call and air their problems. The series was co-produced by the radio station, Europe 1, in whose studios some of the scenes were set. The producers have made a striking effort to recreate a 'real-life' setting, giving the series an almost documentary flavour. This is evident not only on the technical side but also in the language and gestures typically used by radio journalists. On the other hand, the stories themselves are almost totally unrealistic. They are comedies of manners, halfway between the American sitcom and the French 'feuilleton', although there is obviously a desire to lampoon the radio phone-ins that are used as public confessionals and, more broadly, the ways in which people are manipulated by the media.

In *Allô Béatrice* there is also a vein of the 'golden-hearted feuilleton' with all its classic themes: a heroine who becomes famous but remains the simple little girl she used to be, and the heroine who tries to extricate herself from trouble by dreaming up outrageous stories, and yet always comes out on top at the end.

In the episode analysed, the first in the series, with the ironic title of 'Sister Béatrice of the Ratings', the journalist in the radio studio receives a call from a divorced artist, Joseph Arnaud. The court has deprived him of custody of his daughter and he threatens to commit suicide unless someone helps him. Joseph has kidnapped his daughter and hidden her in Béatrice's house. His aim is to force Béatrice to help him, using the medium of radio to ensure that the child is returned to her father's care. Béatrice cynically falls in with this trick. She sees the case as a marvellous opportunity to launch her new programme and exploits it to the full. In this she succeeds, adroitly manipulating two men who are close observers of the whole affair. One is her ex-husband, Antoine, who still loves her. The embodiment of common sense and conformism, he warns her against the risks of the venture. The other is one of Béatrice's colleagues, Olivier, a journalist who is courting her. He is a careerist who, for purely selfish professional reasons, offers to be her accomplice in promoting the success of the operation. Compared with these three men – stupid Joseph, over-cautious Antoine and cynical Olivier – the heroine stands out for her enterprise, astuteness and imagination. It is a cast of stereotypes. But there is also the conflict between the ambitious, career-minded winners, Béatrice and Olivier, and the sentimental 'pure souls', Joseph and Antoine – in the case of Antoine, someone who is slightly ridiculous in his jealousy and fears.

In this first episode, the first set of values is linked with the role of the media, presented as manipulators of public opinion and social institutions. At a certain point, Joseph tells Béatrice that his aim in climbing onto a roof and threatening to commit suicide was certainly not 'to turn you into a little idol of the masses, the consoler of men bereaved, Sister Béatrice of the Ratings . . . ' Although this was not the scriptwriters' intention, the satire is blunted as the story takes the line of thrills and sentiment. Media manipulation is in the end made to seem a legitimate weapon of defence for an individual if institutions refuse him something to which he is entitled in justice.

A second set of values is the lauding of career-mindedness and individualism. The characters who come out on top are Béatrice, Joseph and Olivier, the co-manipulators and co-mystifiers, although their motivations differ: the two journalists have professional reasons for doing what they do, Joseph emotional reasons. The only character who opposes them, Antoine, is depicted as weak and a figure of fun. But the value that this episode extols above all others perhaps is 'fellow feeling', a word used by Béatrice in the first sequence in reply to a viewer who has called in to discuss his marital problems. Relations with my wife have broken down, he tells Béatrice, although there is still a measure of fellow feeling between us. To which Béatrice answers: 'cultivate that like a rare flower'. One cannot ask too much of life. Being madly in love, passion, success at work, friendship: these are things that one cannot always have. Fellow feeling is a good second best. Béatrice is separated from her husband, but they are still accomplices, friends, ready to do each other a favour when needed. In short, fellow feeling is seen as one of the arts of living.

Les Cinq dernières minutes (*The Last Five Minutes*)
This is one of the very earliest series to have been shown on French television (Antenne 2). It began in 1958, and perhaps because of its longevity and the length of episodes (about 85 minutes) it is somewhat reminiscent of certain American series (*Colombo*, for instance). At the time of our research it was being shown once weekly, repeats alternating with new episodes. The main character is a police superintendant, Cabrol, a paternal and authoritarian but human figure. He relies a good deal on intuition in his work, but he is methodical and meticulous in checking the details of each piece of evidence and each theory. It is a police series, but *Les Cinq dernières minutes* does not in the least abide by the traditional rules for that genre. It is more of a documentary: Commissaire Cabrol's investigations will reveal the guilty person at the end (in the last five minutes in fact, as the title indicates), but in the meantime the viewer learns something about an unfamiliar social and working environment. In this respect the police-story plot could be said to be just a pretext. The setting and the social atmosphere of the place of the crime are described with precision, the questioning of suspects and witnesses becomes bogged down as it meanders through their past and motivations . . . And there is absolutely

Jacques Debary in Les Cinq derniers minutes

none of the mythology of the genre. Violence is never depicted, there are no car chases, clashes or epic conflicts between policeman and criminal. The psychological dimension prevails.

The episode analysed, 'Crime sur mégahertz', is a little like *Allô Béatrice*. The environment is a commercial radio station. Here again, the radio broadcasting studios and the technical and professional aspects are reconstructed accurately and in detail. Pat, a sexy girl DJ on a commercial radio station (broadcasting rock music and ghost stories) is killed. The suspects are a young radio technician called Luc, the radio station boss who was the girl's lover, Meinhart, her husband Paul, a man named Petrovic who is mentally unbalanced and has attacked her in the past, and members of Pat's family who have always disapproved of the work she does. The treatment is similar to that of many other episodes in the series: a series of *coups de scène*, new suspects coming into the story all the time, people assumed to be guilty, their possible motives, real or apparent evidence, a plot that is revealed only in the last five minutes. All the characters who seem likely suspects at the beginning – Luc, Meinhart, Pat's father – are shown as innocent at the end. Paul, the character whose part is initially written in such a way as to make him likeable to the policeman and to the viewers, is disclosed as the guilty party. The two main sets of values are – by the nature of the genre – in sharp opposition to each other. There are the values of the negative characters, among whom are the victim herself and the radio environment, in other words those who delight in manipulating the public, the 'microphone-addicts' who use and abuse power for their own ends, who compensate for their own frustrations by doing violence to their listeners and thus set dangerous mechanisms in motion. At the end they will be punished. Pat is killed. Paul, in spite of his intelligence and coolness, is the killer and will be found out. Above all the values are centred on the character of Cabrol, a policeman who not only knows how to ask questions but, through his understanding of each person's secret motivations and frustrations, can also help the people he questions. Without undue haste. Indeed, one might wonder whether all this is not an eulogy of slowness (the guarantee of a good police force?).

The story unfolds smoothly and gradually, the sequences are not long (only 8 out of the 42 last more than 3 minutes), but their internal pace is often slow. There are few changes from long shots to close-ups or vice versa; the camera moves, but not the characters. The truth emerges, but only slowly . . . And there is something that prevents a clear-cut distinction being made between good and bad, that prevents a final judgement; there is almost a nostalgic desire for an impossible fraternity. Between the two poles, the positive and the negative, there are intermediate positions, characters who, depending on the twists and turns of the plot, will finally converge towards one pole or the other. One of these positions is that of the young people who live from day to day in this pirate radio atmosphere. Their parents have not been able to care for them and they are still shaken and uprooted by the experience of 1968. Many of these young people might still be able to cope, to find the right path. As in the case of Luc.

The French 'feuilleton'

The 'feuilleton', or soap opera French-style, is a genre that reached French television screens fairly late in the day. At the beginning, in the 1950s, most fiction serials transmitted by ORTF were American and British productions, the majority being children's programmes.[3] The first French 'feuilletons' appeared in the late 1950s and were usually shown on Sundays at about 7 p.m. They were family stories and designed for family audiences. They differed from American and European serials in the length of individual episodes. Examples of these productions were *Le Tour de France de deux enfants* (Claude Santelli, 13 episodes in 1957, a second series in 1958), *Le Fils du cirque* (Bernard Hecht, 1960), *La Déesse d'or* (Robert Guez, 1961). In this running-in period, television schedules had not yet settled down, the times at which the 'feuilletons' were shown varied, and on occasions there was no continuity between two series.

The period of maturity and expansion began in the 1960s. The rush to acquire television sets led to a substantial increase in ORTF's resources (from television licences) and budgets. The output of fiction, especially series and 'feuilletons', increased accordingly. In 1963 there were 136 hours of 'feuilletons' and series, 29% of which were produced by ORTF, often as co-productions with film companies like

Gaumont or Pathé and with Telefrance, a company set up specially for the purpose of producing television programmes. By 1966, the transmission of serial fiction had already more than doubled (319 hours) and the percentage of imported programmes had fallen from 71% to 59%. In 1964, when the second channel came into being, ORTF set up a 'Service des Feuilletons' headed by William Magnin, whose work was to co-ordinate all productions and co-productions. In the meantime television scheduling had stabilised. The pattern was to show a family 'feuilleton' on Sundays just before the news (one of the most popular programmes was *Thierry la Fronde*, with four series between 1963 and 1966), and a 15-minute 'feuilleton' broadcast daily from Mondays to Fridays, this too scheduled just before the evening news: *Le Temps des copains* (1961), *Janique Aimée* (1963), *Rocambole, Rouletabille, Comment ne pas épouser un miliardaire* in 1966. Series made up of 30-minute episodes were shown on Thursday, Saturday and Sunday afternoons for children and in the evenings for adult audiences. These included *Belphégor* (1965), *Cécilia médecin de campagne* (1966), *Les Saintes chéries* (1966), *Jacqu le croquant* and *L'Homme de Picardie* (1969).

The year in which the growth in French-made soaps reached its apogee was 1971. Production covered the whole range of genres that best typified the 'génie français': sentimental intrigue (*Noelle aux quatre vents, La Demoiselle d'Avignon*), a panorama of an environment or a period of history (*François Gaillard, Mon fils, La Maison des bois*), a running series of a hero's adventures (*Les Nouvelles adventures de Vidocq, Quentin Durward, Arsène Lupin*).

A genre that was very popular with audiences in those years was the family saga, usually set in the past (*La Famille Boussardel, Les Thibaults, Au Plaisir de D., Les Dames de la côte,* etc.). The format was a mini-series of 6 or 8 episodes, with each episode lasting 60 to 90 minutes.

The golden age, however, was to continue for little more than a decade. French output of fiction reached its high point in 1971 (with 43% of the fiction on the air being home-produced). In the meantime, however, the schedules had expanded considerably (the third network started transmitting in late 1972) and the volume of fiction being shown increased in proportion, from 362 hours in 1971 to almost 800 hours in 1980. Original fiction production was unable to keep pace and, by 1980, it had fallen back to 27%. To make up for this drop in production there was a rise in imports, especially of American programmes, and repeats, both of which were increased four fold over a period of only a few years. When TF1 started to put on *Dallas* in 1981 on Saturdays at 9.30 p.m., there were no French high-quality programmes to compete with it. The tendency towards extending broadcasting hours continued apace (with regional programmes and breakfast television), there were ever more imports and repeats and there was stagnation in the home production of programmes. It is against this background that one should view and appreciate the decision reached in 1985 to create *Chateauvallon*, the '*Dallas* à la française'. This was intended at the same time to strengthen the existing policy of co-producing with other countries, especially with Italy and West Germany.

In this varied and chequered history it is not easy to discern any genres or narrative styles that stand out strongly enough to have left a clear-cut imprint on French production of fiction for television, in other words anything comparable in significance and continuity to the British soap opera. The most popular and perhaps the most genuinely French genre might be said to be the story with a historic setting, and in a sense this is a potential source of effective competition against imported programmes.

This does not mean, however, that – leaving aside the historic fiction genre – France should not produce fiction having a clear-cut French identity, with its own special features that distinguish it from fiction produced elsewhere. The four series analysed in the course of our research are all very different. The question we asked ourselves in our analysis was whether they had any features in common justifying a belief in the existence of a national tradition, a 'French style' of making television, and whether that style might be linked with France's cultural tradition in a broader sense. We feel that four points are worthy of note.

1) All these stories are firmly rooted in reality. They have what might be called a documentary component. The viewer is placed in the position of someone watching a news story or report. Many scenes in *Chateauvallon* were filmed in a real newspaper's printshop and office.

The radio studios in *Allô Béatrice* are in fact Europe 1's own studios. The episode of *Les Cinq dernières minutes* analysed was also filmed on the premises of a real radio station. Arles and the Camargue in *Le Paria* are shown just as they would be depicted in a travel documentary. In other words, the settings are realistic. The characters, too, are realistic – as already pointed out – in that they behave in the way people in their profession actually behave, using the same gestures and vocabulary. Finally, a number of real-life events with which the audience may be reasonably familiar are incorporated into the story. In *Les Cinq dernières minutes,* for example, the property scandals surrounding a politician in the South of France are clearly taken from real-life events. The press baron in *Chateauvallon,* Boulard, has something of Robert Hersant. The stories being told are set in real places and in very specific social environments, micro-universes of a readily identifiable career or profession that the viewer will, if he follows the story, get to know better. Here we have what we might call the Balzac tradition of the French novel, a tradition that was followed right from the very earliest 'feuilletons' to be produced in France, continued over the years and is still with us today. Examples of this tradition are to be found in the world of lawyers in *François Gaillard* and of boatmen in *L'Homme de Picardie,* both of which were written in the 1960s by Henry Grangé and André Majeur, who also wrote the scripts for early episodes of *Les Cinq dernières minutes.*

2) In French television fiction dialogue is always the key factor in the *mise en scène.* In our four programmes, the tone of the dialogue is very specific: it is the tone often used in French popular cinema, a typical exponent of which is Michel Audiard. It is a lively, cut-and-thrust, stinging, biting dialogue, a game in which the speakers are constantly batting words back and forth. There is a liking for the *bon mot,* the neatly turned witticism and the play on words. The language may sound spontaneous but in fact it is far from impromptu. It is a carefully 'written' language (which does not necessarily mean that it is literary), picking up the way ordinary people express themselves and incorporating dialect expressions, all in a terse and taut format. It is a far cry from the classic eloquence of theatre, which makes use of vocal tone and delivery. The psychological register is often one of mocking humour in which the characters affectionately chivvy each other. The fairly juicy

language, the delicate balance between a measured, serious use of vocabulary and syntax and its mischievous use, are often important factors in the construction of plots and the moral portraits of characters. The dialogue in American serials, on the other hand, is always descriptive and utilitarian.

3) Filming and editing techniques are very different from those used in a product such as *Dallas.* One of the characteristics of *Dallas,* or so it seems, is that so many sequences (almost one out of two) are centred on two characters facing each other over a desk or a restaurant table or in a living room, filmed by the use of rapid two-shots, very carefully 'framed' shots and, finally, with the camera zooming in to a close-up of the character who has come out top in the confrontation or duel. The average length of a sequence in a French 'feuilleton' is very much the same as in America, but in a French series the internal pace of the sequence is slower. Less use is made of cross-cutting and there is more camera movement, with short pan-shots and travelling-shots accompanying a character as they move. There are sequence shots in which variations in depth of field are used for dramatic effect. Unlike *Dallas*, the character is not normally isolated from the setting by using extreme close-ups but is shown as interacting with the environment, even though the shot may be confined to a few tools of his or her trade or familiar objects. Even when two characters face one another, the camera is not always placed dead in front of them (cutting from one to another); often a more oblique angle is preferred. The establishing shot is usually larger. Finally, the use of colour and lighting is different. In French serials (although not perhaps the low-budget productions such as *Allô Béatrice*), the colour components of the lighting are an important factor in setting the scene and defining the action. In *Dallas* the same levels of strong lighting are used for all daylight and indoor scenes; any differences in location and environment are indicated through the use of furnishings and token objects. In French serials, each setting is lit in its own way, and the alternating use of places with warm lighting and those with cold lighting, highly coloured sequences and shades of grey, is a very important mode of expression.

4) The main characters in contemporary television fiction tend to depart from the hero as conventionally portrayed in popular storytelling and even in the television programmes of an earlier period. The

discrepancy is not so great in *Le Paria* and *Les Cinq dernières minutes.* In *Le Paria* the leading character comes from a traditional breed of heroes: the innocent man returning to obtain justice, coalescing around him a clan of good people to combat the evil people. But from the way the story develops in the first episode the viewer only gradually discovers that he is the stuff a 'hero' is made of, since some of his gestures and his way of behaving make him seem unlikable. The same nuances are to be found in 'Crime sur mégahertz' in the serial *Les Cinq dernières minutes.* The main character in the first series of this 'feuilleton' in the 1960s, Commissaire Bourrel, was far closer to what is generally regarded as a hero: an effective policeman who loves his job, always on the ball, the protector of widows and orphans. His counterpart in the more recent series, Cabrol, shows signs of vulnerability: he is tired, sickly even, he is loyal and a good man but he makes mistakes and he is vaguely sceptical about the values which he is called upon to uphold in the course of his job. In *Allô Béatrice* and in *Chateauvallon,* the distance from the conventional hero figure is even greater. In the former, the two leading characters in the episode analysed are ambiguous to say the least; they are cynical careerists. In *Chateauvallon* the characters may be less ambiguous but they are certainly contradictory. They move easily and rapidly from being 'likeable heroes' (the victims of plots, committed to defending their family honour, in desperate search of a fleeting moment of happiness, etc.) to being 'anti-heroes' (plotting against others in their turn, prepared to defend their own interests by trampling on other people's, placing a higher priority on political compromise and money than on their own feelings). In brief, their characteristic is psychological discontinuity. This means that the *coup de théâtre* that is a typical soap opera device is not confined to sudden changes in situation but also includes sudden switches in the stance and attitudes of individual characters.

Notes

1. Research on the production in our project was undertaken by Régine Chaniac. Apart from this, the summary that follows is taken from the

analysis by Jean Bianchi.

2. This is not to say that the script was still being written while the programme was being transmitted, which would have meant that changes could be made to the plot in the light of audience reaction. When *Chateauvallon* went on the air for the first time on 4 January 1985, 13 of the 26 episodes in the first series were in the can and a further 13 were in the editing stage.
3. The programmes for younger viewers included: *Ivanhoe* (Britain), *Rin Tin Tin, Fury, The Wild Horse* and *Black Eagle,* all from the US. Among the series for adults shown in the evening were *Sherlock Holmes* (Britain) and *Destination Danger* (US).

6
The Federal Republic of Germany

Among all the countries covered, it is in West Germany that television has to the greatest extent been assigned the role of educating the public and of cultural leadership. The people responsible for programmes have had a far stronger and more dramatic sense of the identity and responsibility of public television. It may also be the country in which prejudice against popular television serials has survived longest. Indeed, underlying that prejudice there is certainly a hint of a broader and more deeply-rooted prejudice against the medium of television as such, which has been viewed (not just in the early years but until relatively recently) as the 'corrupter' of aesthetic and cultural values, as a 'vulgar' art by comparison with a noble art such as the cinema. Replying to a question on the nature of the film made for the cinema as opposed to the film made for television, this is what the critic A. Meyer had to say: 'We consider the television film as a great devaluation of the genuine elements produced and cultivated by the cinema in the context of a tradition dating back more than 80 years'. And yet German television has performed a decisive function in the promotion of film-making by the younger generation and by the great names of cinema. This function has grown in importance in recent years as the Federal Government has modified its policy on film-making and as the supply of Federal grants for film writers and directors has dwindled. An example of the importance of German television in this respect has been the role played by departments such as ZDF's 'Das kleine Fernsehspiel' and SFB Channel 3's 'Projektionen'. This television policy has been very important, most of all in the field of personal-view documentaries, short films and experimental films in general, but also in the field of full-length theme films produced and co-produced by television to be shown, in the first or second instance, on the large screen, or to be screened simultaneously on television and in the cinema. Over the past few years, the much discussed imminence of commercial television has fuelled fears that public television might be pressurised to abdicate its mission, at least in part, in order to compete. In this context, the 'rehabilitation' of popular melodrama following the success of the mini-serial *Holocaust* and other imported programmes, especially American programmes, has had differing effects. On the one hand, it has strengthened those fears. On the other it has suggested alternative programming strategies: if it is the mission of television to educate the public (among other things), and if it has been demonstrated that the use of Brechtian drama techniques for the production of television fiction has not had the results hoped for, why refuse to accept the evidence, ie that the melodrama and popular series that are so popular with the public may themselves be used to inform and to arouse public awareness of certain problems?

In our research, two programmes were analysed: *Schwarzwaldklinik* (ZDF) and *Lindenstrasse* (ARD), the only programmes that met the stated criteria in the period under review. They are very different from each other in content and production methods. Both are derived from foreign models, the former from American and the latter from British models, but at the same time they are closely linked with German symbols and realities. In the pages that follow, many references will also be made to another mini-series produced by ARD, *Heimat*, a milestone in the history of German television fiction.

Schwarzwaldklinik (Black Forest Clinic)

This is a ZDF and ORF (Austria) co-production. The first 24 episodes (23 in fact, as we shall see) went on the air between October 1985 and February 1986. The making of the second series of 24 episodes was delayed by the death of the director, Alfred Vohrer. In terms of content, *Schwarzwaldklinik* has drawn on three genres that are very popular in Germany: the 'Heimatfilm' (as discussed below); the 'Arztfilm' (stories of doctors and hospitals) and the traditional family serials of the *Forellenhof* type. While recognising that the German 'Heimatfilm' is far removed from the Western genre and that the

'Arztfilm' is far removed from both *General Hospital* and *M*A*S*H*, the way in which these traditional genres have been merged is very 'American'. The serial is set in a clinic in the Black Forest. All or almost all the stories are played out inside this ultra-modern hospital, and almost all the main characters are doctors and male and female nurses. ZDF publicised *Schwarzwaldklinik* in a trailer for the 1986 Cannes International Television and Video Market (MIP-TV) as a 'compelling story' of 'hope and pain, suffering and joy, of love and life, and death': its emphasis is 'on action . . . its plots do justice to any adventure series or cops and robbers saga . . . Many of the stories could have been taken from today's headlines. The series does not shy away from controversial topics and complex moral issues like the subject of mercy killing . . . The Clinic is confronted with crises faced in any big city hospital . . . it is a nerve centre of tangled human destinies'. If the blurb bears any relation to the makers' actual intentions, the product as offered cannot be said altogether to live up to all these high-flown promises. Episodes of *Schwarzwaldklinik* are not TV action films in the traditional, 'American', sense; sometimes stories are elevated to the rank of 'controversial topic' when they would be common currency in any big hospital. For example, in one episode a convict from a nearby prison is rushed into hospital for an emergency operation. Here the scriptwriters dramatise situations that have nothing very dramatic about them. Is a criminal's life worth as much as anybody else's life? How should one behave towards him? How much should he be supervised, and what will happen if he takes advantage of the situation and escapes? And so on. In another episode a young male nurse is accused of stealing from an old lady, his friend, on her death bed. The director of the hospital comes to his defence, many people dislike him, but in the end his innocence is proved and there are great celebrations. In the meantime a young man, a conscientious objector, has problems with one of his patients, a gruff old general who is not such a bad old stick when it comes down to it. . . Even so, there are a few truly controversial episodes like the one containing a highly realistic rape scene, which triggered off so much protest that in the end it was officially listed as pornographic material. The worried producers then withdrew one of the next episodes because it contained scenes of violence. In view of the general tone of the stories being told, which are aimed at a broad cross-section of viewers and go out early in the evenings and at weekends (Saturdays at 7.30 p.m. and Sundays at 8.45 p.m. on alternate weeks) these two episodes can only be seen as serious scripting misjudgements, and it is hard to understand how they could have been made.

Schwarzwaldklinik is in fact a family story, the story of a hospital – which after all is a large family. It is also a family story in a narrower sense in that it recounts the troubled relationship between the head physician, Professor Brinkmann, and his son Udo, who works as a doctor in the same clinic, together with their stories, their wives deceived, lovers dismissed and new loves, jealousies and betrayals. The lead character is Brinkmann père, the senior consultant, a surgeon at the top of his profession and a kind, sentimental man with great human qualities, always prepared to listen to the problems of those working for him, all the more human for his one (forgivable) fault, a weakness for women. But here again, everything remains in the family. His mistresses are invariably nurses, and the most recent – Christa – has had an affair with the son, Udo, before falling in love with the father. In the episode analysed, Prof. Brinkmann is going away, officially to attend a conference on the island of Sylt but in fact because Christa is spending her holiday there. Their love affair is just starting up. While the two are in Sylt, Brinkmann's ex-mistress Elena has a serious car accident. She dies soon after she is rushed to hospital. Udo thinks back over the circumstances in which his mother died ten years before, when Brinkmann was also away at a conference. On the very evening when his wife was breathing her last he was in a hotel room with Elena – was it to discuss a scientific paper? The episode concludes with a bitter confrontation and clash between Udo and his father.

Schwarzwaldklinik has been produced on a substantial budget (the 24 episodes cost DM 11 million) and with great professional expertise, as is only right and proper for a programme intended as the German answer to *Dallas* and also for export. In this respect the producers' hopes were borne out, at least in part. Paramount has paid almost DM 5 million for the rights to the series in the American, Asian and Arab markets (ZDF will also receive a percentage of the profits if Paramount manages to sell the rights to one of the three leading American networks – although this has not yet happened). ZDF has also sold *Schwarzwaldklinik* (but not all 24 episodes in every case) to Italy (RAI 2), Great Britain (Channel 4), France, Belgium, Switzerland, Finland and South Africa.

The product has undoubtedly been packaged with meticulous attention to detail. Each episode opens with a panoramic aerial shot of the green countryside and forest, zooming in onto the clinic in a manner reminiscent of the opening of *Dallas*. But with *Schwarzwaldklinik* the credit titles are in Gothic script, of course, and framed as in an old print or a picture postcard from the good old days. The camera work is professional, 'clean-cut', without rough edges, but at the same time it is linear and lacks inventiveness, perhaps for the very reason that the production has been made with one eye on the international market. The concern seems to be to avoid errors or a personal, individual style that might make it less easily and universally readable. The photography is not just unoriginal, it makes a particular effort to be derivative, 'quoting' from other tried and tested models that are immediately recognisable. For example, the hospital scenes are taken from American soaps such as *General Hospital*, the scene of Elena's car accident is derived from the made-for-TV action film and has a thriller-type sound track; it is also derived from the German series produced to educate the public about the causes of road accidents, *The Seventh Sense*. Scenes of Christa and Brinkmann on holiday on the island of Sylt are like holiday and nature documentaries. The two lovebirds stand kissing at the rudder of a boat, almost as if they were posing for beauty shots; behind these two bronzed, fit people who exude happiness a German flag flutters in the wind. In short, some of the sequences are merely a collage of clichés, no different from the filmed material put out by firms that specialise in public relations.

There is nothing haphazard about the decision to set the story in the Black Forest. In so doing, *Schwarzwaldklinik* is linked with the 'Heimatfilm', in other words the type of films (that came into being in Nazi times and were rediscovered in the 1950s and the 1970s – see below) that evoke in the viewer a strong sense of belonging and identification. 'Heimat' – literally 'Home' – has all the connotations of 'roots', having a house and a family in a very specific, well loved place. This need for a 'Heimat' is deeply imbued with a yearning for what

Gaby Dohm and Klausjürgen Wussow in Schwarzwaldklinik

Elias Canetti has called a symbol for almost every German, the forest as an archetype of shelter. Expressed in terms of human relations, it is equivalent to a sense of community. Archetypes such as the forest were passed down for centuries via the oral tradition of folk stories before they were 'deep-frozen', transformed into stereotypes by the mass communications media and the advent of cheap printing in the 19th century. The process of fixing and simplifying the symbols and archetypes continued with the introduction of photographic reproduction technologies for wide-scale distribution – to a point at which the stereotypes became clichés. The archetypes of the forest, the dark forest, and the clichés of the Black Forest are those that most commonly recur. And this is the heritage on which the film industry too has drawn. While it is true – as we shall discuss below – that the 'Heimatfilm' came into being during the Nazi regime and was in consonance with its nationalist ideology, it is no coincidence that it has survived the collapse of that regime: it has survived for the very reason that its roots are embedded in German tradition dating far back into the past.

Quite apart from history and tradition, there is a far more topical and practical, perhaps even utilitarian, link between the Black Forest and *Schwarzwaldklinik*. The way the success of *Schwarzwaldklinik* has been exploited by the producers themselves is striking: when *Schwarzwaldklinik* first appeared on the television screen on 21 October 1986, the protracted opening sequences – made up of no fewer than 17 pictures of the Black Forest – were faded out and a pretty announcer, dressed in a traditional 'Black Forest' costume, immediately came onto the screen. Using the most persuasive of ad-language, she offered viewers all the goods that ZDF was putting on the market to coincide with the launch of its new series. Among these products was a glossy coffee-table book on the Black Forest, described as an ideal present for the Christmas that was fast approaching. And barely had that Christmas season ended when the Black Forest tourist board recruited Klausjurgen Wussow, the actor playing the part of Professor Brinkmann, for a publicity campaign to revitalise the image of the Black Forest, so corroded by acid rain and tree disease. Thus *Schwarzwaldklinik* succeeded in restoring to the Black Forest at least some of its former reputation for magical beauty, even if tourists now visit it not so much to rediscover the forest as to see where Brinkmann and company are filmed on location, just as the Ewing ranch in *Dallas* has become a mecca for tourists. When in January 1986, 1,200 medical students staged a protest demo in that very place, they finally captured the attention of the media which they had been unable to obtain when they had demonstrated in the large towns.

Schwarzwaldklinik has beaten all the records: 24.6 million viewers (a 62% share of the television audience) by the end of the first week (during which, on a one-off basis, no fewer than four episodes were transmitted). By January 1986 the figures were over 28 million per episode, an unprecedented success. Today almost 50 million Germans have seen at least one episode in the series. *Dallas*, at the peak of its popularity, reached about 22 million viewers (just over 50%) per episode. Have the pupils outstripped their masters? Just as the production of *Chateauvallon* was halted when its leading lady was killed in a car accident, so production of the second series of *Schwarzwaldklinik* has been held up by the death of Alfred Vohrer, who has directed almost every episode. Facts such as these are more significant than any figures in revealing how the pupils, bright though they are, have nonetheless remained European; it's hard to imagine *Dallas* being stopped for similar reasons.

Lindenstrasse (Linden Street)

Very different from *Schwarzwaldklinik* is a production that has achieved only partial success, at least in terms of popularity with audiences: *Lindenstrasse*, produced by ARD. Right from the start the plan was for the serial to last for 200 episodes or more. Here again, ARD opted for a production system closer to the American (as the producers of *Chateauvallon* had done): electronic cameras were used and most of the filming was in a fixed studio location. This influenced the narrative structure, which had to be woven around stories that can be scripted, rehearsed and shot quickly and at low cost: four days' work to produce one 30-minute episode, three hours to tape and edit a 3-minute sequence, keeping down all the other post-production costs as well. The producers managed on the whole to keep to this schedule, but at the expense of quality. For a long initial period the editing and lighting left much to be desired. The decision to try out unknown actors and amateurs gave rise to major problems. Some had difficulty remembering their lines, with the result that the mistakes and gaps had to go on the air because there was no time to reshoot the scenes. The total cost of the first 52 of the 30-minute episodes of *Lindenstrasse* was DM15 million, compared with DM11 million for the 23 episodes of *Schwarzwaldklinik*, each of 45 minutes. The cost per minute for *Lindenstrasse*, DM9,615, was only just below the DM9,662 per minute that it cost to make *Schwarzwaldklinik*. The costs were inflated before production by the construction of an ultra-modern 1,500 m^2 sound stage, complete with 13 sets, plus all the outside locations. A comparison of the costs for the two series is clearly in favour of *Schwarzwaldklinik*, since a good deal of its cost was recouped through sales (almost half, i.e. DM5 million, from the sale of rights to Paramount), whereas *Lindenstrasse* had been intended for German audiences, even though its producers had taken British productions as their model. *Coronation Street* and *EastEnders* in particular were cited by its co-producer with WDR, Hans Geissendörffer, who had lived in London for a number of years. In fact *Lindenstrasse* is perhaps closer to *Brookside* than to other British soap operas in the sense that its characters, with a few exceptions, are white-collar rather than the working-class characters in most British soaps. If the German serial has anything in common with the models mentioned by Geissendörffer it is perhaps in its narrative structure, its use of a large cast, the interweaving of different stories, the fact that all the characters live in *Lindenstrasse*, with certain leading characters emerging more prominently than others, and the main subject of the soap opera being their affairs and those of their families.

Above all, whereas the stories in *Coronation Street* are set in the realm of everyday folk (the kind of people who keep smiling despite their troubles), in *Lindenstrasse* we are in a world of highly coloured melodrama. On the fourth floor of number 3 in the street live Franz and Henny, both of them teachers, with their two daughters Tanja and Meike. He is serious, romantic, peaceable. In short, he is dull, especially for a woman like Henny who dreams of adventure and grand passion and is highly ambitious. Henny moves up to the fifth floor to live with Stefan, her daughter Tanja's athletic tennis teacher. Tanja goes with her mother, while Meike stays with her father. Franz is in the grip of despair and takes to drink, neglecting the home and his little girl. To force her parents to come together again, Meike tries to commit suicide (previously she has tried to attract their attention by falling sick; in an attempt to catch a cold she has shut herself in the refrigerator and has almost died of hypothermia). In the meantime, Henny's relationship with Stefan, already 'disrupted' by her daughter Tanja, a second Lolita who exerts all her wiles to seduce Stefan, takes a turn for the worse when Stefen deceives Henny with another woman. Months go by and Henny seeks a reconciliation with Franz, but by now he hates her, he wants to move away and get a divorce. Henny takes her own life. And the melodrama continues, with Henny's father attacking Franz who is by now on the verge of collapse himself because of his ruined marriage, his feelings of guilt and his inability to look after his daughters even though they need him. He is needed above all by the little Meike, with her big eyes and her rosy cheeks – a new Red Riding Hood in a cruel world, a stereotype of sweet innocence.

On the second floor of the same house in Lindenstrasse live Hans and Helga Beimer, both of them in their forties, with their 16-year old daughter Marion and their 14-year old son Benny. Hans is a golden-hearted social worker who helps everyone to the best of his ability, supported in turn by his wife, who is equally unselfish. Happy in her role as a housewife, she is a perfect stereotype of the good mother in the best tradition of German family serials, the exact opposite of Henny. The writers have obviously wanted to point up the contrast between the Beimers and the couple on the fourth floor, Franz and Henny, who would fit perfectly into an American soap. The message is clear: Henny commits suicide at 35, whereas Helga is 45 years old, simple, without extravagant ambitions. Her only worry is that she is fat (but her husband, luckily for her, doesn't care). The only real problems for Helga and Hans are caused by their children. Benny has a crush on Tanja, who lives upstairs, but she treats him scornfully and with insults. He runs away to Portugal and refuses to come back home. Marion too, a quiet, serious girl, quite unlike the sexy Tanja, has problems with affairs of the heart. She goes on holiday to Greece with Vasily, the son of an immigrant couple who run the Greek restaurant in *Lindenstrasse*. The holiday ends badly since she, the stereotype of a young intellectual, is more interested in instructing him in the glories of Athenian culture, while he is interested in only one thing, going to bed with her. Marion is equally unfortunate with other loves later on. Indeed, everything happens to her. More than once she comes home with her clothes in tatters, her face bleeding and in her eyes that sad and distant look that, by dramatic convention, is worn by someone who has just been raped. Often she shuts herself away in her room for days on end while outside her parents rack their brains to understand what can have happened to her. Not much, usually. But one day, while her parents are in Portugal looking for Benny, Marion (despite having been told not to by her parents) goes for a cycling tour with her boy friend, at last finding true love. The boy is knocked down by a car and dies before her eyes, and she is injured. Despairingly and in a state of shock and depression, she contemplates suicide. Not even her father, who has always been so wonderful as a social worker, is capable of helping her . . . And so on and so forth.

As is obvious in view of the emphasis placed on the personal and often the very intimate aspects of the characters' lives, there is ample occasion for grand (and often gross) melodramatic effects and all the necessary cliff-hangers at the end of each episode. It is equally obvious that the scriptwriters (Geissendörffer himself and Barbara Piazza, a former social worker – a circumstance of which great play was made in the promotional campaign, to project an image of *Lindenstrasse* as a social-minded soap opera) surrendered too readily to the facile temptation of the crudely melodramatic. Many of the scenes they show are orgies of tears and blood and in the long run are altogether unrealistic and counter-productive because they go beyond any dramatic convention. All too often minor incidents are hyped to appear more sensational than is warranted. Inured by the implausibility of the scene when Marion comes home late, her blouse torn and her face bloodied, looking just as if she had been raped whereas in fact no such thing has happened, by the time viewers come to the close-up of the dying Henny they are no longer involved. And on occasions characters that have been consistently built up as stereotypes (and the whole of *Lindenstrasse* is in the final analysis a gallery of stereotypes) suddenly, and for no apparent reason, break the conventional codes of behaviour for those stereotypes, confusing the viewer. It seems unlikely that the authors should deliberately have departed from narrative convention in this way, all the more so since it is always counter-productive.

Perhaps the reason may partly be indecision before the event, in other words the (conscious or unconscious?) choice of a hybrid genre. On occasions the writers apply the rules of situation comedy, at other times the rules of soap and melodrama. This is fairly evident in the portrayal of the character of Henny. On the one hand it strikes a comic note, for example when showing her fixation with organic foods and jogging; on the other hand she is played in a tragic key, as she cries with tears of rage out of her unscrupulous selfishness and with tears of sympathy as the mother of an unhappy little girl who has tried to commit suicide. By the end her personality is so confused and contradictory that the viewer is inevitably left bewildered. Not surprisingly, the programme has been relatively unsuccessful, never reaching more than half of the audiences who watched *Schwarzwald-klinik*.

From 'the alienation effect' to melodrama.

The concern to educate and inform the public that was referred to at the beginning of the section has had a decisive influence on the schedules of German public television, certainly in the early years but also later, probably right up to the end of the 1960s. For instance, it meant that audience ratings did not have an undue influence over production choices. Even so it has, perhaps paradoxically, had the effect of legitimising the serial format. According to certain critics, for instance, 'an author may not be able to draw the viewer into his ideal world in a single television play, but it may be possible in a serial production'.[1]

For an understanding of the production and programming of fiction in the German Federal Republic, the structure of television in that country must be made clear. Each of the eleven Federal states (*Bundesländer*) has its own broadcasting station, except three states in northern Germany which are served by Norddeutscher Rundfunk. The nine stations are grouped to form a programmes cooperative, ARD, which transmits its own programme on Channel 1, ARD also produces five regional programmes for Channel 3.[2] Finally, the eleven states jointly run the second national channel, ZDF. In terms of programming, ZDF is a centralised body, but in production terms this network has the same Federal structure as the country. *Lindenstrasse* was the first serial to be co-produced by all the ARD stations. Normally the only co-produced programmes are news programmes and other information services, while each station is free to produce whatever it wants. Programmes made by individual stations are also broadcast via other ARD transmitter stations, which thus operate as the first nationwide network. Bayerischer Rundfunk of Munich has on more than one occasion refused to transmit programmes, on the grounds that they were inappropriate for Bavarian audiences, particularly those that lampoon Bavarian ways and traditions. The police series, *Tatort*, is a co-production, but not in the accepted sense since each episode is made independently by individual regional stations. *Tatort* can be defined as an 'umbrella' series, a national container. The only thing the episodes have in common is the basic idea of the plot. There has been a crime, and a police officer is called in to solve it. Even so, had it not been for the success of *Tatort* the nine partner stations would have been unlikely to have taken the path to true co-production of fiction serials. It has been rightly pointed out,[3] however, that the key to the success of this serial, which has now been on the air for over 15 years, lies in the very lack of standardisation of the episodes of which it is constituted. Each policeman in the serial lives and works in a different city, having his own style and his own political opinions, just as each city has its own separate problems and its own criminal fauna. Over the course of the years, eight police officers have gradually faded out and others have come onto the scene to deal with new types of crime and different social contexts. Because of the flexibility of its structure, with differing realities reflected in turn, the serial has reached and satisfied many types of audience. Inevitably *Tatort* has been the programme involving the largest number of writers and directors.

Another effect of the decentralisation of production is the high percentage of productions sub-contracted to outside companies, often only average to small in size. This in turn is the reason why serials, except for police serials, tend to consist of a few episodes – 3 to 6, only in exceptional cases as many as 13. It is a point we shall discuss in more detail shortly.

German serial production can be grouped under two main headings. The first and undoubtedly the best is the police series, the second is the mini-serial play, with episodes usually lasting about an hour, shown on a weekly or multi-weekly schedule. The first type of serial abides by the conventional rules of the genre, with fixed characters, specific settings and an indefinite number of episodes. They are also all on the crime theme except for *Drombusch*, which recounts the adventures of an ordinary family in Darmstadt. Among the best known in this genre are *Der Kommissar Derrick, Der Alte, Ein Fall für Zwei* and naturally the forerunner of the genre, *Der Kommissar* (1969-76, 97 episodes), with Eric Ode as the leading character. This ZDF production has perhaps been the most successful serial ever to be transmitted in Germany, reaching an audience which in the years of its prime topped 30 million. It was the success of this serial that persuaded ARD, in the late 1960s, to launch *Tatort*, and in turn the success of *Tatort* was a challenge that induced ZDF to bring out *Derrick* in 1974. These three serials topped the audience ratings, easily outdoing the two American serials most popular with German audiences, *Columbo* and *Kojak*. The format of the German series was inspired by the American crime series, especially in the early stages. Over the years, however, the episodes were rooted more and more firmly in the German social scene. They covered not only subjects like drugs – almost a compulsory theme for police stories today in every country – but also issues such as property development scandals, immigrant workers, youth protest and pollution. Obviously the attention devoted to certain topics arose not just from sociological and cultural motivations but on the whole from a desire to capture the viewer's interest by telling stories related to topical events, the kind of stories that are headlined in the newspapers. Whatever the motivations, however, these are the factors that distinguish the German programmes from their American competitors. The same is true of the stress placed on the inner workings of characters' minds rather than the action. It is hardly surprising that the police stories sometimes resort to melodramatic motifs, perhaps barely sketched in but always recognisable. The director of *Schwarzwaldklinik*, Alfred Vohrer, had previously directed countless episodes of *Derrick* over almost a decade. Herbert Lichtenfeld, the scriptwriter for *Schwarzwaldklinik*, had written the script for many episodes of *Tatort*.

Both Lichtenfeld and Vohrer, besides their respective contributions to the two police series, had all the right credentials to work on *Schwarzwaldklinik*. Lichtenfeld is also the author of many stories serialised in illustrated magazines, while Vohrer had directed many films in the melodramatic genre, including film versions of many highly popular kitsch novels by Johannes Mario Simmel and Heinz G Konsalik.

Under the other fiction programme heading, as we have pointed out, come the serial plays in a small number of episodes. They are generally adapted from literary classics and inspired by historic events. Examples of this type of programme are Theodor Fontane's *Von der Sturm*, Thomas Mann's *Buddenbrooks* and *Felix Krull*, and *Mozart*, a biography. But there are also original scripts based on contemporary stories: Like *Schwarz-Rot-Gold (Black-Red-Gold)*, a tele-story in three instalments about high financial crime; *Tod eines Schülers (Death of a Student)*; *Unser Walter*, the story of a Down's Syndrome child; and other 'lighter stories' about daily life like *Hans und Hof* dealing with rural problems, and cheerful Bavarian tales like the Münchner Geschichte stories. In most instances these are mini-series but there have also been attempts to produce long series like *Ein Herz und Seine Seele (A Heart and its Soul)* produced by the WDR (Westdeutscher Rundfunk). The latter is the story of a reactionary father who comments on politics ironically; equally ironically the father is capable of self-criticism. Inspired by the American sit-com *Archie Bunker*, which was itself based on the BBC's *'Till Death Us Do Part*, it was written by Wolfgang Menge, a well known television writer. The series was interrupted, partly because of the problems caused by its very length (actors were unwilling to commit themselves for too long a period; the author fell short of ideas) and partly also because the producers realised that the main character had been totally misunderstood. Although described by the scriptwriters as reactionary, racist, small-minded like his American and British models, the public eventually grew to love this character.

In the history of the intellectually and socially committed literature of Germany, a significant chapter is that of the tele-films and series produced by Rainer Werner Fassbinder. The fact that an author like Fassbinder was offered the possibility of working in the television

Hanna Schygulla and Gottfried John in Acht Stunden sind kein Tag

medium[4] was in itself relevant not just for all the positive and negative lessons that could be learned from this experimentation, something that could never have happened in other countries and could no longer happen in Germany today, but also because Fassbinder's work, or at least some of it, ended by serving as a point of reference in the debate between the school that sees television as having a 'cultural' mission and the advocates of 'popular' television. Some people hoped that Fassbinder would reconcile the two schools of thought, although they were to be disappointed. WDR, the largest and most active station in the ARD network, commissioned Fassbinder to make *Acht Stunden sind kein Tag (Eight Hours are not a Day)* in 1972. According to Peter Märthesheimer, who at the time was an editor in WDR's drama and entertainments department headed by Günther Rohrback, *Acht Stunden sind kein Tag* is a conscious attempt to use the 'bourgeois' genre of family story so popular in Germany in order to convey social and political messages of a progressive nature to a mass audience. Fassbinder seemed to be the obvious choice, especially as he was well acquainted with the work of Douglas Sirk, the outstanding director of Hollywood melodrama in the 1950s. A key factor in this stategy was the creation of 'hybrid heroes'. In the serial in question, the actors looked the part of blue-collar workers, at least as far as their clothes were concerned, but otherwise displayed all the characteristics of white-collar workers: courage, decisiveness and intelligence, 'not mere objects of history but also . . . subjects who . . . could take fate into their own hands.' *Acht Stunden sind kein Tag* was the first family serial to be produced in West Germany which consciously adopted the stylisation of a US television soap. Although it had been intended as an experiment in Brechtian alienation, ironically it became the first step towards what was finally to be a perfect blend of the German family genre and the American soap, without which a product such as *Schwarzwaldklinik* would never have been evolved. According to some critics, who quote the deliberately mannerist, almost expressionistic, camera style and the actors' formal language ('Hochdeutsch'), together with a *mise en scène* that enables the viewer, but not the character, to see and evaluate conflicts, Fassbinder succeeded in expressing visually a Brechtian sense of spatial distance and separation. Other critics disagreed strongly. Some of them, in reviewing Fassbinder's television work, found it excessively mannered and employed terms such as 'formalistic rubbish', using 'effects for the sake of effect' and 'artificiality'. They pointed out that Fassbinder's deliberately artificial restructuring of reality does not necessarily translate into an exposure of the complex social conflicts underlying the surface realism of everyday life.[5] The production of *Acht Stunden sind kein Tag* was halted after the fifth episode. Another very controversial case was *Berlin Alexanderplatz*. When a critic wrote in *Bild Zeiting* that the play was 'dark, you can't see anything', WDR issued releases explaining that it was an 'aesthetic dark', not a technical error, although the lower lighting level of the television screen might have made the 'dark darker'. To which the critics replied that if you make a 13-hour feature film, one that can be shown only on television because it is far too long to be shown in the cinema, creating pictures that would be beautiful on the large screen but are almost black on the small screen amounts to an 'aesthetic error.'[6]

In the late 1970s, pressure from the people within television who had tried to oppose the spread of popular programmes shown in prime-time virtually died away, and with it the desire to create something like the Brechtian alienation effect by recourse to advanced video technology to manipulate the television image, such as the chroma-key. These broadcasters felt out of touch with a public they had sought to enlighten and educate. At the same time, there was growing pressure from politicians (one of whose strengths was the power of the regional parliaments to allow or disallow applications for an increase in television licence fees). According to the politicians, one of the duties of public television was to meet the needs of a mass audience (the people who pay their licence fees). The dilemma of how to entertain and educate a mass audience at one and the same time is still unsolved; indeed, it has become a more dramatic issue as the day draws nearer when public television has to face the competition of commercial television. Experience shows that information programmes, however topical and controversial their subject, cannot compete in terms of audience ratings against entertainment programmes, especially in prime-time.

This was the background for the decision by WDR, which was after all the station that had commissioned *Acht Stunden sind kein Tag*, to buy the rights to the American serial, *Holocaust*.[7] And it is certainly ironic, as Michael Hofmann observes,[8] that public television should have imported a mini-serial produced for commercial networks for the sole purpose of proving that public television was not to be outdone by commercial television – although competition from commercial

Fritz Weaver, Meryl Streep, James Woods and Rosemary Harris in Holocaust

television is still only a future prospect, not yet an existing threat. The purchase of *Holocaust* marked a turning point in the history of television in the German Federal Republic.

From its very beginnings following World War II, one of the main aims that public service broadcasting had set itself was to inform ('enlighten') public opinion about the Nazi regime and the genocide it had perpetrated. But audience interest had always remained on a relatively low level. *Holocaust*, on the other hand, became the focus of national controversy even before the first episode went on the air on 22 January 1979. It was *Holocaust*, even before *Dallas* (the first episode of which was to be broadcast by ARD in June the following year), which sparked off a public debate on the television serial drama. Always under fire, this was viewed by critics and broadcasting officials alike as a minor genre, one that was quite unsuitable for conveying an adequate picture of the complex realities of everyday life because of its tendency to simplify and use stereotypes. The enormous emotional impact of *Holocaust* on the public forced many people to reconsider this view. Although it had been shown on the third, regional channel, 30% to 40% of German households (between 10.4 and 14.4 million people) watched each of the four episodes, and from 3 to 5.6 million viewers watched the studio phone-in discussion after each episode. It should be noted that the great efforts deployed to 'upgrade' the product made it a 'serious' event. Each episode was preceded by a documentary by way of introduction and historical background, and it was then followed by a discussion among experts, politicians and journalists. To ensure that the programme was discussed in depth in schools, the regional school authorities and other bodies distributed information material for teachers and pupils. The respectability of *Holocaust* was endorsed by Heinrich Böll, who declared that after *Holocaust* the enlightened representation and the emotional representation of conflict could no longer be said to be mutually exclusive.[9] And certainly, after *Holocaust*, productions dabbling in Brechtian dramatic techniques were to vanish from prime-time television. The events surrounding *Holocaust* seem to suggest that the issues raised by the importing of American serials related not so much to the conflict between American value systems and one's own national values and identity as the conflict between commercial television and public service television, at least in West Germany.

It was in this new climate that *Heimat* came into being, the German reply to the American challenge of *Holocaust*. And that reply came from WDR, the same station that had imported the American serial. Nor was that all: *Heimat* was made by editor Joachim von Mengershausen of WDR and director Edgar Reitz, the men who had put the work of Christian Ziewer onto the small screen – as we have seen (see note 6), perhaps the most advanced cinematic attempt to use Brechtian dramatic techniques ever made in Western Germany. Although Reitz had always maintained that the inspiration for his family saga had come from *Holocaust*, the influence of *Roots*, which had been a great success with the German public, was just as evident, not only because the English word 'roots' perfectly renders the implications of the German work 'Heimat' (see the discussion above in connection with *Schwarzwaldklinik*). Like the producers of *Roots*, Reitz preferred to use little-known actors, even amateurs who spoke the regional idiom, to create a sense of authenticity. Marita Breuer, who played the female lead, was virtually unknown before her role in Reitz's serial made her a household name.

Heimat tells the story of a modest family living in a backwoods village from 1918 to our own days. It is the history of Germany as seen through the eyes of its central character Maria, a symbolic figure who bears the weight of her family's sins and sinners, people who were unrepentant after 1945 and who devoted all their efforts to creating their own little 'Wirtschaftswunder' (economical miracle). Maria was shown by Reitz as being a suffering mother figure, the symbol of a Germany defeated and destroyed, somewhat as Helma Sanders-Brahms did in her film *Deutschland bleiche Mutter (Germany Pale Mother)* – a sort of compromise, perhaps, since the time had not yet come when there could be a return to the altogether discredited term 'Vaterland'. As Hofmann reports, when Gustav Heinemann, the President of the Federal Republic of Germany at the time, was asked in the early 1970s whether he loved his fatherland, he replied: 'I love my wife!'

To assess the implications and importance of Reitz's *Heimat*, it should be borne in mind that during the Nazi regime the term 'Heimat' had been the very symbol of Teutonic nationalism, and the Third Reich had exploited the 'Heimatfilm' genre to the full. It was to flower again in the 1950s but did not survive the cultural criticism of the early 1970s. Reitz's *Heimat* restored the respectability of the genre. Reitz could tell that story with great authenticity because he had been born and had grown up in the region in which the events were set. He knew its dialects, usages and customs, he was familiar with every tiny mannerism of his people. This is what enabled him to tell his story without compromising its credibility. His is an emotional defence of the 'little people' of the Nazi epoch. Many of the characters managed to profit by the opportunities offered by the regime, but they were humble folk who had never had much from life.

When, in one of the episodes, a little boy asks a question about the concentration camps, his family remains silent. *Heimat* avoids any discussion in depth of the problem of genocide. 'The persistence of the melodrama might indicate the ways in which popular culture has not only taken note of social crises,' wrote Thomas Elsaesser, ' . . . but has also resolutely refused to understand social change in other than private contexts and emotional terms.'[10] And there is no doubt that the melodramatic form does not lend itself to conveying abstract concepts regarding the collective guilt of a people. What it celebrates above all else is the subjective viewpoint. The melodramatic form may have made it possible for *Heimat* to restore credibilty to the standard excuse that the German people has already been punished enough by all it has suffered during and after World War II.

It took no less than five years' work to produce the eleven episodes of *Heimat*, indicating the difficulties encountered by Reitz and Mengershausen in coming to terms with the genre of melodrama. It is true that when the idea of the series was mooted they had already turned their backs on realism and Brechtian drama, but at the same time they were not yet prepared to take the opposite path wherever it might lead. Thus they attempted something a little like naturalism, something poetic at its best, something very close to crass sentimentalism at its worst. It is almost a whispered melodrama. While the makers of *Roots* launched their serial as a story of 'terror and death' and 'love and triumph', the producers of *Heimat* were to tone down the words from 'triumph' to 'success', although they assured the public that in *Heimat* there would be 'love', 'unhappiness' and 'simple humour' in sufficient measure to supply the audience with a steady flow of tears. When you watch *Heimat*, notes the critic Peter Buchka, you never know whether these tears come from your emotion, your laughter or your mourning. Perhaps, observes Hofmann, they are above all tears of self-pity.

Notes

1. Werner Kliess at Teleconfronto 1983. This chapter is based on research conducted by Michael Hofmann on behalf of the CSS project.
2. In March 1986, ARD embarked on a national satellite-transmitted programme, *Eins Plus*. In the same way, two of the regional programmes mentioned can be received nationwide via satellite. In late 1984 ZDF in turn launched an international programme, also via satellite, in conjunction with Swiss and Austrian television (SRG and ORF).
3. Silvana Abbrescia, in her paper at Teleconfronto.
4. The best-known programme is perhaps the last: *Berlin Alexanderplatz* (1980), from the novel by A. Doblin. *Acht Stunden sind kein Tag* (1972) is discussed in the text. The others were: *Welt am Draht* (1973), a story in two episodes, Fassbinder's only excursion into the world of science fiction; *Angst vor der Angst* (1975), the story of a woman who goes mad out of a fear of becoming mad; *Bremer Freiheit* (1972), the story of Geesche Gottfried, a woman from Bremen who killed 15 people and was hanged in the market place; *Ich will doch nur, dass Ihr mich liebt* (1976), the story of a man who reveals in every gesture he makes his failure to understand that the secret of love is to give of one's self; and *Bolwieser* (1977), based on a novel by Oskar Maria Gref about a couple in a small town in southern Germany. It may be of interest that while the ratio between original works and adaptations in Fassbinder's work for the cinema was 2:1, in his work for television it was 1:5. Regarding Fassbinder's television work, see the essay by Thomas Thieringer in Tony Rayns (ed.), *Fassbinder* (London: British Film Institute, 1979), as well as the book edited by Giovanni Spagnoletti for Teleconfronto.
5. See the essay by Thieringer cited above and the essay by Manuel Alvarado in the same volume.
6. A more 'Brechtian' and more intellectually rigorous contemporary of Fassbinder in those years was Christian Ziewer, the director and author of *Liebe Mutter, mir geht es gut* (1973), *Schneeglöckchen blühn im September* and *Der aufrechte Gang* (1977), which were also successful with viewers. The first two programmes achieved a 32% share of the audience, the third 25%.
7. Breaking with the past, when purchases had to be agreed by all broadcasting stations in the ARD network, WDR took the initiative of acquiring *Holocaust* on its own.
8. As with the reports by the other research groups, the full text of Hofmann's report can be obtained on application to the Consiglio Italiano

per le Scienze Sociali.

9. Michael Hofmann points out the analogy between *Roots* in the US and *Holocaust* in Germany (and earlier in the US as well): the controversy that arose when the two programmes came out brought the 'highbrow' advocates of 'cultured television' into conflict with the 'middlebrow' advocates of a popular television, the type of television that speaks to the person in the street. 'Because it had tackled the themes of the monumental injustice and atrocities of modern history,' observes Hofmann, 'the image of melodrama has earned its promotion from the ranks of escapist soap opera to those of a serious dramatic work.'
10. Thomas Elsaesser, 'Tales of Sound and Fury: Observations on the Family Melodrama', in Christine Gledhill (ed.), *Home Is Where the Heart Is* (London: British Film Institute, 1987).

7
Italy

For the Italian share in the research project, single episodes were taken from the following five mini-series: *Voglia di volare (Longing to Fly)*, *. . . E la vita continua (. . . And Life Goes On)*, *Quei 36 gradini (Those 36 Steps)*, *Casa Cecilia – un anno doppo (Cecilia's House – a year after)* and *La piovra (The Octopus)*. The latter does not really fit into the category of 'family stories' – it was included primarily because it was the only one to sell well abroad and was also the most narratively 'open', i.e. it was closer to a serial because the initial series was followed by *La piovra* 2 and 3 (*La piovra* 4 will soon follow). However, care was taken to select an episode in which family story elements are strongly emphasised: in the episode the marriage of Commissioner Cattani breaks up, the relationship between Cattani and Titti begins, and Cattani's daughter rebels against her parents' decision and decides to remain in Sicily with her father.

Voglia di volare (Longing to Fly)
The main characters of this mini-series are David, a forty-year-old Alitalia pilot, and his wife Barbara, who is separated from him and lives in Rome with their fifteen-year-old daughter Andreina. The episode studied (the fourth and last) presents the story of four relationships either undergoing difficulties or not being fulfilled: that between David and his wife; that between David and his girlfriend Cristina (they have split up); that between David and his daughter (they do not communicate successfully and he is devastated by her attempted suicide); and finally the relationship between Andreina and Stefano, a long-standing boy-friend whom she currently rejects. The problem of

the relationship between father and daughter dominates and it provides a tortuous and tormented set of experiences for David, who is incapable of shaking himself free. After his daughter's attempted suicide he goes on leave and gives up flying. There are no shortage of symbols and metaphors – no doubt he will start flying, living and loving again at the end of the episode, especially as just before the end all the problems are resolved. After the death of David's father there is a rapprochement between the pilot and his wife, which seems to herald a decision to return to each other (she creates the possibility of the rapprochement by attending the funeral). Having surmounted her difficulties, Andreina establishes normal relations with her father (again it is important to note that it is always the woman who plays the active role in resolving problems); finally to the great delight of Stefano, who has persevered through everything, his relationship to Andreina is restored. The only relationship not to continue is that which lies outside the family, i.e. the one between David and Cristina.

As a result one critic was able to write that *Voglia di volare* could be considered ' . . . a moral piece because it puts in the foreground the failure of all the irregular family situations which have repercussions on children's lives', and according to the Catholic magazine *Famiglia Cristiana*:

> *Voglia di volare*, despite its picture-story superficiality, indirectly constitutes an encomium for family unity . . . It is positive, or rather it is among the more positive offerings provided nowadays by public or private television. But how far we are from absolute values and how sad it is that we must content ourselves with the morality of this domestic tele-novela. There is no analysis of the causes of such a breakdown, generally summed up in the immaturity of the father, the chief character. Apart from the alarm that might be engendered as regards the safety of international flights entrusted to such immature pilots, the tele-romance solves the affair in terms of magical psychology: suddenly the father matures and everything falls into place.

It is a story without pretensions which could have been told in bubble captions or as a picture story and yet it is told with a certain charm and also with a certain attention to the psychology of the characters. Andreina and her mother Barbara, in particular, are two convincing, well-acted characters who only occasionally are improbably scripted, such as when the childish and naive thirteen-year-old Andreina says to her father 'But when will you give up exploiting the women whom you have close by?'. There is also a degree of humour in the conversations of all the children in the programme, whereas David's character proves to be dull and stereotyped.

The production is not particularly imaginative and the pace sometimes slackens, but it is not slipshod. Predictably, considering that the subject is not especially original, the script here and there slips into the banal (for example in the meeting between Andreina and her father's girlfriend) and indulges in the use of the melodramatic (for example when David returns to his parents' house), occasionally surrealistically so. In the last scene David, having returned to piloting his DC-9, finds the ghost of his father in the cockpit (but the camera angle makes him appear as if he was sitting on the clouds just outside the aircraft). The father tells David to 'hold fast . . . not to be afraid . . . I shall always be near you . . . ' David, emotionally touched, weeps, but suddenly afterwards, finally calm, replies to questions from his co-pilot about what is happening to him: 'No, everything's OK. I'm not crying any more now.' Thus the story ends in the style of pure melodrama, and a television critic described the serial as ' . . . a tear-jerking hotchpotch, containing love, sickness, death, reconciliation and cures, a sort of *Kramer v. Kramer* with a touch of homegrown provincialism'.

. . . E la vita continua (. . . And Life Goes On)

This is a family saga which makes a nodding reference to the *Dallas* type of programme without really imitating it. As in *Dallas*, the vicissitudes of life depicted are those of a wealthy family which is divided and unhappy, but there is no central figure like JR in the Italian production. Furthermore, whilst the clashes between the chief characters in both programmes are often dramatic, violent and public, in . . . *E la vita continua* they are more internalised and less immediate. In *Dallas* wealth is the object of contention, in . . . *E la vita continua* wealth is merely the setting. *Dallas* is a story not yet concluded – what we see on the screen is taking place today or perhaps tomorrow – whereas the Italian production tells of the past and was conceived in terms of the spirit of 'How we were'.

Radiocorriere billed . . . *E la vita continua* as ' . . . thirty years of Italian history presented through the vicissitudes of a family of Lombard industrialists', but history is merely used as a backdrop, it does not provide the motor force of the narrative. To take the episode studied, for example, the historical setting chosen is 1968 and the climate that of student unrest. The opening conversation between two students – Laura and Vittorio – whom we presume to be politically aware, consists of slogans and clichés which could have been written by journalists who wished to give a flavour of the period but didn't necessarily understand the issues at stake. And yet whilst this conversation is taking place, in a university lecture theatre actual footage, borrowed from the RAI archives, of May '68 in France is shown. One cannot help feeling that the Director (Dino Risi) wished to ridicule, or at least to treat with ironic indifference, that political climate and those characters. The 'trial' to which a lecturer is subjected by his students is realistic enough but his character is scarcely credible, being lost in a sort of human and ideological limbo, and in general characters and dialogues are highly stereotyped. The result is hardly history.

This is unfortunate because the choice of a plot based on real events and linked to periods in which societal happenings had far-reaching effects created the scope for a more thorough and credible treatment. The reconstruction of the social events of the 1950s and the reports of political and economical happenings still do not succeed in providing an intelligible account of Italy's recent history – the spirit and style of the programme are close to those of an almanac. On the other hand this might well have been the intention of the producer and the scriptwriters – simply to portray so many stories rather than history itself. The cast is international and over 100 locations were used not just in Brianza (where the programme was set) but also in Cannes and Berlin.

All this having been said, and despite the slogans with which the mini-series was introduced, . . . *E la vita continua* is above all else a family story and it is as such that it should be viewed and analysed. The ingredients are all there – love and passion, conflicts between generations, a wide range of characters with intertwining narratives and many dramatic events. As in almost all family stories produced by Italian television the situation at the outset of the episode in question is typically that of a broken family, and in this one the emphasis is on the relations between adults and young people rather than between adults. There are three stories that interlock: the relationship between Laura and Vittorio, that between Laura and her mother, Silvia; and the relationship between Vittorio and his father, Saverio.

Silvia is a managing woman, cold, sure of herself; caught up in the rhythm of her work which only allows her to give brief spells of attention to her daughter, she is essentially selfish. Laura deals with her mother on her own ground by flattering her: you are the liberated woman, I have always admired you for it, you have had your affairs, now leave me to live mine. Similarly, Saverio is a successful businessman. Between him and his son there is essentially no conflict but Vittorio feels that his father has never had a high opinion of him. He is distressed over this although he is determined to defend his own independence – but this is only revealed when his father rushes up to 'save' him. Thus whilst Silvia's role is unchanging, Saverio rediscovers

Virna Lisi, Tobias Hoesl, Jean Pierre Marielle in . . . E la vita continua

his paternal love in a moment of crisis when he abandons his own affairs in order to help his son. Meanwhile, Laura, who is having an affair with the lecturer, learns from her mother's example to survive her own disappointments in love and to face life standing on her own two feet.

Despite offering a story which would give a psychoanalyst a field-day, the screenplay is good – tidy and realistic. Again however, as with other Italian series, the melodramatic moments detract somewhat from what are otherwise quite credible conversations and situations. For example, in order to 'wean' his son off heroin, Saverio takes Vittorio off to the country where they stay for eight long months. On the day of victory where the son says 'I'm cured' he and his father chase each other across the meadow yelling and Vittorio shouts: 'yes, spank me, spank me as you used to do when I was little!' – a nostalgia for an authoritarian father (in the old days, when fathers used to spank, certain things did not happen), or for a childhood dreamed of as innocence? The drug question has been handled as an exclusively 'private' affair without any reference to the wider social problems involved and the script indulges in some common misconceptions. Vittorio is shown in Greece smoking a 'joint' (as if to say: beware, they start with a joint and end up with heroin, mainlining and desperate), and the drug pusher is a physically repellant 'creature', drooling, with crooked teeth and an evil smile.

The director, Dino Risi, is well known for several films he made which belong to the genre of Italian light comedy and which depict Italian life in the 1950s. He obviously enjoyed the unusual opportunity of working on what is effectively a six-hour long film. The fact that the film was subsequently stretched to eight hours may account for a certain loss of rhythm and occasional slowness.

Quei 36 gradini (Those 36 steps)

Set in a mansion block in the Parioli quarter of middle/upper-class Rome, this mini-serial recounts the lives of the joint owners of the building and of the other people who are connected with it. It is the most 'Italian' of the mini-serials under examination, partly because of the decision to make the characters talk in dialect. It is also possibly RAI's most successful attempt to create an original fiction series which neither apes American programmes nor follows earlier Italian models.

The central character is that of Pietro, the caretaker of the building, a man in his late forties, unmarried. Pietro is secretly in love with Signora Matilde, who lives in one of the apartments of the building, after separating from her husband. Pietro and Matilde have at least one thing in common, namely Rosa, a young girl whose mother abandoned her (asking Pietro and Matilde to look after her) in order to run after her lover, Mariuzzo. Pietro is so fond of the child that when one year later suddenly the mother shows up again (she has in the meantime married Mariuzzo) and tells him she wants the child back, he is shocked. And so is Matilde. Rosa too does not appear especially pleased. At about the same time, Dora, a Countess, moves into one of the apartments of the building which she has bought. An arrogant and unscrupulous woman, the Countess soon succeeds in kicking other tenants out and buying their apartments. She makes no secret that she aims at owning the whole building. Pietro, beside hating her as a person, sees her as a threat – he has always regarded that building as *his* place and hates the idea of the old tenants leaving. The Countess, moreover, has made no mystery of the fact that she plans to get rid of him too, eventually.

Like *Voglia di volare, Quei 36 gradini* also belongs to the 'all heart and sentiment' tradition but manages to avoid many of the pitfalls of the genre. It is a far more sophisticated and less stylised production, the events recounted are more complex and varied, the direction is meticulous and some of the characterisations are extremely well drawn and scripted. It is also a pleasant surprise to have a programme which despite being intended for a mass audience, contains a basic pessimism which the happy ending of some of the story lines does not disguise.

Particularly well drawn are the characters of Pietro, the caretaker, Rosa the little girl and the Countess, a negative character who, however, often livens up what would otherwise turn out to be flat and predictable situations. Dora, moreover, brings into the story class antagonism, an element not often found in this kind of programme. For example, there is a conversation between Dora and Pietro where she tells him that there is going to be a minister among her party guests and at the same time she tries to discover Pietro's political opinions. He replies that if that man is a minister then at least one thing is for certain, namely he, Pietro, didn't vote for him. Compare this conversation with the scene between Saverio and the garage mechanic in . . . *E la vita continua* where the mechanic kisses Saverio's Jaguar and exclaims 'You beauty . . . I would marry you. Happy the rich, who have no worries!'.

Overall, however, it is the nonconformist portrayal of the family which is most striking about *Quei 36 gradini*. Pietro and Matilde do not succeed in communicating and they only meet up again as a result of the obstinate determination of Rosa, who has picked them as her chosen parents. It is the little girl, not the adults, who creates the new (informal) family. Relations between Rosa and her real mother have broken down despite the genuine efforts of her new stepfather Mariuzzo (presented as a 'good mafioso') to win the girl's friendship. The love between Carla and Aldo, who keep parting and then laboriously (and without passion) keep making it up is overshadowed by the memory of his wife leaving him and then dying in a Boston hospital. In the breakdown of Matilde's marriage she is presented in a strong, honest and positive light. Pino's family breaks up and, on his release from prison, he seems to begin to rebuild a sort of family with his sister Carla. The two are linked to Pietro because they used to own one of the apartments in the Parioli building.

Where there are moral statements about families being made in this production the conclusions are somewhat equivocal. Positive value is given to the birth of new family circles (Matilde-Pietro-Rosa; Carla-Aldo-Pino) but they are informal and arise out of the ashes of other families which have broken up. On the other hand, the commentary Pietro provides on all these stories is conformist and steeped in popular (Roman) good sense. In fact, the true protagonist of *Quei 36 gradini* is the extended unorthodox 'family' of the block of flats – as one critic expressed it:

> The block of flats is a 'staging post' between the drama of solitude and the relationship of conflict with the world, the point where it is possible to bring people back into harmony among themselves and each one into harmony with himself. The point of reference and guarantor for this 'harmony' is Pietro, the caretaker. He constitutes the 'viewpoint' from which the story is told.[1]

Thus, through the voice of the caretaker/guardian of souls – Pietro – the intermingling of the lives in the Parioli building provides a focus for outlining a picture of the simplicity of life, of popular wisdom (particularly evinced through the character of the little girl) and of the strength of traditional feelings. The story lines are all credible, permeated with sadness and resignation.

Casa Cecilia – un anno dopo (Cecilia's House – A Year After)

Unlike the other programmes examined, *Casa Cecilia – un anno dopo* does not present a broken family, extra-marital histories, generational conflicts or human dilemmas. According to the producers, the intention was to present a 'normal' family – the Tanzis – facing '. . . the ordinary problems of any middle-class Italian family'. It was also intended to keep a balance between the humorous and the serious but it is the humorous that predominates – intentionally in the case of the parodies of old slapstick film comedies but sometimes unintentionally. For example, in a programme which sets out to tell the life of a 'normal' family it is more than farcical to have the family woken in the middle of the night by intruders, supposedly thieves, to then hide together in the same bed (there are 5 of them), pulling the sheet over their faces and waking up in the morning to find the house burgled.

This lack of consistency in the style of the programme is not helped by narrative inconsistencies, poor acting, dull dialogue, slovenly production and a plot that often lacks credibility. Cecilia, the wife, is a dentist, Aldo, the husband, a writer of romantic novels (she is the true boss, he a poor idiot) and the children are colourless and merely serve to continue the conformist values of their parents. The absence of contemporary references is striking; there is nothing modern about the house furnishings; despite the presence of three adolescents there are no signs of youth culture and there is no opposition to the parents coming from the children. Instead the parents' disapproval is feared, as in the case where the 18 year-old daughter has been earning pocket money by copying music scores (she hides the money) and the parents appear amazed that she should be capable of it.

All in all the programme is best summed up by the unquestioning philosophy that is articulated by Cecilia and Aldo's remarks in the final sequence: '. . . in our family everything ends in pleasantness and cheerfulness because we mean well' and '. . . after all, nobody can deny that we are a normal family!' Among so many conventional characters, Busotti, the producer of photo-stories (the eldest daughter is acting in one of them, something that truly shocks her parents), stands out as a solitary and ironic transgressor, who possesses the quality of not taking himself seriously: 'Isn't it true that in life all of us are clowns?'

La piovra (The Octopus)

This is the story of a lone police commissioner, Cattani, who has been posted to a small Sicilian town, where his predecessor has been killed by the Mafia. Cattani is an honest and resolute man. Cautiously, but firmly, he starts collecting evidence against the Mafia and their local and national accomplices. He falls in love with Titti, a drug addict, the daughter of an aristocratic family, whose former lover is sent to jail by Cattani after he makes an attempt on the commissioner's life. Else, Cattani's French wife, eventually decides to return home. At the very last minute, when she is about to board the plane, their daughter Paola decides that she would rather remain in Sicily with her father.

La piovra will be remembered as an important event in the history of Italian television fiction. It proved, contrary to the opinion held by many broadcasters, that a programme dealing with 'serious' issues can, when it is well done, get an audience as large as those of international soccer matches (*La piovra 1* was watched by 15 million people, *La piovra 2* by 21 million); and also that in order to compete successfully with *Dallas*, RAI did not need to 'copy' American programmes, but should and could instead make an intelligent use of the best tradition of Italian cinema. Finally, it proved that when a programme is produced according to the highest quality standards, it can be competitive also on foreign markets. In Italy, *La piovra*, in addition to being very popular with the public, won wide acclaim from critics and intellectuals.

Because of the objectives of our research, understanding the true reasons for such a success was the main motivation that guided us in our analysis of the programme. We wanted to verify the arguments underlying most of the comments and praise that the programme elicited from critics. In particular: was it true that *La piovra* represented an example of 'serious' (i.e. educational) television and that people liked it *in spite of that*? Or, according to others, that it was successful *precisely because of* those qualities? Furthermore, is it true that *La piovra* is not television really, but rather a product that is essentially cinema more than anything else – and if so, was this a decisive factor in its success?

Leaving aside for the time being the latter point, the other points boil down to one question really: is *La piovra* a programme about the Mafia? If not, what is it about?[3] The fact that the director of *La piovra 1* was Damiano Damiani, who has directed other films on organised crime, corruption and other politically sensitive issues, would seem to confirm that *La piovra 1* is indeed about the Mafia above all. On the other hand the script is by Ennio De Concini, the author of some of Italy's most successful popular television and cinema comedies. The very idea of putting together two such unlikely bedfellows is indicative, it seems to us, of the producers' strategy. The product was meant for television. The choice of Damiani would guarantee that a subject like the Mafia would be dealt with realistically and seriously; while on the other hand De Concini's style and experience were the ingredients that would put the programme on the wavelength needed to win appreciation from a mass audience. It was an unlikely marriage and yet it worked, by integrating in often unpredictable ways two different interpretations of facts and their political and human implications. This is especially true in the case of the episode we analysed. As one member of the audience research group put it: 'I wasn't quite sure whether it was a family story in which somehow accidentally the Mafia was brought in, or vice versa. . . . ' However, such ambiguity was not perceived negatively by most viewers and may even have contributed to raise the level of appreciation. On the other hand, Damiani and De Concini approached the subject from angles which had more in common than one might have imagined and which came closer to each other as the work progressed. 'The possibility of creating a story which would be human, private, intense, outside any social dimension – that was my main interest at the time,' De Concini said in an interview when asked about *La piovra*. 'I was fascinated with the idea of this man locked into a difficult situation like only a policeman's can be, with his marriage about to break down; a man who, in a land which is not his, meets and falls madly in love with the heiress of a great family, destroying his own family, his profession, himself and the woman he loves . . . something damning and sublime.' But if that was indeed De Concini's idea of the film, it never came true, because, he said, for the first time in his career he found himself confronted with a reality 'so violent and so absorbing that private concerns could find no space in it' and Cattani's own problems 'could only fade when compared with that of the Mafia which, even *against my own will*, eventually took over the whole story, maybe rightly so.' Thus it would seem that De Concini found himself involved, without having planned it, in what he later described as an educational and political endeavour. 'My nature,' he said, 'so much more inclined to privilege feelings and private histories rather than public events, was taught a lesson that it has not yet quite managed to absorb. . . . '

The irony of it is that Damiani himself was looking at *La piovra* more as a tale of the private vicissitudes of a man who also happened to be doing a 'particular job' (a policeman's job), than as a story of the Mafia. Which is probably why the teamwork proved to be so nearly perfect. In the end, it is Cattani's own private drama, more than his 'particular job', that will capture the viewer's imagination and emotions. This,

Michel Placido and Florinda Bolkan in La piovra

incidentally, was inequivocally confirmed by our research on the audience. The discussions of the audience groups focused on Cattani's marriage and love affair much more than on any aspect of his work as a policeman. 'He should have devoted more time to his family and less to his work' would be a typical remark. Some Sicilian policemen, asked about *La piovra 1* by a journalist, said that the way in which Cattani's life and work had been portrayed was unrealistic. And Michele Placido, the actor who impersonated Cattani, said in an interview after the screening of *La piovra 2:* 'I believe that a policeman like Cattani does not exist in real life.' But then why did people like him so much, he was asked. 'Because,' he answered, 'people like to imagine that, as in the film, somewhere, in some remote corner of our corrupted country, there is an innocent and just man who is looking for others like him. Each viewer feels he is one of them.'

Cattani does indeed seem to fit the classic model of the hero – courageous, fighting alone for a just cause against all; human, therefore vulnerable. Our hero believes in the cause for which he is fighting; however, unlike the classical model, he does not really believe that his cause can win. He is anything but a dreamer, and he is experienced enough to see what his weaknesses are, therefore he will resort to cunning more often than to force. In the end, he will be defeated, and defeat will also destroy his private life. The story is open-ended only in the sense that the fight goes on, but it offers the public no hint whatsoever that Cattani may, at some point, defeat his enemies. On the other hand the producers could have hardly done otherwise, lest the story lose credibility – in a country like Italy, where the Mafia is eternal, heroes like Cattani can win a battle, but not the war. It is no accident then if *La piovra 2* is much more of a thriller than *La piovra 1*. With no Victory nor Happy End in sight, a massive dose of intrigue and action had to be injected in order to keep the Hero busy and to entertain his public. Maybe then it was just as well that *La piovra* should have been conceived from the beginning above all as the story of a man and only secondarily as a film about the Mafia . . . And yet Cattani exists and makes sense as a character only because of the Mafia; his vicissitudes would hardly have been emotionally shared by such a large audience had the film not been *also* a film on the Mafia – not a Mafia made of fictional godfathers, but one with connections in the business world and in the world of politics, which the public (if not all, at least part of it) could recognise as belonging to contemporary Italy. One can agree, of course, with remarks made by some magistrates, who said that in real life things are much worse than those described in *La piovra*, or by some sociologist, who did not like the way in which complex problems had been presented by the producers of *La piovra* – a way, they said, that was too sensational, too spectacular, too 'American'. Thus, according to Pino Arlacchi, Italy's leading expert on the Mafia, *La piovra* 'is not really about the Mafia, but about the struggle of a lone man against power and corruption: it is a theme that is as old as cinema — when you scratch under the surface, the mechanism is the same one they used in *Rambo*. . . . ' Other sociologists and media experts hold an opposite view. Thus Gianfranco Bettetini believes that while the fictional representation of the Mafia can only offer an abridged view of the problem, it may be more effective and convincing than a documentary: the very fact of using the traditional models of fiction means giving up the tools of in-depth analysis in favour of stereotypes, but it can help focus attention on some crucial aspects of reality. Fiction can exploit the expectations of viewers accustomed to entertainment programmes in order to make them aware of a problem and of its likely consequences. . . .

De Concini, who is no sociologist but knows the power endowed on those who write for popular television, agrees. Twenty million Italians watched *La piovra 2*, he remarked, therefore the audience included also people who normally would not read the daily press. 'Let's then realise what it can mean, to this kind of public, to see that the head of the secret services is a man linked to the Mafia', especially when it is RAI who is saying so, the 'official' television, which people tend to identify with government and power.

Family, politics and society in Italian television series

With the exception of *Casa Cecilia* it is clear that all the programmes studied share at least one element in common: they all portray broken families or families in some sort of difficulty. In *Voglia di volare* the chief character is separated from his wife; in . . . *E la vita continua* the two young protagonists are both children of separated parents; and in *Quei 36 gradini* two marriages break up and some of the new unions which are formed carry the warning signs of future crises. On the other hand one can argue that a harmonious and happy family would not provide an effective starting point for stories likely to capture the viewers' attention – the only programme (*Casa Cecilia*) that does offer this is, significantly, not credible and whether or not this was the producers' intention it ends up offering a parody of family life.

The sample used in the research, whilst small, is representative. A much larger research project conducted by Milly Buonanno[3] shows that the 'family in crisis' is the dominant model for all RAI's family productions. This, according to Buonanno, is a reflection of the present state of Italian society, where '. . . changes in the family – being still a fairly recent phenomenon – are more acutely perceived and more open to interpretation when seen in crisis.' Another plausible, albeit less supported, hypothesis offered by the same writer is that the model of the family-in-crisis:

> owes much to its narrative vehicle and especially to the linear time pattern of Italian TV fiction which, moving on in a few instalments to the final conclusion of the stories, favours the portrayal of family situations and relationships at a stage of rapid (and therefore often explosive) transformation; whereas the long duration and repetitive and slightly cumulative timing of the American series and serials favours a portrayal of family life in terms of greater permanence and stability.

This observation has some (but only partial) validity if applied exclusively to the institutional permanence and stability of the family in American series such as *Dallas* and *Capitol* – otherwise it is fairly obvious that these programmes too are about families in crisis.

As shown by Buonanno's research some of the most striking qualities of family and personal relationships portrayed in Italian series are:

– the absence of passionate love
– the strong emphasis placed on highly introverted families

– the intimate dimensions and psychological insights which make 'the dynamics of relationships and feelings the real mainspring of the stories'
– a positive connotation of breakdowns, which often result in the subsequent development of a stronger emotional relationship or, at least, the opening of a dialogue between parents and children.

It is these aspects in particular, rather than the presence or absence of crises, which seem to afford the characteristic and most significant differences between Italian and American television family dramas.

Another significant difference between American soaps and Italian series is to be found in the portrayal of the respective roles and relations between the two sexes. There are, for example, no JRs in Italian stories. In Italian programmes the weak person is always the man – it is he who has a crisis of identity, a crisis in his career, a crisis in his family and a crisis in his extra-marital affections. In *Voglia di volare* the pilot David trusts his own safety to his daughter and to his ex-wife; in . . . *E la vita continua*, though in the end the father (Saverio) will be able to give evidence of great dedication and self-sacrifice, he earlier beats his head with his fists and begs his son's forgiveness whilst he is shut up in his Jaguar; Cecilia's husband is a naive fool; all the men in *Quei 36 gradini* are weaklings, moving amongst women who are sure of themselves and courageous in their solitude – 'Your wife is stronger than I: what strength!' says Pino to Aldo. This weakness holds true for both the main and the minor characters, the one exception being Mariuzzo, the mafioso husband of Rosa's mother, who does not seem to be overwhelmed by doubts about life and who in his relations with the little girl shows more intelligence and human warmth than the mother seems to be capable of.

Thus the figure of the strong and courageous man is practically non-existent in these family stories (the commissioner Cattani might appear to be an exception, but his strength is restricted to his professional work as a policeman – the same cannot be said of his relations with his wife and other women). It is worth noting, however, that the 'weakness' of all these men is hardly ever given a negative connotation. The strong characters are all female: the wife, Barbara, in *Voglia di volare*; Silvia and Laura in . . . *E la vita continua*; Matilde, the

Countess, Aldo's wife, Carla and, of course, little Rosa in *Quei 36 gradini*. These women are portrayed as strong, emancipated and independent and not at all in keeping with the popular image of women in the 'average' Italian family. Instead of lazing in the kitchen with one eye on the television set, these women work, have professions (Cecilia is a dentist for example) and are sure of themselves.

Another interesting aspect of these stories of families and personal relationships in crisis is that the problems of adolescent children are often foregrounded. The characters of these young people are not those of scintillating personalities brimming over with intelligence and force of character (with the exception of the very young ones, e.g. Rosa and the daughter of the Commissioner Cattani); instead they have all been caught at that stage in their life where there is a slow and painful transition to an emancipated adulthood. On the whole young people are presented with affection and sympathy, albeit with a certain degree of condescension. In *Voglia di volare* the young people are presented realistically (largely due to the dialogue) and with humour; in . . . *E la vita continua* Laura is quite rebellious and goes off to Greece with her lecturer against her mother's wishes. It is questionable, however, that Laura is being all that rebellious because, as she shrewdly points out, she is leading her life just as her mother did before her. In fact, what is striking about all these programmes is the absence of genuine conflict between parents and children – as Milly Buonanno writes:

> . . . the parents, while not giving up their authority formally, nonetheless are not authoritarian figures; the children, while not being submissive, are not rebellious figures.

In these Italian stories, the plot basically revolves around interpersonal relationships between members of the family (formal or informal) and between the latter and other characters bound to each other by love affairs or friendship (therefore always pertaining to the private sphere). In American stories, the interactions between family events and 'external' events for characters (in general in the world of business or of work) are more numerous and, above all, more organic from the narrative's point of view. Nonetheless, they do not result in a vision of the outside world and its problems broader than the one provided by

Italian series and their self-centered family stories. The opposite is true. Italian series do pay attention to such things as the social context and current affairs, which instead are largely neglected by American productions. This even applies to *Capitol* which, though set in the Washington of politicians, is basically a telenovela about the power struggles and intrigues of two families which tells us little if nothing (on the contrary, may even disinform us) about the politics of the United States.

With the sole exception of *Casa Cecilia – un anno dopo*, all the other Italian series contain some reference to social reality. Sometimes, these references are only sketched, as in the episode of *Voglia di volare*, in which the camera pans over the conditions of life in a Roman suburb; in others, the reference is more tangible and may become an integral element of the story. In this way the problem of drugs becomes the core of the plot of the fourth episode of *Quei 36 gradini*. *La piovra* is a case apart, for obvious reasons since the Mafia and corruption there play such a central role.

Violence, which for obvious reasons permeates the story of *La piovra*, is also present in other series, but only marginally and briefly, touching without truly involving the main characters – there only because, violence being part of our society, producers apparently fear that without it their stories would be labelled as unrealistic. In the episode of *. . . E la vita continua*, a group of students beat up the lecturer and we are told about terrorism and the international Mafia, but how could a story which proposes to cover 'thirty years of Italian life' ignore such events? Violence occasionally links us to the past (the 'crime of honour' in Sicily, in the story of a minor character), but more often it is modern, urban, inescapable, seen as a 'disease', an image which fits in well with the overall aura of nostalgia and lightness in these series. The central setting of these stories is the city, which however, is never really a protagonist, and in most cases is shown only briefly. An exception is the fourth episode of *Quei 36 gradini*, with a fairly effective representation of the urban environment, the pretext being the search for the young drug-addict. Here undoubtedly, the drug addiction is seen also as a social problem, and not just individual and private as in *. . . E la vita continua*. Even the French lawyer robbed in the centre of town and Matilde's husband, robbed in the discotheque (where he was given drugged champagne), contribute to creating the image of a hard and hostile environment.

Apart from this episode of *Quei 36 gradini*, the urban environment is represented by short 'postcards': a cupola beyond the rooftops, a market, the view over the railway bridge, the panorama of suburbia. However, these Italian stories are clearly set in an urban environment and an urban culture; the very typology of the characters belongs to that culture. The city is the present, hence it is real: the countryside is the past, visited or revisited in a romantic or nostalgic key. It may be a return to one's roots, as was David's journey to his home town in *Voglia di volare*, but it is always and only a transient return, generally caused by external events rather than inner needs; or it may be a place of temporary refuge, seen as such because it is 'different' and sufficiently remote from the usual urban environment – besides, it implies an idea of starting afresh, of regeneration and simplicity.

For this reason, Saverio takes his son to the country to wean him off drugs, and Carla goes to the country when she decides to end her relationship with Aldo (in *. . . E la vita continua* and *Quei 36 gradini* respectively). The city is perceived resignedly by certain characters, as a lesser evil ('You know what, I've had enough, I'm going back to my village'), and never as a modern city.

It is true that *. . . E la vita continua* shows us a modern Italy, the world of high finance, industrial enterprises and even the soccer market, but it is also true that often the country shown in these stories is a country which, in many aspects, is still standing on pre-industrial values. Success, ambition and money are portrayed as negative values, having harmful effects on the family and the quality of life. A scrupulous script-writer will include an oaktree or a flock of sheep in a country scene, in order to make it more realistic, and so the script-writer of these Italian stories will cite contemporary events such as violence, terrorism or drugs; but there is almost always a certain detachment between these external (almost foreign) events and the stories told, which emphasise the private, introverted dimension of human relationships. Consequently, certain events or citations might be inserted in the script because they are topical or fashionable and therefore capable of sparking the interest of the public, only to be then treated inadequately or altered. For example, the ecological theme in the last episode of *Voglia di volare* is reduced to a pictoresque scene: the grandfather, a libertarian and a jolly fellow, while on the train takes advantage of the absence of some hunters to throw their guns out of the window and set free some canaries and pigeons.

The Italy portrayed in these series is not an Italy populated by poor people, by workers and proletarians. It is the Italy of the middle and upper-class bourgeoisie – businessmen, bankers, or bank clerks, pilots, teachers, doctors, where home helps and waiters appear in secondary roles; a country without housewives. In *Quei 36 gradini*, Pietro is a door keeper, a commoner of pure Roman extraction, but, all things considered, even he is not badly off. In short, these are all stories of well-to-do Italians even if light years away from the billionaire luxury of *Dallas* oil magnates.

Finally, the Italy we discovered in the series analysed is an Italy which neither considers nor worries about issues such as politics and sex. The latter is present but never directly represented, only inferred (among the series analysed, the most explicit scenes were in *La piovra*). This is not surprising, since these are RAI productions aimed at a large audience, broadcast at peak evening hours; and besides they are family stories with a strong focus on the parent/child relationship, or love stories which favour introspection and a psychological dimension. Furthermore, isn't it true perhaps that the Italian woman is first of all a mother and only secondarily a lover? We are very far from the amorous intrigues which animate certain American family sagas. In the words of Virna Lisi, the main character of . . . *E la vita continua*: 'This television film presents real women and mothers – we've had enough of these fake American dolls who never age despite their children and the difficulties of life.'

The absence of politics in Italian series is more significant, since Italy is a society where, in the last forty years, the level of political conflict has been very high; and moreover, political cinema has produced many good, realistic and courageous films. Consequently, there has been no shortage of topics and materials nor the instruments and know-how necessary to represent them.

Then why is the world of politics and political issues so noticeably absent from Italian television fiction? Possibly because broadcasting in Italy is not just controlled, but rather ruled, if not (for all practical purposes) 'owned', by politicians. Let us just note that:

1) Italian series up to now have been produced exclusively by RAI (exceptions can be counted on the fingers of one hand and in any case, from this point of view, they are not different from those produced by RAI);
2) the time allotted to politicians in RAI's programmes is subject to very strict rules;
3) RAI is a highly politicised bureaucracy – meaning that the appointment of RAI's executives is decided or must be approved by political parties.[4]

Such a system can work (and it does work) only if based on a tacit code of self-censorship. Thus if the official policy is that political statements can be made only in the time slots allotted to politics, an unwritten rule calls for the elimination or edulcoration of political opinions in all other programmes. If these premises are correct, it is possible to assume also that the producers of fiction do not wish to break the rules of the game. Of course, one might agree instead that script-writers and producers simply feel that the audience of fiction is not interested in politics; or else, yet another theory, that politics in Italy today, in the parties, in government and in Parliament, does not lend itself to dramatic representation. The same cannot be said for those deviations and aberrations of the political system such as the Mafia, corruption and terrorism; these are phenomena that indeed escape from the narrow universe of politics and enter that of great crimes or great mysteries, which are so much more congenial to fiction. In the series studied, references to politics were few in number and fleeting in nature. Take the dialogue between Pietro and the Countess in *Quei 36 gradini*, which perhaps remains the most genuine and most direct of all, even if the word 'PCI' (Italian Communist Party) is pronounced neither by Pietro not the Countess. In other cases, the dialogue draws from clichés (one of Silvia's lovers in *. . . E la vita continua* is a communist journalist and when Silvia's mother visits his luxury apartment in Milan, she asks: 'And so this is the communist?') or worse, turns into generic man-in-the-street philosophy, with phrases such as: 'The law is always against the underdog.' The minister who honours the countess' party with his presence appears very stereotyped (rightly so, perhaps, in this case). But even these are only brief flashes. In all these series, politicians and politics are conspicuous for their absence, the only exception being *La piovra*, again for the obvious reasons mentioned above.

However, in conclusion, despite it all, our initial observation still holds good: on the whole, in Italian series, one can find references to the social reality of the country, not presented in American family stories. According to some critics, this kind of consideration is irrelevant because American stories such as *Dallas* can do without explicit references, since 'they (themselves) are American society, they make blood and oil flow', while Italian series are stories where society is nothing but a back-drop.[5] It seems almost superfluous to note that there is more than just 'blood and oil' in *Dallas*, *Dynasty* and their kins: there are power struggles, success, beautiful houses and gorgeous women, and whiskey flows second only to oil. Needless to say, these are all implicit social references, but even these, and others, all added together show us only one side of America, the America of *those* families and even so only partially. It is not enough to watch *Dallas* and the feats of JR to know the United States. These American series tell us nothing about the political and social problems of the country where they are supposedly set.

True, in Italian series people are shown what they need to know in order to place the story in context, but hardly anything more. The technique can be described as a postcard, the student movement postcard, etc, with a postmark so the public can date them, but very little, apart from the flat image, which might in some way act as a guide to their interpretation. Nonetheless, even if one agrees with those critics who claim that in these series Italian society is there only as a back-drop, viewers can get at least a glimpse of that society.

Television fiction, Italian style

While attempts have been made elsewhere in Europe to respond to the challenge of *Dallas* with the production of programmes drawn from that American model, this has not been the case for Italy. Ironically, however, there has been more heated debate in Italy at events such as the first two Teleconfronto conferences in 1983 and 1984 about the consequences (real or presumed) of the mass consumption of American telefilms than there has been in the rest of Europe. Furthermore, RAI is the only European state broadcaster to conduct a feasibility study on the problems of producing popular serials able to successfully compete on the international market.[6] These days, it would appear that RAI has given up the attempt to make soaps or serials and has concentrated instead on the production of 'films in instalments', a choice which has its roots in the history of RAI's fiction production.

The marriage between RAI and cinema is a successful union which has lasted for nearly thirty years (1960 saw the production of the first 'film in instalments' – Giacomo Vaccari's *Mastro Don Gesualdo* – and 1964 the creation of the 'Servizio programmi filmati'). It experienced its critical pinnacle in 1977 and 1978 with gold awards at Cannes for *Padre padrone* and *L'albero degli zoccoli (The Tree of Clogs)* respectively. In the following pages, however, we shall restrict ourselves to those RAI programmes which were produced specifically for television.

There are three distinct periods in the history of Italian television fiction. The first runs from 1954 to 1963, when electronically produced *teleromanzi* ('telestories') predominate; the second runs until the end of the 70s, through which transitional period occurs the progressive decline of 'telestories' and the gradual return of film stock in the production of television fiction; the third sees the definitive triumph of film.

Nineteenth-century European literature provided much of the basic material for Italian television drama productions throughout the 1950s and 60s – in fact out of 307 adaptations of literary works, over 60% were foreign (73% if purchased films are included). From the 1970s fiction series became increasingly contemporary and secular, and foreign literary adaptations have virtually disappeared in recent years. Thus in Italy over a thirty-year period one sees a significant shift both in terms of style – from electronic recording back to film shooting – and in terms of content – from literary historical dramatisation to contemporary drama.

There are a number of factors that have contributed to this

transition:

a) however prolific nineteenth-century authors, the plundering of some 500 of the most suitable titles virtually eroded the available literature;
b) the modernisation of Italy – particularly in terms of public habits and taste – means that nineteenth-century dramatisations, while still proving to be entertaining, are increasingly outmoded;
c) most important of all is RAI's loss of monopoly position.

The significance of this loss is that private stations brought into the home new images, which were not necessarily more realistic than those of nineteenth-century dramatisations, but were different enough to change the public's expectations. Through the importation of programmes, RAI had already broadcast such images. However, it was not 'diversity' itself that was significant; the turning point was caused by the sheer volume of new programmes offered by a rapidly expanding private television system. RAI, while continuing to fulfill its public service obligations in terms of its cultural and educational scheduling, at the same time met the competition of the private stations by substantially increasing the volume of fiction.

In 1986 telefilms and *teleromanzi* represented 12.3% of total programming, more than twice as much as in 1961, and in the same period the share of films grew even more dramatically, from 2.8 to 12.9%. Cultural and educational programmes withheld pressure better than some feared and also improved their relative standing, climbing from 6.8% in 1968 to 10.4% in 1986. Theatre lost some ground (from 2.6% to 1.2%), while ballet and classical music together have done slightly better and today seem to have found a rather stable position, with a share of approximately 2% of the total programming. At the same time the growth of some popular genres like variety and quiz shows has been less significant than some might have expected (8.1% in 1968, 13.7% in 1986). These data contradict early predictions which were made about the dire effects of competition from private networks. Actually, if we look at absolute figures rather than percentages, it will become even more apparent how the growth of mass culture genres was only marginally fed with losses from the other genres. Instead, *that growth was made possible by the increase of total hours of programming*, that jumped from slightly less than 4,000 in 1961 to approximately 14,000 today. Even theatre which, as we saw, declined in percentage terms, has actually improved its standing. It passed from 130 hours in 1961 to an average of 170 hours in the period 1980-85, which is significant if one considers that it had dropped substantially in earlier years (71 hours in 1971, 65 in 1977). Also, news broadcasts have grown substantially in the past six years, although their share of the total programming has declined. In 1986, news broadcasts and other news services (sports not included) represented 15.6% of the total, down from 23.3% in 1968.

Since private networks in Italy today are not yet entitled to broadcast live, and therefore are unable to produce news broadcasts and live coverage of sports events among other things, the confrontation between RAI and the private networks was bound to take place in the fields of fiction and light entertainment. As mentioned before, RAI responded to competition by increasing its fiction programming. Thus, RAI 1's fiction output climbed to 1,227 hours in 1986, from 274 in 1974. Films alone account for almost half of that growth. The rate of growth has been especially high for those genres, like films and telefilms, which represent the main components of private networks' programming. Not surprisingly then, the fierce competition between RAI and the private networks on the international market has led to sharp increases in the price of these products. This was inevitable, given the relatively modest volume of RAI's in-house production of fiction programmes. The high percentage of re-runs in the programming of fiction by RAI and the private networks is indicative of the difficulties with which both state and private broadcasters are confronted. In 1986, 46.9% of films scheduled by RAI were re-runs. Less than 9% of all fiction broadcast by RAI (not including re-runs) in the past two years was produced or co-produced by the corporation. At present, the production capacity of all three channels of RAI totals less than 200 hours a year.

What is striking about the programmes produced by RAI is that, in spite of RAI's almost total dependence on imports for genres like serials and series, no effort has been made so far to produce them. The strategic choice of RAI was to concentrate on what can correctly be regarded as a national skill, namely film-making. The fact that a film is then chopped up in several parts (hence the term 'films in instalments') does not essentially change its nature. RAI's occasional after-thoughts, like showing two instalments in the same evening, are in this respect significant. Many of the programmes, however, can be properly described as mini-series and are billed as such.

Actually all Italian television fiction did was to adopt some of the styles and techniques of American programmes. Thus some critics have pointedly remarked that the way the narrative materials were assembled in *La piovra* is typical of police stories (e.g. the cyclical structure of some of the episodes, with a murder as a prologue and again a murder near the end). Cliff-hangers, freeze-frames, the way in which lengthy prologues and titles are edited, are other examples. On the other hand Italians have not given up making a large use of flash-backs, which are rarely found in American serials, but which are functional to the often introspective narrative style of Italian fiction.

In the initial stage of our research, one of the attempts we made as we sought to establish significant criteria of comparison between American and European fiction, was to build a suitable definition of 'pace', or 'rhythm'. One of the arguments one often hears when people discuss American television fiction and the hows and whys of its worldwide success, is that the 'pace' of US serials is substantially faster than that, say, of Italian fiction. Italian telefilms, some critics would typically say, are too 'slow' – which is why, the argument continues, somehow axiomatically, they are less fun to watch than imported programmes. At the theoretical level, one can think of a number of elements (such as the duration of sequences and frames, editing, camera movements, the use of light and sound, the 'tension' built into characters and situations, etc.) which can contribute to the speeding up or the slowing down of the pace of narration. We did try to identify and to measure them in our detailed analysis of some of the programmes. We reached the conclusion that it was impossible to build a model which would allow us systematically to measure the various factors and their correlations. Nonetheless, some of the data produced by these exercises are worth mentioning and may offer some food for thought to those interested in picking up the thread where we dropped it.

Thus for instance we took the first 114 shots[7] of two American serials and three Italian mini-series, with the following results:

Programmes	Total duration in minutes (of the 114 shots)	Number of sequences	Average duration (in seconds) of shots
Dallas	18′	7	9″
Flamingo Road	13′	8	7″
. . . E la vita continua	17′	8	9″
La piovra	26′	12	14″
Casa Cecilia	25′	12	13″

According to these data, . . . *E la vita continua* is the Italian programme, among those analysed, which comes closer to the American model. *Flamingo Road* is by far the 'fastest' of the five, with 114 shots tightly packed into 13 minutes, and the lowest average duration per shot (that *Flamingo Road*'s narration is fast moving would probably coincide with the viewer's intuitive evaluation), and *La piovra* the slowest (but we know from our audience research that viewers perceived it differently). If one takes as a base for comparison a given time duration – the same for all programmes – instead of the number of shots, results do not change substantially. We took the first 13 minutes of each programme. In that span of time, *La piovra* has 6 sequences for a total of 63 shots and thus appears to be much 'slower' than *Flamingo Road* (8 sequences and 114 shots). In short, we would agree that 'pace' is not a significant factor in determining audience appreciation. Otherwise we could hardly understand why the data listed for *La piovra* are virtually identical to those listed for *Casa Cecilia*, something which totally contradicts both our intuitive judgement and all available audience appreciation ratings.

The detailed analysis (frame by frame) of the five programmes (camera work, dialogue, sound, special effects, etc., were among the factors considered) also failed to produce significant results. The analysis confirmed that Americans are much more fond than the Italians of close-ups (82 in *Dallas's* first 144 shots, 40 in . . . *E la vita continua*) and of shot-reverse shot (78 and 50 respectively). It also confirmed that Italians shoot on location to a much greater extent than Americans do. Shooting on location does, of course, cost more. It is fairly obvious that the added cost can be acceptable, from a producer's point of view, when all you are doing is a 6 or 8 episodes mini-series, but would be prohibitive for programmes like *Dallas* or *Capitol* which consist of hundreds of episodes. And again, more generally, one can afford to borrow some technical standards from cinema when the programme is a mini-series, but one can hardly do the same systematically when the programme is an open-ended serial. From this point of view, the end result in the two cases is bound to differ also in terms of quality, *all other conditions (and in particular professional skills) being equal.*

All too often critics of the American model fight their battle under the banner of cultural values, as if European broadcasters unwilling or unable to reassert national identity through their programmes had no alternative outside that of producing poor copies of the American model. This attitude can occasionally cause some rather paradoxical effects, like when, for instance, certain choices are explained as if they were made in compliance with national standards and policies. This may be the case of course, but is irrelevant, given the fact that under present conditions American techniques (both in production and marketing) are simply not applicable in European countries, if for no other reason than that the market is just not there. Also, the two models, the American one and the national one, are not necessarily absolute alternatives, but may co-exist.

This was essentially the point made in 1982 by the 'Feasibility study on the production of serials/series', an in-house RAI report, better known as 'Rapporto Fichera' (see note 6 above). The report argued that it was about time for Italy, too, to move on to standardised, i.e. industrialised modes of production, because: a) the television market was becoming increasingly international, and b) Italy should operate on that market as a producer as well, and not be progressively reduced to the sole role of consumer. Accordingly, the production of fiction, (although not only fiction) should abide by the rules of industrialisation/ serialisation. In order to achieve that, it was necessary to modernise and rationalise the production and distribution processes. Because RAI's structures were inadequate for embarking on this type of production (either directly or through the traditional device of sub-contracting all or part of the work), the Report recommended that the task should be entrusted to a new organisation, an associate company which, while in partnership with RAI, would be granted independent management.

Not only was the Fichera Report never published, but it was not even put on the agenda of the Board of the Corporation. Copies of it, however, were circulated both in and outside RAI in semi-clandestine form (parts of it eventually were published in some media magazines) and widely discussed. The report was eventually shelved. It can be reasonably assumed that the RAI leadership and politicians felt that the proposals put forward in the report would have shaken RAI's internal balances of power. Besides, the report 'disturbed' some categories such as film directors, who saw themselves threatened by Massimo Fichera's apparent belief that their role would need to be re-defined (in favour of the producer) in the new division of labour called for by industrial production techniques. Finally, the report was adversely affected by the fact that it dropped right into the middle of the debate on American cultural colonialism which was going on at the time, a debate that focused mainly on television fiction. Thus in the end too much stress was laid on fiction and little attention was paid to the fact that the 'industrialisation' advocated by Fichera would apply to television in general (including, for example, documentaries, educational and science programmes) and not to fiction only.

Notwithstanding the fact that the Fichera Report was shelved, RAI has nevertheless increased its fiction production, and has even made some attempts to produce American-style action telefilms. Yet, given the financial and organisational constraints, it is inconceivable that these efforts might develop into the regular production of serials or series. According to Sergio Silva, head of Struttura 1 of RAI 1, who in recent years has produced some of the most successful Italian mini-series, there are no particular reasons why Italian series should not exceed the customary four or six episodes, apart from the vague notion that four may be too little and more than eight too long and too boring ('Besides, there are not many gripping Italian subjects that could prove to be winners against US products'). Yet today the trend is toward tightening up programmes, with episodes of one hour and a half, and/or the Monday instalment following immediately after the Sunday one, to hold the audience. According to Silva, it would have been conceivable to produce a 12 hour long *Piovra 1*, but that would have required an enormous effort. The production capacity of Struttura 1 of RAI 1 is about 35 hours yearly, plus 15 hours of co-productions. Above all, in order to adopt the American 'quantitative' strategy, it would be necessary to begin by acquiring the mentality which stands behind that strategy, something not altogether impossible but which today does not exist. The Americans, Massimo Fichera points out, invest large budgets also in average products (deliberately average), while in Italy work on an average product is done on an average or low budget. Silva agrees:

> What impresses in the Americans is the concentration of energies that they bring to bear on every production – everything is squeezed out. The actors may be mediocre, but they are professionals; and the programmes are well made, better on average than European ones. Let's not forget that it was they that invented the cinema, which is a big industry, with huge financial turnover, all of which cannot fail to be reflected in the product; besides, they have always operated in a highly competitive situation and this too has not been without consequences on the quality of the goods delivered. This professional/industrial dimension does not exist in Italy . . .

Economic factors are not the only ones that have prevented Italy from entering that 'industrial dimension' (which was central to the proposals put forward by the Fichera Report) – cultural factors, or rather one should say cultural prejudices, have weighed negatively. The tradition of the 'cinéma d'auteur', to give one example, is not one to encourage talented young directors and script-writers to agree with the rules of popular television fiction. Instead, it results in looking down on the 'industrial' product from the dais of high culture, forgetting that Americans do not produce only *Dallas* or police stories but also, to stay within the field of fiction, TV-movies which deal with political and social topics. Inevitably then, when Italians have tried to produce American-style series, they have ended up mainly by imitating (in most cases unsuccessfully) their technical characteristics (action, cliffhangers, freeze-frame), without really tapping their national know-how, i.e. the tradition of Italian cinema. No wonder then if these attempts (like *Caccia al ladro d'autore*, *Fiumicino International Airport Atelier*) turned out to be flops.

At the same time, American imports, after years of indiscriminate pillaging by both RAI and the private networks, can no longer supply the Italian market as they used to, either as far as quantity is concerned (the demand far exceeds the supply), or from the standpoint of quality. It is significant that Silvio Berlusconi's Fininvest, whose success on Italian screens was linked for years to *Dallas* and other American serials, should have decided to start their own productions. According to estimates made by Berlusconi's staff, their target as from 1988 is some 40 to 60 films per year, including co-productions in their various forms. The objectives seems to be to set up a production machine that operates both as a traditional film industry (producing films for the big screen) and as a producer of television programmes. Berlusconi has formed a consortium with Maxwell, Sedoux, Beta Film and a Spanish group (along the lines of the RAI-ZDF-Antenne 2-SRG-Channel 4 consortium) which should ensure from the outset access to the international market; another company, 100% Italian, Italia International, will allow Berlusconi to operate on the international market, mainly through co-productions, independently from the consortium. It is a very ambitious programme. The days when Italian private broadcasting was a semi-clandestine operation run by amateurs are long gone. The first productions of the consortium will be *Gli indifferenti*, from Moravia's novel (with Vanessa Redgrave and Laura Antonelli in the cast) and *Scandal* (based on the Profumo scandal). The first production of Italia International, *Casanova*, with Richard Chamberlain, has already been broadcast. It will be followed by *White Whale*, a biography of Hemingway, and *Anastasia*, a four-hour, 8 million dollar colossal, directed by Marvin Chomsky, who directed *Roots*, and a cast of famous names including Rex Harrison and Olivia De Havilland. If these selections are indicative of those that are to follow, then the strategy seems geared to stories and events well known outside their country of origin, in order to make the product readily marketable.

However, these films, while prestigious, cannot solve Berlusconi's main problem, namely that of meeting the day-to-day demand for fiction programmes by his three networks. Thus Fininvest is moving ahead also with several productions aimed at the domestic market: mini-series and mini-serials, in the best tradition of Italian light comedy, a menu composed of great love stories, some adventure, an appropriate dose of realism, etc. One point worth noting is that some of these stories are intended for young people, a target audience so far virtually ignored by RAI's fiction programmes. The first episode of *I ragazzi della III/C*, a mini-serial about the daily life (at school and outside school) of a group of teenagers, was broadcast on 17 January 1987. *I ragazzi della III/C* will be remembered not only because it was the first programme of Berlusconi's new production strategy to go on the air, but because it scored a *higher audience than Dallas* (over 7 million). . . .

However, quite obviously, series like *La piovra* and *I ragazzi della III/C* (to mention two programmes, belonging to two very different genres, among the many domestic programmes that have done better than imports), cannot alone match the demand for fiction from RAI and the private networks. Nor can RAI and Berlusconi continue to rely on imports as in the past, for the reasons mentioned above. The good-quality fiction (of the kind produced by Sergio Silva), which we described as 'films in instalments' because it owes more to cinema than to television, has climbed to the top of Italian audience ratings; but it has also reached, or is about to reach, the limits of its growth: its share of the schedules is relatively modest and cannot be expected to grow significantly. What, then, lies ahead?

Until now the competition between RAI and the private networks on one hand, and between national programmes and imported ones on the other, has been fought mainly in prime-time. Prime-time means big budgets, popular actors, high (i.e. cinema) quality. That was phase one, the most aggressive one, because it is where audience ratings count most. But in the long run what will count, as in any war, is the broad front, that is, not only prime-time but also the afternoon and early evening audience. 'Then we will have the organisation to tackle phase 2,' says Sergio Silva. 'We will have to get to work on this audience as well: hundreds of hours for a mass audience . . . ' Silva does not believe that in order to win phase 2 RAI should produce telenovelas (their audience is marginal, he says), nor tele-films, which cost too much, nor *Dallas*-type serials, which cost less than American mini-series but are anything but 'cheap'. What we need, Silva argues, is large-scale production, at very low cost, for a strictly national audience: for instance, sitcoms. That would mean working mainly in studios, with a minimum of outdoor locations, electronic cameras, low post-production costs, and so forth. In short, what that would amount to in practice, assuming that Silva is right, would be a rehabilitation and a reconversion to a true television format, as distinct from the cinema format – the format of the early days of Italian television (see above). RAI shelved it some twenty years ago. But then of course, if it were to come back today, the motivations and the objectives would be very different from those of the early days.

Notes

1. Marcello Frediani, *11 Sabato*, 19-25 January 1985.
2. It must be made clear that our comments here and in the following pages are about the first series (*La piovra* 1) except when specific reference is made to the two other series produced so far. *La piovra* 4 went into production in February 1988.
3. Milly Buonanno, *Marriage and Family* (Verifica Programmi Trasmessi, ERI, 1985).
4. Thus the map of political affiliations or leanings of RAI's staff will approximately mirror that of the Italian Parliament. If RAI's President is a socialist, then inevitably RAI's Director-General will be a Christian Democrat; and since the Christian Democrats are the party of relative majority it is only 'natural' that the Director-General should have more power than the President.
5. Silvana Silvestri in *Il Manifesto*, 3 April 1984.
6. The study is known as the 'Fichera Report', from the name of the man, Massimo Fichera, Deputy Director-General of RAI, who promoted it. 'While in France television continues to sail on unconcerned,' noted Michèle Mattelart (*Réseaux*, April 1985), 'omitting to do any research on its mode of operating, present or future, preferring to rely on the talent and intuition of programme directors, RAI has embarked on a study centred on the question: "Is there a way to start industrial production of fiction to

provide an alternative to the dominant production of the United States?" RAI was forced to address this question because of the competition from private broadcasters who upset the balance between supply and demand of programmes, until then controlled by the state television. By filling up the air with entertainment programmes, mainly serialised fiction, the private stations laid bare the void that existed as regards national production of the genre.'

7. The choice of working on 114 shots rather than any other number was fortuitous. 114 shots corresponded to a duration of 15 to 25 minutes, depending on the programmes, which we thought was sufficiently representative of the episode as a whole.

8
Summary and Conclusions

Dallas, and American serial fiction in general, is always the loser when competing with fiction produced by European countries; but, to continue the sports metaphor, it wins the indirect challenges. If, in each country, national programmes occupy the top positions in the audience ratings, the public's second choice *never* falls on programmes produced by other European countries. American is the *lingua franca* of the European market of television fiction.

This is perhaps the most significant overall finding of our survey. Before examining these results, it may be useful to briefly recapitulate the main guidelines of our work as well as its limits. As our survey progressed the subject we studied gradually became more specific, and to some extent even changed. We had to acknowledge that some of our premises were influenced by the political and ideological climate created by the debates on cultural imperialism which we had sought so hard to avoid. In the comparison between American serial fiction on the one hand and European fiction on the other, we attributed to the latter a homogeneity which was not truly there. Instead we had to take into account a reality which was *much more diversified than we had expected.* The differences encountered in the definition of the sample have been discussed in the introduction. At this point, it is perhaps important to underline how the non-homogeneity of the sample stems mainly from the presence of British (but also Irish) serial fiction, which presents very different characteristics from the fiction of other countries. Programmes such as *Coronation Street* or *EastEnders* have no equivalent elsewhere and are very different from the mini-series or serialised films that characterise the production of countries such as

Italy and France.[1] These differences are anything but accidental. They reflect the tastes and culture of the various countries and the characteristics of their programming schedules. Thus, for instance, unlike in other countries, in Great Britain the working class is the privileged protagonist of serial fiction and can recognise itself (but in the past tense, i.e. nostalgically) in minimalist and everyday stories such as those of *Coronation Street*. Again, to offer another example, while many films[2] will be found at the top of the audience ratings in France and Italy, they hardly appear at all in the English ones.[3] In order to define once and for all the area we covered, let us say that, for each country, our choice fell on those programmes most representative of that country's serial fiction production, televised in peak viewing hours and with a good audience rating. Obviously this type of choice could only emphasise the *different* models and cultural matrixes of the countries studied.

On the other hand, we also know that *Dallas* is not truly representative of American serial fiction, much less is it a model of production planned according to the best ground rules of 'how to produce a successful programme', as all too often it has been made to appear.

In the light of such a varied universe as that of the world-wide production of serial fiction, whose internal diversifications are much deeper than they appear to be at first glance, our initial methodological resolutions ran aground when faced with a reality which could not be classified so as to permit a strictly scientific comparative analysis. If we insist so much on this observation, it is because we are convinced that it has implications which extend beyond the field of methodology.

The first implication is that, if we put ourselves in the public's shoes, the comparison is no longer between two or more cultures, for example between the United States on the one hand and Europe on the other. In other words, as far as the public is concerned (except for the marginal groups of intellectual élites) it will never be a matter of choosing *between two cultures*, but, rather more prosaically, the choice will above all be *between different genres* which coexist in the world of television fiction. And if a certain product is then associated with a certain country, this is due only to the fact that some programmes are exported and others are not. In the United States, television movies which deal intelligently with problems of social importance are *also* produced. But these television movies are mainly for the domestic market, they are not so much known abroad and therefore cannot contribute to the idea a foreign audience has of American television. We believe this point is of fundamental importance in order to understand the characteristics and functioning (communication and the absence of communication, the exchange flows) of the television fiction market in Europe.

A second implication which springs from the first is that if one wishes to talk of comparison and comparative judgement between different schools of television fiction, in many cases it can be wrong, from the audience's point of view, to speak of competition. The public may equally appreciate very different television programmes, because these programmes play complementary roles in the gratification of tastes and the fulfillment of needs which for the public at large can be quite dissimilar. In order to cite an example taken from the world of Italian television, the audience might appreciate *Quei 36 gradini* through a process of identification with the characters and problems of its own everyday life, just as it might appreciate *Dallas* or another American series by identifying with 'universal' characters and situations. In the second case, the degree of escapism and its potential will probably be higher than the first. However, it is obvious that 'popularity' and 'escapism' cannot be considered synonyms and only in certain cases do they coincide. Similarly, the audience appreciation of a programme such as *La piovra* will depend, for a certain type of public, on it being considered a sociological analysis or a political denunciation, while others consider it simply a thriller. One can presume that the second intepretation will offer more 'escapism' than the first.

In fact, the debates which rage over serial fiction in general, and American fiction in particular, conceal much more serious controversies, namely those on the validity of television as an art form or a means of communication. It is quite natural that 'old' countries with centuries of history and an established cultural tradition were slower to assimilate a new, 'popular' medium such as television. Even when it was accepted, this happened partially and gradually at first; the programmes in which television was merely a means of spreading traditional genres (theatre, music, documentaries) were accepted more readily than those made specifically for television, among them telefilms and soap operas which, more than others, possessed the characteristics of that popular culture disliked by highbrow critics. The people in charge of programming, namely the so called 'gate-keepers', were often, especially in the past, highbrows themselves. In some countries (the case of Germany is emblematic) audiences were kept under supervision for a long time and their choices coerced. The expansion of television schedules, the limits of national production from a quantative point of view and lastly the logic of the market, have gradually forced many doors to open, thereby fostering the public's encounter with popular programmes. It is at this point that the mechanism of audience ratings begins to make its weight felt. Their importance in the decisions taken by those responsible for programming is a relatively recent phenomenon.

The conflicting relationship between the elite classes and this new medium has not followed the same paths in every country.[4] In Great Britain, Ireland and West Germany, the culture/television dichotomy was more clear-cut and deep-rooted than elsewhere. In West Germany, a country in which prejudices against popular television series survived perhaps longer than in others, the lengthy and difficult battle between the epigones of Brechtian *Verfremdungseffekt* and the soap opera ended in victory for the latter, thanks also to Fassbinder, whose *Acht Stunden sind kein Tag*, at the beginning of the 70s, was the first family series made in West Germany to consciously adopt the stylisation so typical of American melodrama. In Italy the battle was never even engaged because, unlike other countries, the majority of Italian intellectuals during the formative years simply took no interest in television. A late awakening occurred, when the damage was already done, as a reaction against the spread of private broadcasting. Perhaps France is the one country which, more than any other, has been capable of investing this new medium with certain characteristics of its own culture, without dramatising the dichotomy between tradition and modernity (as in Ireland) or between cultured and popular television (as in West Germany). It is a recent fact that, after years of co-existence between the two rival models of cultured television and 'escape' television, preference now goes to the latter. As concerns the American model in particular, we noted that *Chateauvallon*, the

'French *Dallas*', is at the moment an isolated episode, produced at a time when the Texan saga was at its peak and there was great concern (above all political) over the effects of Yankee pre-eminence on the television market. What's more, the fact that *Chateauvallon* was not sold abroad to the extent expected and that, in the countries where it was televised, it obtained only a modest success, should discourage similar attempts. As far as Great Britain is concerned, it is important to remember the opinions expressed in the past by many critics, convinced that the *serial form* illustrates perfectly the 'corrosive effect of television' (an opinion and a concern voiced also by the Irish at the beginning of their television experience); these critics, in fact, recommended the Pilkington Committee on British Broadcasting to:

> include a special mention of the effect of dramatic programmes . . . especially those in serial form . . . we are emphasising . . . that the main impact of television on values and attitudes derives from such programmes.

According to this point of view, the serial form is dangerous because it is ambiguous; it does not offer reassuring solutions, definite endings or clear-cut good/bad dichotomies – the heroes are manichean, unsettling characters.

If these were, in fact, the problems, then the diffusion of the American model of serial programmes, bearers of values all the more ambiguous because alien, could only make matters worse. In fact, despite the language similarities, it is no chance occurence that the greatest resistance to the 'made in USA' product was recorded in Ireland and Great Britain. During the October 1986 – April 1987 season in Ireland, out of a total of 28 episodes of *Glenroe*, 12 topped the bill in the weekly audience ratings, 12 were second and 4 third. Out of the 28 episodes of *Dallas* televised during the same period, none came first in the ratings, only 3 came second and 5 third; it is also significant that *Glenroe's* position has improved year after year: from an average of 4th position in the weekly charts for the first 10 programmes in 1983/84 (first session), to an average of 2.5 in 1984/85 and 2 in the following year, up to 1.7 in 1986/87. In Great Britain it is extremely difficult to find an American programme in the first 5 places of the

BARB charts of the 100 most viewed programmes[5] and in general the quota of American programmes in the Top 100 is not more than 20%. In other countries similar charts do not exist and therefore any comparisons would be inaccurate. However, in Italy between 28 June and 17 October 1987 for example, the American quota in the most popular 100 programmes (despite the massive supply of American programmes by the private networks) was less than 25%. It is useful to point out that, apart from *Dallas*, in 59th, 64th, 68th, 88th and 93rd place, the programmes were always films (the most popular: *Rocky II*, 9th, *Serpico*, 14th), while the series with the best ranking was *Little Roma* (22nd), an Italian production.

Obviously a quota of 20% such as the one recorded in Great Britain, even if not to be sneezed at, is not sufficient to justify exaggerated fears over the dangers of American cultural 'colonisation'. Nonetheless, that quota, even if modest, appears far too high up the charts for the establishment of English television. The most severe critics believe the programmes from the other side of the Atlantic to be 'rubbish', at the same time admitting that, if English television production has reached such high standards, it is thanks to the Americans. This would be an obviously contradictory position were it not for the high opinion that the English producers have of themselves. Therefore, these contradictions are recomposed in a strict yet immodest logic: 'We produce a load of crap, but when it's good, it's better than that produced anywhere . . . Could we beat the Americans at their own game? I suppose it's possible, but . . . I doubt they will ever beat us at ours.' (Linda Agran).

How can one talk of 'high standards' when the material in question is 'rubbish'? And is it rubbish only because it is American and not when it belongs to others? And who can claim the right of primogeniture? Does the merit or demerit of having invented a certain way of producing television belong to the Americans? Or is it that television works at its best when certain rules are applied, the Americans being the first to have learned and exploited those rules?

A further query follows close on the heels of these: can a certain way of considering and producing television (seen as aberrant from the point of view of an ideal of culture) be adapted to objectives which differ from its natural ones, for example, cultural and social objectives, not just entertainment? We will attempt to answer this, or if not answer at least supply information useful to the debate, by examining what we consider to be two emblematic examples, namely Ireland and West Germany. The serial form, and specifically in this case the soap opera, has its own rules and a logic inherent to its open structure, a fact unerringly underlined by the Irish critics at the dawn of the television era in their country: these rules include ambiguity, the impossibility of offering indisputable definite solutions, or in short, amorality. If we consider the attempt made by the Irish to adapt the soap opera to didactic ends – a paradoxical situation since its promoters were aware of its alleged 'perverse' nature – then the results of such an attempt were both inevitable and steeped in irony. Serials, like other programmes, were thought of as a vehicle to enhance the distinctive traits and values of Irish society and culture, but the result was a product very different from the one proposed. The subject matter included problems and topics not generally debated elsewhere because considered either taboo or too troublesome, thereby attracting the barbs of conformist critics; and the narrative, self-deprecating style favoured a critical revision of the past. In fact, the period in which Irish television was born and developed was marked by rapid innovations in society. Television ended by participating in this liberalisation process, even at times in the front line.

Different, but no less emblematic, is the case of West Germany. For years, ever since its debut, one of the objectives of West German television was to inform the public about Nazism and the genocides committed by the regime. But the response of the public was always disappointing. Instead, the emotional impact of the American mini-series *Holocaust*, televised in 1979 by WDR (the same network that commissioned *Acht Stunden sind kein Tag* from Fassbinder) was enormous. Its success is all the more remarkable because *Holocaust* was televised on a regional channel. *Holocaust* became a serious topic for debate in the media as well as in the classroom. On television it was presented in a showcase situation, with a carefully researched documentary as introduction to all episodes and with a discussion by prominent scientists, civic leaders, and journalists as a follow-up to each episode. To ensure an in-depth discussion in high schools, the regional centres for political education and other non-partisan educational institutions provided abundant background materials for teachers as well as study guides for students.

To top this wave of respectability, Heinrich Böll, the famous German author, declared that after *Holocaust* an enlightened and an emotional representation of social conflict had ceased to be opposites. With regard to the German audience he thus confirmed in dignified language what David L. Wolper had already pronounced in the promotional style of hyperbole: 'American television audiences are yearning for information – but in an entertaining, dramatic and emotional form.'

And so melodrama, a genre always criticised in a country that had constantly looked upon popular television suspiciously, won its promotion from the rank of 'escapist' soap opera to that of serious dramatic work. The analogies with *Roots* in the United States, and *Holocaust* first in the States and then in West Germany, have quite rightly been pointed out. What happened in West Germany with the programme *Holocaust* exemplifies how conflict and the ensuing choices are not so much between what is American and what is European culture, but between television genres, or between different ways of producing television. This is certainly true for the public, and also as we saw in the case of *Holocaust* for the critics. The fact that during those years, in Germany, the serialised melodrama was seen as an American product or at least as an imported product, does not invalidate this observation.

Obviously, one must ask oneself what the public's reaction would have been and what sort of success the programme would have had, if every effort had not been made to 'enable' the product with debates, historical documentaries and other initiatives; in other words, if *Holocaust* had been treated by the programme executives just like any other mini-series, allowing the public to decide its merits according to the quality of its production, without embellishments or didactic incentives. In fact, *Holocaust* was presented in West Germany in a container-programme, in which the mini-series acted as a magnet, but without which it would not have had the impact it did. A somewhat similar case happened in France: *Heimat* was also presented in a container-programme, even if a little different from the West German one. However, these observations relative to the promotional strategy and its contribution towards the success of the programme, even if well founded, would in no way invalidate the success of a programme like *Holocaust* in a country such as West Germany.

This confirms the fact that the difference between television 'made in USA' and European television is not so much a question of contents, 'popular' on the one hand, 'serious' on the other, but rather of narrative style and packaging of the product: in brief, the difference is mainly to be found in the ways in which one conceives and produces television. *Holocaust*'s success in Germany has shown that melodramatic fiction can carry out pedagogic tasks more effectively (from the point of view of reaching a wide audience and not, obviously, from the point of view of completeness of information or depth of analysis) than programmes openly, or even only surreptitiously, didactic. This is an art, or perhaps should we say a skill, in which the Americans are masters. If this is so it is undoubtedly also due to the fact that in order to discover and judge television, they did not stand on the podium of high culture as is often the case in Europe (albeit more so yesterday than today).[7] Certainly, it is perfectly normal for something like *Holocaust* to be more popular than a documentary on genocide, but it is by no means an accident that, in order to deal with a subject such as genocide, the Germans should spontaneously use documentaries and the Americans instead a mini-series. However, what needs to be underlined here are not so much the differences between melodrama and didactic programmes, as much as the differences between European and American melodrama or, more precisely, American export melodrama.

As has already been pointed out, one of the main differences between American and European programmes can be found in their narrative styles (the American being more conversational and direct, the European being more descriptive and didactic) and the way in which they are produced and packaged. This does not mean, however, that the contents are the same, if one takes the word 'contents' in its broad sense. The themes and situations may be the same, but in general their *treatment* will vary as well as the perspective and the emphasis on values.

Contrary to European fiction many American programmes are free from references to real situations (social and political) and often even to time, thereby favouring a symbolisation of characters and situations and this, in turn, increases the audience potentially able to identify with the stories told.

In many American series the contents (and in this case we mean, above all, the plot) are a pretext, upon which are grafted the various dramatic ingredients necessary to win over the public. In European series the 'pretext' is itself a dramatic element. *Schwarzwaldklinik* was popular with the Germans because it showed environments and evoked collective memories deep-rooted in the history and culture of the country (beginning with the locality, the Black Forest, and all that it symbolises). The fact that its producer followed the American model in more than one way, including the promotional strategies, may have contributed to its success, *but this has not been proven*. Suffice it to note that the series' American slant *alone* was not sufficient to ensure the success of *Schwarzwaldklinik* in other countries, where there was no identification with these contents. In France, for example, *Heimat* was more successful than *Schwarzwaldklinik*, perhaps because it was inserted in a container-programme watched by a large audience, but doubtless also because the history of the German people under Nazi rule, narrated according to the most classic rules of melodrama, could emotionally involve the French public, or at least interest them, much more than the stories of people in a large hospital in the Black Forest.

Our research has shown how the production of European fiction presents strong national characteristics which reflect the cultural and social identity of the country, its history and its traditions. This is true also for those programmes such as *Schwarzwaldklinik* and *Chateauvallon* based on the American model. A French 'feuilleton' is unmistakably French. An Italian television dramatisation is unmistakably Italian. One could say: but an American tele-film is also unmistakably American! That is true. What then is the difference?

There are two answers. The first is that truly American television programmes, those programmes which tell the audience what the United States are like, how the Americans live, talk and work, do not generally appear on European television screens. The second answer is that, when in Europe a programme is called unmistakably 'American', the reference is mainly to brand, a trade-name, that immediately reveals to the audience the style, the know-how of the producers (more than the story, the problems). A typical example is *Capitol*, a programme set in Washington and about politicians but which, nevertheless, tells us nothing of the American political system – it simply narrates the affairs of two families fighting each other, intrigues and conflicts which could take place in any other big (and rich) capital: politics in *Capitol* is really nothing but a pretext. The same could not apply to the Mafia in *La piovra*. In short, when we say that a programme is unmistakably German, or Irish, or Italian, it is because it *tells us something* (informs us, even if often in a superficial manner) about that country. Instead, American programmes for export contain all the stereotypes, not so much of American life but rather of those traditional values of anti-American propaganda: money, power, violence, ambition, intrigue, etc.

However, these *also* happen to be essential ingredients in the packaging of a popular melodrama. Evidently the Americans are not the only ones who resort to these ingredients or expedients. But they have an advantage over we Europeans: they know how to use them without guilt complexes, without the scruples and limits imposed, more or less unconsciously, by cultural legacies. And therefore they use them more effectively.

On the other hand, what meaning should one attribute to the word 'stereotype' when applied to a society such as the American one which, in its role of 'melting pot', recognises in pluralism its own special *raison d'être*? The American television audience is not monocultured, as are the audiences in most European countries. Hence the need for American television to universalise these stereotypes, or to create universal stereotypes, in order to involve all the components of the public. In fact, the 'melting pot' has worked mainly from an institutional or social point of view, and has only superficially impinged on the various cultural identities that co-exist in it. Consequently, while it is true that stereotyping is among the canonical rules which govern the production of 'feuilletons' and melodrama in all countries, the character Pietro in *Quei 36 gradini* is perhaps more 'Roman' than JR is 'Texan'.[8] If we compare two family sagas, *Dallas* on the one hand and . . . *E la vita conitinua* on the other, we can see how, together with the daily events of that Lombard family, salient moments of Italian life periodically appear, like terrorism, for example, even if only in the background. In *Dallas*, we are not even told who is the President of the United States in this or that period of the life of the main characters, and no mention is made of events or problems pertinent to American society. Even if events or problems *are* mentioned, it is in such a fleeting fashion as to pass unobserved, or in any case, they do not involve the Ewing clan. The stories are both timeless and dimensionless; even *Dallas*, the city, is to some extent an abstraction. At the opposite end of the scale are the French series, where some of the stories often assume documentary overtones, and where references to political affairs are not uncommon. So, by watching the character Boulard in *Chateauvallon*, the French audience will immediately think of Robert Hersant, the press magnate and Silvio Berlusconi's partner in La Cinq. JR, instead, is only and always JR. Consider again Ireland and West Germany, countries in which television fiction programmes are, more than elsewhere, pervasively permeated by the national ethos. In Irish productions one will find the unsolved and painful theme of the transition from a rural society to an industrial one; in the German ones the difficult reconciliation process between past and present, the search for the meaning of life in a modern industrial society. When compared to these European products, American serials (or at least the fiction most widespread on foreign markets) appear a washout, lacking in 'genuine' contents, in short, pure entertainment. If indeed *Dallas* is like *Genesis*, as has been suggested, then *Dallas' Genesis* has no heroes or drama.

If these premises are accepted, and if indeed the main problem is to defend the cultural heritage of Europe, we could ask ourselves whether indeed one hour of good fiction cannot, by itself, transmit certain values (of national identity, of knowledge and awareness of the problems of contemporary society) and count for more than 10 hours of telenovelas or *Dallas*.

Nowadays, in some European countries like Italy, the danger of falling standards of tastes and values does not come from fiction. If considered in the global panorama of television, when fiction is of good quality it can even aspire to a place among educational and cultural programmes, in a broad sense. The real danger comes from variety programmes and their marriage with advertising and sponsorship. Needless to say, this is no outside enemy: variety shows are a genre where competition from imported products is almost nil.[9] However, the success of American fiction in many European countries cannot be attributed only to the quality of these programmes nor simply to a deterioration of public taste. This increase of imports stems from the combined effect of two factors: 1) the increase in the total hours of programming of fiction; 2) the impossibility of national production exceeding a certain level due to structural and financial limits. While the production capacity of RAI does not reach 200 hours of fiction per year, fiction transmitted by RAI passed from 274 hours in 1974 to 3,687 hours in 1986, an increase of over 1,300% in 13 years (re-runs included).[10] If we add to that the hours of fiction broadcast by private networks we would obtain astronomical figures. Thus while the fall in values and tastes cannot be held responsible for the invasion of imported fiction, they may well represent eventually one of the results of such a massive intake of that fiction. But to say that we will have been 'colonised', by an 'external' enemy, would amount to denying the evidence. The sharp increase in programming hours has thrown open the doors to the 'enemy' who, following market laws, had no difficulty or remorse in crossing that threshhold.

The point to be stressed here is that only a relatively small number of European programmes entered through those doors, due to the above-mentioned limits of our production capacity. But it is even more significant that only a minimal part of those programmes that entered obtained high audience ratings in the importing country.

In all the countries studied (Italy, France, West Germany, Great Britain and Ireland) and presumably also in others, national fiction normally comes first in the audience ratings.[11] *Dallas* and other American series normally do not go higher than second place at best. The only exception is France, but only for a short period and due to the absence of national competition during that period.[12] This appears to suggest that the penetrating force of American culture conveyed by television has shown itself to be weaker than expected. Quite apart from audience ratings, our research has also shown how television series in European countries have preserved strong national traits, a distinct and original social and cultural identity, basically uncontaminated by the American model. These conclusions contradict certain fears, repeatedly expressed in the past, regarding the consequences of the dominance of American productions in the schedules of European television. However, audience ratings also tell us that immediately after national programmes, the public's preference lies with American programmes, and not with programmes produced in other European countries. The evaluation which springs to mind when reading these conclusions is that, while American is now consolidated as the 'lingua franca' of television fiction, the export of European programmes to other European countries is hindered by a certain number of obstacles, and that, anyway, European television series are not popular with the public of countries other than that of the producing country.

These are the elements to be considered and the starting point from which to discuss the future of European television. An increase in national production, due to existing constraints, cannot alone solve a problem which is not so much, or only, a problem of production, as much as one of distribution, in a broad sense; of identification, transfer of contents and narrative models. The various forms of co-operation, including reciprocity agreements, can force entry into other markets and can contribute in de-provincialising both the public and the market of certain countries. Yet the fact that they are being shown does not in itself ensure popularity, even if the choice of subject and actors takes into account the expectations of viewers from countries other than that of the main producer. Furthermore, in an attempt to create 'Europuddings' tasty to every palate, according to the definition coined by Werner Schwaderklapp of ZDF, these programmes risk being neither one thing nor the other; standing apart from the American model but at the same time betraying the national ones. These considerations are not applicable to the so-called 'colossals' which, by definition, are world puddings before they are 'Europuddings' since they were programmed from the start for the international market, with huge budgets. By definition then, they must be immune from the ambitions and temptations we would otherwise find if the objective was that of creating or preserving a European identity.[13]

It seems to us, in fact, that the problem lacks a definition rather than a solution. On the basis of what our field survey has uncovered, it is difficult to agree with the pessimism of M. Jack Lang – former French Minister for Culture – when he states that Europeans 'passively accept the dominant American model, almost hypnotised by it . . . and so kill the European spirit, which represents diversity of nations, of provinces'. The American model is not accepted, much less accepted passively; if anything it is imposed by the market; we find it in the imported programmes which crowd our screens, but not in national programmes. These continue to present significant differences from country to country, so much so that these differences (and not American competition, or not only American competition) are one of the causes, and not the least, that hinder a more ample circulation of fiction programmes in Europe. For the same reasons it is basically difficult to agree completely with Schwaderklapp. Having declared himself hostile to 'Europuddings', Schwaderklapp said he favoured 'programmes which express an authentic national reality', and added, as if it were a logical consequence, that these programmes could be distributed in other European countries. We have evidence to suggest exactly the opposite: *the more a programme has a national flavour, the more difficult it will be to export it.* This will probably be the most controversial of our conclusions. In fact, Schwaderklapp's opinion is shared by others, and undoubtedly some programmes have been successful abroad (in other European countries) due to the fact they were very Italian or very French; but these cases are more often than not unsupported by statistical data which would allow comparisons with other programmes, and they represent *exceptions*. The very Roman environment of the *Quei 36 gradini* is the reason behind the difficulty in selling it to other countries; not to all other countries, for example perhaps not to Spain or Portugal, but certainly to many others. The Danish public, faced with the alternatives of *Dallas* and a story set in Copenhagen, in which it can identify with the situations and characters, will choose the latter. But between *Dallas* and *Quei 36 gradini*, it will probably choose *Dallas*: it is more immediately understandable, it amuses, requires less effort and rings universal bells, and therefore 'works' anywhere – or almost.

Is it possible to beat the Americans at their own game? What can one say, for example, about a solution which would rinse national wine in the river of Television For All, in order to make it more 'universal', more appetising to different publics? The attempt has been made in some cases, and the most famous is *Chateauvallon*. However, it was not sufficient in this case to invent a family saga seasoned with power struggles and intrigues. There is intrigue and intrigue, and the ones in *Chateauvallon* are very French indeed. This 'American style' series when shown abroad proved to be a letdown, when one compares its very limited success with the expectations of those who launched it as the 'French *Dallas*'.

However, let us suppose that similar initiatives meet with success. Should we be pleased? What if those who, over all these years, have denounced the danger of American cultural colonisation and called for a European 'answer', were to acknowledge that there might be a contradiction between policy aimed at defending European identity and a policy aimed at selling European programmes all over the world, from Peru to Algeria, as with *Dallas*?

It seems to us that two points can be made and one question raised which may offer a way around such a dilemma. The first point is that Europe is turning into a market where a growing number of deals between West European broadcasters take the form of co-production agreements. This was not so until recently. In the past, co-productions represented a relatively small part of television exchange. In the last few years however, co-productions (co-financing, pre-sale rights, reciprocity agreements) have been growing consistently. This trend has been especially visible in 1987.

The second point is that American series are no longer as popular as they used to be, and that fewer of them make it to the top of the audience ratings. It is significant that in Italy Silvio Berlusconi's three private networks, which owed their success throughout the past ten years to the massive and often indiscriminate scheduling of American programmes, are now slowly but increasingly replacing them with domestic productions and European co-productions. A number of factors can account for the drop in popularity of American series. One is over-exposure – at least as far as Italy is concerned. Another one is that the 'American way of life' is no longer widely accepted as everyone's dream – as Europe has grown more affluent and more self-confident, the American myth has declined. Finally, in the case of Italy, the excellent work done by Sergio Silva and others at RAI has proven beyond doubt that domestic productions can beat American programmes. Berlusconi's networks are now following RAI's path, strongly encouraged by audience ratings: for example, in recent months American series scheduled on Sundays have scored an average share of 14%, while the average share of in-house productions and co-productions has been 35%.

The one question which must now be raised is whether exporting to non-European markets in general, and to the American market in particular, is likely to continue to stay on the agenda of European producers as an important, albeit admittedly long-term, objective. As one of Berlusconi's aides said when we interviewed him recently:

> Of course not. America can be found in Europe. A programme co-produced by three European countries can, if good, yield the same amount of money in Europe that we would make by selling it to an American network. With one difference on top of that, namely that here we would be dealing with people we know well and work well with, while dealing with Americans is like dealing with out-of-space aliens.

Actually, one might argue, the point is well taken but almost irrelevant, since we should have learned by now that European programmes do not go down well with the American public.

The Italian case is an extremely interesting one, in the sense that Italy is a country which appears to be shifting away from a situation of over-dependence on, and over-exposure to, American programmes to one where both public and private broadcasters are investing increasingly large amounts of money into domestic productions and European co-productions. At the same time one should note that the Italian case is not (or not yet) representative of the situation existing in Europe as a whole. There is, of course, at least one very good reason for this, namely that because of the competition between RAI and the private networks, Italian broadcasters are much more market-minded than other European broadcasters. Sergio Silva's main intuition and innovation when he was put in charge of Struttura 1 of RAI 1 was marketing, a notion which public broadcasters traditionally tend to ignore (with the exception, perhaps, of the British). Silva was the first person to start thinking systematically in terms of a European audience and to start raising money for his own productions outside Italy, through co-production deals.

As mentioned already, Berlusconi decided that it was about time to follow his example. In 1987, Fininvest produced 70 hours of fiction (cinema and television), allegedly for a total cost of 70 billion lire, 40 of which were raised in Europe through co-financing agreements (or pre-sales, as was the case in a deal with West Germany). During the same period, Fininvest invested between 5 and 6 billion lire in co-productions outside Italy. It is virtually impossible to know how much RAI as a whole has invested in co-productions in 1987 outside the ECA (European Co-productions Association); we are therefore assuming that 30-40 billions would not be too far from the truth. In 1987 the ECA itself spent 50 billion lire.

Thus today the Italians are playing a pivotal role in Europe's television market, a market where co-financing is rapidly becoming the main channel for the dissemination of television fiction. Even the British, albeit half-heartedly, have shown interest. France is, after Italy, the country most likely to play an active role, partly because competition between state and private television there is quickly developing along patterns which resemble those of the Italian model. As the turnover of co-production grows bigger, more broadcasters from more countries will want to buy shares of the new business. It is also possible that the Americans may also try to move into the game, not only on an occasional basis (they have already co-produced RAI's *Il cugino americano* and Berlusconi's *Mamma Lucia*), in order not to lose the European market – although one can venture to predict that even so they will not succeed in holding on to the dominant positions they have held until now.

At the time of writing we must limit ourselves to taking good note of these developments which are too recent to be fully evaluated. We will have to wait until the end of 1988 and 1989, when many of the new programmes will have made it to the screen, to assess the full extent and importance of this new market. In particular it will be necessary to monitor these developments in terms of: a) economics; b) the results of the dissemination of national programmes outside their country of origin; c) the quality and content of the programmes.

If the scenario we have just outlined is fully realised, we will need to return to the question raised earlier about national and European identities. Would their dilution represent one of the conditions for co-productions to succeed with a European (i.e. multi-national) audience? If it is true, as we pointed out, that the more a story is rooted in local (social and cultural) situations the more difficult it will be to export it, how will co-production deal with that problem?

The first, intuitive answer to these questions would seem to be that there is no way co-productions can resolve the contradiction we described above, between a policy aimed at preserving national identities and one aimed at creating a wider market. In other words, co-productions may succeed in freeing Europeans from their dependence on American imports, but that could imply watering down the national characteristics of European fiction.

However, when we put the question to an Italian broadcaster, he responded as follows:

> All the fiction we produce should draw from real life, from what are the true and authentic characteristics of our society and daily life . . . Naturally then some of these programmes (e.g. *Quei 36 gradini, I ragazzi della 3/C*) will not be exportable. But so what? We will still want to produce them, because our audience likes them, as evidenced by the fact that they score higher ratings than *Dallas*. As for co-productions, again we must draw from real life, from true characters and situations, but choose those among them which are familiar or also recognisable elsewhere – this is the case with the mafia in *La piovra* but not with Pietro and the Countess in *Quei 36 gradini*.

His observations are pertinent and interesting. Admittedly, they did shake some of the beliefs we carried with us when we entered his office, which is fair enough – a researcher who is not prepared to acknowledge that his or her hypothesis was wrong is not a true researcher. Nonetheless they did leave us with some semantic doubts; for example, do the words 'recognisable' and 'universal' have different meanings? When Europeans engaged in a co-production single out characters and situations which are recognisable in more than one of their countries, are they doing something basically different from what an American producer does when he or she is working on universal stereotypes? One final thought: it would indeed be nice to believe that there is still enough room for creativity and diversity in our Western civilisation to allow for substantial differences between American universal stereotypes and European ones. . . .

Be that as it may, the opinion just quoted should be studied carefully because it can tell us something about the future strategy of European broadcasters, a strategy aimed at two markets, namely the domestic market and the European one – the latter being essentially not a market in an orthodox and traditional way, i.e. a place where people sell and buy goods, but rather a place where producers would be co-financing joint ventures.

Notes

1. Great Britain also produces mini-series and we could obviously have included them, preferring them to other programmes, if our only problem was to satisfy a need for homogeneity; but a homogeneity obtained this way would have been of little significance since the mini-series in question do not represent that part of British television fiction most popular with the public.
2. There are films in the top positions of the German television charts, but to a lesser extent.
3. In the classification of the 20 most popular programmes in April 1987, there is only one film (15th place), as against 7 series, 1 news programme, 1 sports programme and 8 variety or comedy shows (the total is less than 20 because one serial (*Bergerac*) and one show (*Clive James on TV*) appear twice, with two different ratings. During the same period, in the first 20 places of the French charts there are 9 films and one TV-movie.
4. Naturally the following observations refer to the sample of five countries we studied, and therefore they are not automatically generalisable, nor are they exclusive.
5. Among the few exceptions there is *Joe Kidd* (a film), in 4th place during the 2nd week of January 1987. The BARB charts include all programmes, therefore also the news and sports programmes. However, the first 20-30 places are nearly all fiction programmes. Coming back to the American problem, in May 1986, *Dallas* was between the 6th and 8th place. Top 100 Charts published by *Electronic Media.* (Source: Auditel.)
6. The expansion of the programme schedules (increase in the daily hours of transmission) and the increase in channels provides the public with a high density supply in which it is difficult to navigate because many

programmes, due to their contents, length and quality are very similar to one another. This is the reason for the importance of the time slot, which can favour some programmes instead of others. The insertion of a programme in a container may represent a way to guide and capture the public, as an alternative to, or in concomitance with, other promotional strategies. Naturally, in all these cases, it is not the public who decides and chooses. At most the public can approve or disapprove of the choices of the programmers, by conceding or withholding viewing.

7. Among the European programmes analysed, an example of surreptitious but effectively didactic fiction is *The Riordans*, an Irish programme which was also fairly successful with the public: the actors were asked to behave like *real* farmers and the stories were shot in *real* farms, because, between the lines, ideas on good agricultural management were to be propagandised.
8. Perhaps it is no chance that in American stories, regional or local traits are only briefly outlined, while in European stories they are accentuated or exaggerated; this occurs because the differences between an American citizen of Italian origin and one of Greek origin are more marked (and less attributable to a common cultural matrix) than the differences between a Roman and a Milanese.
9. Of the 100 programmes at the top of Italian audience ratings in the period 28 June-15 October, 1987, 25 were variety programmes; *Fantastico 3* was in 3, 5 and 6 place. (Source: Auditel.)
10. Fiction televised by the French ORTF passed from 362 hours in 1971 to 800 hours in 1980.
11. Particularly significant is the case of Fininvest's *Canale 5* which, after having elected itself godfather and distributor of American fiction in Italy, has acknowledged the limits of this strategy and has begun its own productions. The result is that the series *I ragazzi della III/C* (televised at the beginning of 1987) obtained a popularity rating higher than *Dallas*, which had been the most striking example of the success of *Canale 5* for a long time.
12. However this is an exception which confirms the rule. The data relating to the French series analysed for our research are compared to those of *Dallas*. *Dallas*' share in 1984 was 28%, in 1985, 22.5%. *Chateauvallon's* share in 1985 was 30.7%, *Allô Béatrice*'s share in 1984 was 37.7%, the share of *Les Cinq dernieres minutes* in 1985 was 32.5%. The average share of *Le Paria* was only 13%, but should be compared with the usual performance of fiction programmes on FR3.
13. In the *Segreto del Sahara*, RAI's latest 'colossal', Salgari's citation is only an affectation, an Italian stamp stuck on a purely international package.

BIBLIOGRAPHY

A trawl through the trade and commercial press will reveal a huge number of articles about television soap operas. For example, the BFI's reference library reveals dozens of file cards listing articles in: *American Cinematographer, Broadcast, City Limits, Hollywood Reporter, The Listener, Radio Times, Screen International, Television Today, Television Weekly, Televisual, TV Guide, TV Times*, to list the more obvious. Some of these articles offer substantial and useful information. Also, there are a large number of 'fan' publications and books about the lives of the characters in the soaps. Below, we have simply listed the more academic publications about soaps and also the wider contextual works we have drawn upon during our research.

AA.VV, '*Dallas* et les séries télévisées', *Réseaux*, CNET no.12, 1985.
Robert C. Allen, 'On Reading Soaps: A Semiotic Primer' in E. Ann Kaplan (ed.), *Regarding Television: Critical Approaches – An Anthology* (Los Angeles: AFI, 1983).
– *Speaking of Soap Operas* (Chapel Hill, N.C.: University of North Carolina Press, 1985).
Manuel Alvarado, 'Eight Hours Are Not a Day' in Tony Rayns (ed.), *Fassbinder* (London: BFI, 1976, with Afterword in 2nd edition, 1979).
Ien Ang, *Watching Dallas – Soap Opera and the Melodramatic Imagination* (London: Methuen, 1985, originally published as *Het Geval Dallas* (Amsterdam: Uitgerverij SUA, 1982)).
Michael M. Arlen, 'Smooth Pebbles at Southfork' in Michael M. Arlen (ed.), *The Camera Age: Essays on Television* (New York: Farrar, Straus and Giroux, 1981).
Jacques Aumont, 'Une esthétique industrielle (à propos de *Poldark*)', paper given at conference *La ripetitività e la serializzazione nel cinema e nella televisione* (Urbino: July 1983).
Jean Bianchi, *Comment comprendre le succès international des séries de fiction à la télévision? – Le cas 'Dallas'* (Laboratoire CNRS/IRPEACS: Lyon, France, July 1984).
Pierre Bourdieu, 'The aristocracy and culture', *Media, Culture and Society* vol. 2 no. 3, 1980).
Pat H. Broeske, 'Love in the Afternoon', *Cinema Papers* no. 52, July 1985, p.17.
Charlotte Brunsdon, '*Crossroads*: Notes on Soap Opera', *Screen*, vol. 22 no. 4 Winter 1981, pp.32-37, re-published in E. Ann Kaplan (ed.) *Regarding Television: Critical Approaches – An Anthology* (Los Angeles: AFI, 1983).
– 'Writing about Soap Opera' in Len Masterman (ed.), *Television Mythologies: Stars, Shows and Signs* (London: Comedia, 1984).

– 'Feminism and Soap Opera' in Kath Davies, Julienne Dickey and Teresa Stratford (eds.), *Out of Focus – Writings on Women and the Media* (London: Women's Press, 1987).
David Buckingham, *Public Secrets – 'EastEnders' and its Audience* (London: BFI, 1987).
Peter Buckman, *All For Love – A Study in Soap Opera* (London: Secker and Warburg, 1984).
Milly Buonanno, *Matrimonio e famiglia* (Rome: RAI-VPT, 1985).
Omar Calabrese, 'I replicanti', *Cinema & Cinema* no. 35/36, April-September 1983.
Muriel G. Cantor and Suzanne Pingree, *The Soap Opera* (Beverly Hills: Sage, 1983).
Francesco Casetti, *Un'altra volta ancora* (Rome: RAI-VPT, 1984).
– (ed.), *L'immagine al plurale* (Marsilio Editori, 1984).
Mary Cassata and Thomas Skill, *Life on Daytime Television. Tuning in American Serial Drama* (New Jersey: Ablex, 1983).
James W Chesebro, 'Communication, values and popular television series. A four year assessment' in Gary Gumpert and Robert Cathcart (eds.), *Intermedia, Interpersonal communication in a media world* (New York: OUP, 1979).
Ivano Cipriani (ed.), *L'Europa del telefilm* (ERI, 1987).
Mike Clarke, *Teaching Popular Television* (London: BFI/Heinemann, 1987).
Richard Collins and Vincent Porter, *WDR and the Arbeiterfilm: Fassbinder, Ziewer and others* (London: BFI, 1981).
Zayda Martinez Cornielles, 'Aproximaciòn al verosimil temporal de la telenovela', *Video Forum* no. 12, 1981.
Gerard Cornu and Brigitte Chapelain, '*Dallas*: A Serial For World Consumption' in Peter Ayreton (ed.), *World View 1984 – An Economic and Geopolitical Yearbook* (London: Pluto, 1983).
'*Coronation Street*' in Edward Buscombe (ed.), *Granada: The First 25 Years* (London: BFI Dossier Number 9, 1981).
Antonio Costa and Leonardo Quaresima, 'Il racconto elettronico: veicolo, programma, durata', *Cinema & Cinema* no. 35/36, April-September 1983.
Stephen Dark, 'Home is for Healing', *Primetime* vol. 1 no. 3, March-May 1982, pp.12-13.
– '*Dynasty*: All In The Family', *Stills* no. 11, April-May. 1984, pp.28-29.
Douglas M. and Wollaeger K., 'Towards A Typology of the Viewing Public' in Richard Hoggart and Janet Morgan (eds.), *The Future of Broadcasting* (London: Macmillan, 1982).
Chris Dunkley, *Television Today and Tomorrow. Wall to Wall 'Dallas'* (Harmondsworth: Penguin, 1985).
Richard Dyer (et al) *Coronation Street* (London: BFI, 1981).
Umberto Eco, 'Tipologia della ripetizione', paper given at conference *La ripetitività e la serializzazione nel cinema e nella televisione* (Urbino: July 1983).
Madeleine Edmondson and David Rounds, *The Soaps – Daytime Serials of Radio and TV* (New York: Stein and Day, 1973).
Jane Feuer 'Melodrama, Serial Form and Television Today', *Screen* vol. 25 no. 1, January-February 1984, pp.4-16.
Dick Fiddy, 'Soap Wars' in Dick Fiddy (ed.), *The Television Yearbook* (London:

Virgin, 1985), pp.111-112.
Leslie Fiedler, *What Was Literature? Mass Culture and Mass Society* (New York: Simon and Schuster, 1982).
Mark Finch, 'Sex and Address in *Dynasty*', *Screen* vol. 27 no. 6, November-December 1986, pp.24-42.
Christine Geraghty, '*Brookside* – No Common Ground', *Screen* vol. 24 no. 4-5, July-October 1983, pp.137-141.
Luke Gibbons, 'From Kitchen Sink to Soap: Drama and the Serial Form on Irish Television', in Martin McLoone and John McMahon, *Television and Irish Society*.
Christine Gledhill (ed.), *Home Is Where the Heart Is* (London: BFI, 1987).
Nick Goodway, 'Lorimar cleans up with soap operas', *The Observer* Sunday 1 June 1986, p.30.
Giovanna Grignaffini, 'JR: Vi presento il racconto', *Cinema & Cinema* no. 35/36, April-September 1983, pp.46-51.
Stuart Hall, 'Encoding/decoding' in Stuart Hall et al. (eds.), *Culture, Media, Language* (London: Hutchinson/CCCS, 1980), pp.128-138.
Anne Hjort, 'When women watch TV – how the Danish female public sees *Dallas* and the Danish serial *The Daughters of War*' in *Medieforskning* (Denmark Radio, 1985).
Dorothy Hobson, *'Crossroads': The Drama of a Soap Opera* (London: Methuen, 1982).
Horton and Wohl, 'Mass Communication and Para-social Interaction', *Psychiatry* no. 19, 1956.
François Hovejda, 'Grandeur et décadence du serial', *Cinema & Cinema* no. 58/60, 1959.
Michael James Intintoli, *Taking Soap Seriously: The World of 'Guiding Light'* (New York: Praeger, 1984).
Sheila Johnston, 'Street Credibility', *Prime Time* vol. 1 no. 2, Autumn 1981, pp.28-29.
Dave Kehr 'Texas Raunch', *Film Comment* vol. 15 no. 4, July-August 1979, pp.66-68.
Annette Kuhn, 'Women's Genres', *Screen* vol. 25 no. 1, January-February 1984, pp.18-28.
Cristina Lasagni and Giuseppe Richeri, *L'altro mondo quotidiano* (Turin: ERI, 1986).
Geoffrey Lealand, *American Television Programmes on British Screens* (London: BRU, 1984).
Chin Chuan Lee, *Media Imperialism Re-considered. The Homogenizing of Television Culture* (London: Sage, 1980).
Tamar Liebes, 'Ethnocentricism: Israelis of Moroccan Ethnicity Negotiate the Meaning of *Dallas*', *Studies in Visual Communication* vol. 10 no. 3, 1984, pp.46-71.
Tamar Liebes and Elihu Katz, 'Once Upon a Time in *Dallas*', *InterMedia* vol. 12 no. 3, 1984, pp.28-32.
– 'Patterns of Involvement in Television Fiction: A Comparative Study', *European Journal of Communication* vol. 1 no. 2, 1986, pp.151-172 (reprinted in Gurevitch and Levy (eds.), *Mass Communication Review Yearbook*, vol. 6 (Newbury Park, CA: Sage, 1987), pp.480-500).
– '*Dallas* and *Genesis*: Primordiality and Sensuality in Television and Fiction' in

Carey (ed.), *Communication and Culture* (Newbury Park, CA: Sage, forthcoming).
– 'On the Critical Ability of Television Viewers', in Borchers and Seiter (eds.), *Rethinking the Audience: New Tendencies in Television Research* (London: Methuen, forthcoming).
Colin MacCabe, 'Realism and the Cinema: Notes on some Brechtian theses', *Screen* vol. 15 no. 2, Summer 1974, pp. 7-27.
– 'Theory and Film: Principles of Realism and Pleasure', *Screen* vol. 17 no. 3, Autumn 1976, pp.7-27.
Mary Mander '*Dallas*: The Mythology of Crime and the Moral Occult', *Journal of Popular Culture*, no. 17.
Herta Herzog Massing, 'Decoding *Dallas*: Comparing American and German viewers', in Arthur Asa Berger (ed.), *Television in Society* (New Jersey: Transaction, 1987).
Armand Mattelart, Xavier Delcourt and Michèle Mattelart, *International Image Markets* (London: Comedia 1984).
Michèle Mattelart, 'I telefilm americani, i loro valori, i loro modelli culturali, il loro successo', Teleconfronto I, Chianciano Terme, 1983.
– *Women, Media and Crisis – Femininity and Disorder* (London: Comedia, 1986).
Martin McLoone, 'Strumpet City – The Urban Working Class on Television', in Martin McLoone and John McMahon, *Television and Irish Society*.
Martin McLoone and John McMahon, *Television and Irish Society* (Dublin: RTE/IFI, 1984).
Tania Modleski, 'The search for tomorrow in today's soap operas', *Film Quarterly* vol. 33 no. 1, Fall 1979, pp.12-21.
– *Loving With a Vengeance: Mass Produced Fantasies for Women* (Hamden, Conn.: The Shoestring Press, 1982).
– 'The Rhythms of Reception: Daytime Television and Women's Work' in E.Ann Kaplan (ed.), *Regarding Television: Critical Approaches – An Anthology* (Los Angeles: AFI, 1983).
Oscar Morana, 'Porra una aproximación semiológica a la telenovela', *Video Forum* no. 1, 1978.
David Morley, *The 'Nationwide' Audience* (London: BFI, 1980).
– 'Cultural transformations: the politics of resistance' in Howard Davis and Paul Walton (eds.), *Language, Image, Media* (Oxford: Basil Blackwell, 1983), pp.104-117.
Laura Mulvey, 'Douglas Sirk and Melodrama', *Australian Journal of Screen Theory* no. 3, 1977, pp.26-30.
Horace Newcomb, *TV: the most popular art* (New York: Anchor, 1974).
– 'Texas: A Giant State of Mind' *Channel of Communication*, April-May 1981.
Barbara O'Connor, 'The representation of Women in Irish Television Drama' in Martin McLoone and John McMahon, *Television and Irish Society*.
Frank Parkin, *Class inequality and political order* (London: Paladin, 1973).
Jean-Marie Piemme, 'Simulation et dissimulation: le representation du travail dans trois feuilletons télevisés', *Etudes de Radio-Télèvision* no. 18, 1972.
– *La propagande inavouée* (Paris: Union Génerale d'Editions, 1975).
Jayne Pilling and Stephen Woolley 'Cul-de-sac for the Nuclear Family', *Primetime* vol. 1 no. 3, March-May 1982, p.13.
Bill Podmore, '*Coronation Street* – the making of a hit', *The EBU Review* vol. 35 no.

6, November 1984, pp.11-13.
Ann Poliatowski, 'Soap Opera' in Dick Fiddy (ed.), *The Television Yearbook* (London: Virgin, 1985) pp.107-110.
Phil Redmond, '*Brookside* – a socially realistic twice-weekly drama', *The EBU Review* vol. 36 no. 6, November 1985, pp.39-42.
Jane Root, *Open The Box* (London: Comedia, 1986).
Ruth Rosen 'Soap Operas – Search for Yesterday' in Todd Gitlin (ed.), *Watching Television* (New York: Pantheon, 1987) pp.42-67.
Helena Sheehan, *Irish Television Drama: A Society and its Stories* (Dublin: RTE, 1987).
Jean Sickler 'La télévision, va-t-elle résusciter le feuilleton?', *Les cahiers de la télévision* no. 16, 1963.
Philip Simpson (ed.), *Parents Talking Television – Television In The Home* (London: Comedia, 1987).
Julia Smith, 'How to get started – creating a soap opera from scratch', *The EBU Review* vol. 36 no. 6, November 1985, pp.47-48.
Michel Souchon (ed.), 'Anatomie d'un feuilleton: Francois Gaillard', *Les cahiers de l'éducation permanente* no. 57 bis, Terme-Editions 1973.
Giovanni Spagnoletti (ed.), *R W Fassbinder TV* (Sienna: Editori del Grife, 1983).
Lesley Stern, 'Oedipal Opera: *The Restless Years*', *The Australian Journal of Screen Theory* no. 4, 1978, pp. 39-48.
Joelle Stolz, 'Les algériens regardent *Dallas*', *Les nouvelles chaînes*, pp.223-246.
Gillian Swanson, '*Dallas* 1', *Framework* no. 14, 1981, pp.32-35.
– '*Dallas* 2', *Framework* nos. 15/16/17, 1981, pp.81-85.
Laurie Taylor and Bob Mullan, *Uninvited Guests – The Intimate Secrets of Radio and Television* (London: Chatto and Windus, 1986).
Teaching 'Coronation Street' (new edition) (London: BFI, 1987).
S. Tee, '*Dallas*: het gezin van de week', *Skrien* no. 118, May-June 1982.
John Tulloch and Albert Moran, *A Country Practice: 'Quality Soap'* (Sydney: Currency Press, 1986).
Raymond Williams, *The Country and the City* (London: Chatto and Windus, 1973).
– *Television, Technology and Cultural Form* (London: Fontana, 1974).
– *Marxism and Literature* (Oxford: OUP, 1977).
Mallory Wober, 'Cinderella comes out showing TV's Hits are its Myths', *Media, Culture and Society* no. 6, 1984.
Patricia R Zimmermann, 'Good Girls, Bad Women: The Role of Older Women on *Dynasty*', *Journal of Film and Video* vol. 37 no. 2, Spring 1985, pp.66-74.

REPORTS

A twisted yarn: some psychological aspects of viewing soap operas, IBA Report.
Report of the EBU Seminar on the production of Popular Series and Serials for Television held in Chianciano, Italy 3-6 June 1984 in *The EBU Review* vol. 35 no. 6, November 1984, pp.8-25 (6 articles).
Report of the Second EBU Seminar on Popular Serials held in Chianciano, Italy 9-13 June 1985 in *The EBU Review* vol. 36 no. 6, November 1985, pp.30-51 (8 articles).